For Dr Mrinal Bose

Physician, novelist, friend, philosopher and guide

WHY THERE ARE NO NOYONTARA FLOWERS IN AGARGAON COLONY

Praise for Shahidul Zahir

It's good to read works outside the sphere of the Anglophone and the European, not because we perform a duty by doing so, but because, as with these arresting novellas by Shahidul Zahir, they amplify our sense of what fiction can do. Zahir's world is close, sometimes violent, but never claustrophobic. It enables discovery, even love, showing us the curiously moving ways in which human beings assign value to small things, including their own lives. – AMIT CHAUDHURI

In these novellas the political is the personal is the intimate is the lyrical is the ironic is the universal. Perhaps it would be best if you were to read these books which will leave you with unforgettable images of a jamdani of skulls and a flock of sarus cranes as harbingers of a nation in the throes of birth. – JERRY PINTO

Zahir's writing is propelled by an alertness to the inner lives of objects, animals, the landscape, and marginalized people as they collide against the obscene lies created by those in power. Haunting and apocalyptic, his fiction may be about the recent past, but it reads like a literature of the future. – SIDDHARTHA DEB

Short, pithy, compact … unsettling the present and casting a dark shadow on the future. – RAKHSHANDA JALIL, *The Wire*

A rare gift … Zahir synthesises hard-hitting social realism with a surge of surrealist paranoia to forge a style that keeps the reader on tenterhooks. – SOMAK GHOSHAL, *Mint*

Translating a work of this literary value is challenging. It becomes even more difficult when much of its power is associated with nuances of language and local culture. The translation succeeds spectacularly in this regard. The descriptions of places cast a spell that leaves you wide-eyed, like a child listening to stories of faraway places. – DIPANJAN SINHA, *The Hindu*

SHAHIDUL ZAHIR

WHY THERE ARE NO NOYONTARA FLOWERS IN AGARGAON COLONY: STORIES

TRANSLATED FROM
THE BENGALI BY V. RAMASWAMY

HARPERPERENNIAL
An Imprint of HarperCollins *Publishers*

First published in English in India by Harper Perennial 2022
An imprint of HarperCollins *Publishers*
4th Floor, Tower A, Building No. 10, Phase II, DLF Cyber City,
Gurugram – 122002
www.harpercollins.co.in

2 4 6 8 10 9 7 5 3 1

P-ISBN: 978-93-5629-032-7
E-ISBN: 978-93-5629-033-4

Typeset in 11.5/15.7 Adobe Caslon Pro at
Manipal Technologies Limited, Manipal

Printed and bound at
Thomson Press (India) Ltd

Contents

Where Is My Heart's Wanderer?

THE PEOPLE OF GHOST LANE in South Moishundi were caught in a tangle again, and the people of Twin Bridge and Padmanidhi Lane, Wari and Banagram, Narinda and Dayaganj learnt about this difficulty of theirs; they, the people of Ghost Lane, said:

We would like to go back, once again, to the subject of Abdul Karim, because for the last few days, we have been hearing in the moholla that he was going to Mymensingh; but we decided not to pay any attention to that. Then, one Thursday evening, when Abdul Aziz Byapari, the owner of the house on No. 64 in our moholla, that is, Ghost Lane, was returning after buying a packet of hot dalpuris, he encountered Abdul Karim, and he said, 'Hey Miya, come and have some dalpuris.'

Abdul Karim felt embarrassed to accept the sudden invitation to eat dalpuris and said that he got heartburn when he ate them; but disregarding that, Abdul Aziz Byapari said, 'Come, come, it's great stuff. You keep to yourself all the time!'

So Abdul Karim had to accept; he went inside Abdul Aziz Byapari's house and ate dalpuris, and as he gazed at the gathering darkness, he remarked, 'There's no dal in the dalpuri, it's only potato!'

Abdul Aziz Byapari: 'Yes. Just see how the price of dal is rising!'

Abdul Karim: 'Let me bring some dal for you!'

AAB: 'From where?'

AK: 'I'm going to Mymensingh for an outing.'

After that, when Abdul Aziz Byapari asked him what business he had in Mymensingh, he said that he was actually going to Akua, and when Abdul Aziz Byapari seemed not to know where Akua was, he said that he was actually going to Phulbaria. Then, since Abdul Aziz Byapari was similarly clueless about where Phulbaria was, he said that Akua was the name of a place near Mymensingh, and that Phulbaria was near Akua. When he heard that, Abdul Aziz Byapari gave him another dalpuri, or rather potato puri. Abdul Karim ate the second dalpuri, and as he ate it, he once again remarked, 'These bastards make dalpuri with potato! The price of dal is going up, I'll get some dal for you.'

AAB: 'From Mymensingh?'

AK: 'Yes, why do you ask?'

AAB: 'What work do you have in Mymensingh?'

AK: 'I have a friend there, I'm going there for an outing.'

AAB: 'You have a friend in Mymensingh?'

AK: 'Why, isn't that possible?'

Abdul Karim then fell into the inevitable conversational snare. Abdul Aziz Byapari didn't let him off, and giving him the last dalpuri from the packet in his hand, he said, 'Tell me, what's the matter?'

AK: 'Nothing, it's just like that. My friend told me, "Come to my place for an outing," so I thought, since my friend's inviting me, let me go there for an outing.'

AAB: 'How did you make friends with someone from Mymensingh?'

AK: 'I did. I had gone to the Mohakhali bus terminal one day, and that's where I met my friend, the one who has asked me to come for an outing to Mymensingh.'

That night, we, the people of the moholla, tired after the day's work, heard the latest news regarding Abdul Karim's trip to Mymensingh and said, the boy's a damn fool, and we arrived at the conclusion that there was no further possibility of this unemployed son of Khorshed Alam becoming a man. The next day, Friday, after the Jumma prayer at noon, Abdul Karim spoke to Ali Akbar of our moholla, and we found out about it. Ali Akbar had warehouses in Rahmatganj, and when he was returning home after the Jumma prayer, he met Abdul Karim on the way, so he asked him, 'What's up, Abdul Karim Miya, I believe you're going to Mymensingh?'

AK: 'Yes, uncle. Assalamualaikum!'

AA: 'Why, what takes you there, what business do you have there?'

AK: 'Nothing, it's just like that. I have no work there, I just thought I'd go for an outing.'

AA: 'You're just going for an outing!'

AK: 'Yes. What are you going to keep this time?'

AA: 'What do you mean what am I going to keep?'

AK: 'No, I meant, what are you going to keep in the warehouse this time?'

Ali Akbar got annoyed. He said he kept a large number of things as part of his warehousing trade, and then Abdul Karim advised him to keep cane jaggery. He said, 'Keep jaggery. I'm going to Phulbaria, I'll get cane jaggery for you.'

AA: 'But didn't you say you're going to Mymensingh?'

AK: 'Yes, from Mymensingh I'll go to Akua, and from Akua to Phulbaria. There's good sugar cane in Phulbaria, and it produces fine cane jaggery. I'll get jaggery for you from there.'

We thought this intermediate-pass, unemployed Abdul Karim, who we knew to be the king of laziness, was actually taking the moholla folk for a ride, and that he had taken recourse to this ploy after being at his wits' end in the face of his father's continuous complaints and tirades of abuse; there was no substance to all this talk of his, he had never gone anywhere in his life and he would never go. Then, on another Thursday, he again encountered Abdul Aziz Byapari. It was evening, and once again, as Abdul Aziz Byapari was returning home, he met Abdul Karim on the way.

AAB: 'What's up, you're still in the moholla?'

AK: 'Why shouldn't I be here?'

AAB: 'You were supposed to go to Mymensingh!'

AK: 'I'll go there.'

AAB: 'Will you get dal for me?'

AK: 'If you say so, I'll get it.'

AAB: 'But I'm not a wholesaler, Miya, I'm just a shopkeeper.'

AK: 'Why do you need to be a wholesaler? Just put it under your cot and leave it there, and sell it later.'

Then Abdul Aziz Byapari asked him to come and have dalpuris, and once again, Abdul Karim felt embarrassed and Abdul Aziz Byapari pacified him, 'Come, come, even if it's potato puri, it's tasty.' Abdul Karim then entered Abdul Aziz Byapari's house, sat on a chair, and ate potato puris and talked.

AK: 'If you tell me, I can bring dal for you. I'll be going there anyway for an outing, I can bring back two or four maunds when I return.'

AAB: 'Why didn't you tell your father?'

AK: 'There's no point.'

AAB: 'Why's that?'

AK: 'We don't get along.'

Even after that, we in the moholla were of the opinion that Abdul Karim was actually up to mischief; although we couldn't say for certain whether he would ultimately cheat someone, we thought there was cunning in his conduct, and when Abdul Aziz Byapari mentioned his father, it seemed his cunning was revealed and he had nothing left to say in reply then. But even after that, we could not be certain because the next Friday, after the Jumma prayer, he spoke to Babul Miya, the proprietor of the eating house in Raysha Bazar. It was Babul Miya who spoke to him first and thus fell into the trap. When Babul Miya inquired about his proposed trip to Mymensingh, he said that he would leave in the next day or two, and after that Abdul Karim returned to the old subject.

AK: 'I heard that the price of dal has risen, and so you make dalpuris with potato!'

BM: 'Yes, we make it with potato, but the bloody price of potato is no less!'

AK: 'Since I'm going to Mymensingh, if you tell me, I can bring back two or four or ten maunds of potatoes for you.'

BM: 'Oh no, what will I do with so many potatoes!'

AK: 'Why? Don't you need potatoes for your eating house?'

BM: 'I do. I buy them wholesale when the price is favourable.'

AK: 'But I'm going to Phulbaria. Fine potatoes grow there. If you say so, I can bring back potatoes for you at half the price.'

In the face of this pressure, Babul Miya changed his tactics.

BM: 'Why are you going to Mymensingh?'

AK: 'I have no work. I'm sitting idle, so I thought, let me go for an outing.'

BM: 'No work! Why don't you sit with your father in the shop?'

AK: 'I don't want to sell nuts and bolts. I want to be in another line of business, but Abba won't accept that.'

When we heard about this conversation between Babul Miya and Abdul Karim, it occurred to us for the first time that perhaps Abdul Karim was thinking about a means of livelihood. Of course we couldn't be completely certain, because we just didn't want to believe that the eccentric and useless Abdul Karim could actually be doing something. And when we still saw him in the moholla after ten or fifteen or twenty days, we once again thought that he was indeed playing with us in some way; or perhaps, through all this, he was trying to convey to his father that he did not want to remain unemployed. But there was no news of his going to Mymensingh, and he was still in the moholla. We thought that maybe it was because Abdul Aziz Byapari didn't want to purchase dal, and Ali Akbar didn't want to buy cane jaggery, or Babul didn't want to buy potatoes that Abdul Karim didn't go to Mymensingh. After that, he once again ran into Abdul Aziz Byapari of the house on No. 64, and Abdul Aziz Byapari once again invited him to eat dalpuris.

AK: 'Why do you have so much dalpuri?'

AAB: 'What else can I eat? My father and grandfather ate it, so I eat it too!'

AK: 'There's only potato in the dalpuri, I told you I'll get you dal.'

AAB: 'From Mymensingh?'

AK: 'Yes.'

AAB: 'When are you going there?'

AK: 'I'll go. Let's see.'

AAB: 'When?'

AK: 'I'll go. I thought I'd bring back some stuff for you, but I see that you don't need anything.'

Once again, we heard about all this and exclaimed, 'Bloody moron,' because we came to know that, even after so much talk, Abdul Aziz Byapari was unwilling to undertake the dal trade with Abdul Karim. We lost count of the number of days that went by in this manner, but Abdul Karim was steadfast in his desire to go to Mymensingh and Phulbaria. Then, on some Friday, when Abdul Aziz Byapari was returning for the fourth time with a packet of dalpuris at around dusk, he encountered Abdul Karim, and once again he asked him to come and eat dalpuris.

AAB: 'Come!'

AK: 'Potato puris?'

AAB: 'Come, come and eat.'

Then Abdul Aziz Byapari once again raised the subject of Abdul Karim's trip to Mymensingh. 'What happened about you going to Mymensingh?' When we in the moholla heard about this, we had no doubt that Abdul Karim was playing a trick on us, and that we kept getting caught in the trap of the trick that he had laid. Maybe by then the inclination for this game had awakened in us as well, and we thought that we ought to come down on him and not let him get away, and that we should ensure that he was taught an appropriate lesson for playing such nasty jokes on us. But there was more astonishment waiting for us, and after giving Abdul Karim the hot, yellow dalpuris, or rather potato puris, dripping in oil, Abdul Aziz Byapari asked him a question – we were unable to understand why he had not been asked this question earlier, or why we hadn't ever thought about it! After treating him to dalpuris for the fourth time, a question arose in Abdul Aziz Byapari's mind, but when he heard the answer to the question, he was completely dumbfounded. Because when Abdul Aziz Byapari asked, 'What's your friend's name?' Abdul Karim informed him that his friend's name was Shefali.

AK: 'I'll go to Mymensingh now. If you want, I can bring back dal for you.'

AAB: 'Who's Shefali? How did Shefali become your friend?'

AK: 'Why? Isn't it possible?'

AAB: 'Hey, where did you meet her?'

AK: 'I met her.'

AAB: 'Where did you meet her? At the Mohakhali bus terminal?'

AK: 'Yes.'

AAB: 'Did she ask you to visit her?'

AK: 'Yes.'

AAB: 'No wonder your father is always railing against you!'

AK: 'Why?'

AAB: 'A girl whom you don't know at all says, "Come and visit," and you're going by that!'

AK: 'Why?'

AAB: 'Miya, you're an idiot by nature. Don't tell your father all this. If you do, he'll thrash you!'

We, too, thought that actually Abdul Karim was a donkey! But after that, like Abdul Aziz Byapari, we fell into confusion because Abdul Karim was unwilling to accept this censure. He was unwilling to concede that, just because Abdul Aziz Byapari had treated him to dalpuris, or rather potato puris, he had a right to reprimand him.

AK: 'I'll go this month itself, whatever all of you might say.'

AAB: 'Why will you go? To meet that girl?'

AK: 'Yes, but why do you ask?'

AAB: 'Have you ever been outside Dhaka?'

AK: 'Do you think I won't be able to go just because of that? That's not a problem. I'll be able to go. I've written down the address.'

For the people of Ghost Lane, more than the subject of Abdul Karim and his trip to Mymensingh, it was the subject of Shefali that became more significant. The days of the people of the moholla, of South Moishundi and Ghost Lane, were full of perturbation. So the bastard's having a love affair, they said. They thought that it was possible for Abdul Karim to do all this because he was unemployed. The people of the moholla then began to despise the fact that he was having a love affair more than they did the fact that he was idle. They could not forget that Shefali was a girl, and that Abdul Karim had said that she was his friend! As a result, the people of the moholla lost sleep over it: they lay awake in bed, their bodies tired after a whole day's work. The sense of the futility of life and how it had been wasted was about to devour them. They fell into a kind of gloom; they thought that it was better to be unemployed like Abdul Karim! He spent his time lazing around, lolling or lying in bed all day, telling tales about the faraway Shefali – but there was no sign of him going to Mymensingh. If he encountered Abdul Aziz Byapari or Ali Akbar or Babul Miya again, when they asked, 'Aren't you going?' he laid the blame for his failure on them. He said, 'I'll go. I told you I'd get some stuff for you, but you didn't agree!' When the people of the moholla heard about this, they were amazed: 'Do you see what a shrewd bastard this boy of Khorshed Alam has become!' Then, one day, as Abdul Aziz Byapari was returning home after buying dalpuris, he looked for Abdul Karim, but he wasn't to be found. When the people of the moholla heard about this, they began calling Abdul Aziz Byapari a donkey. They said, 'That bloody son of a Byapari only gobbles dalpuris and dances along with this unemployed rascal of a boy!' But subsequently, the people of the moholla changed their opinion and their respect for Abdul Aziz Byapari was restored because they learnt about the story of Abdul Aziz Byapari eating dalpuris in full detail, and they thought that Abdul Karim's cunning ways would now come to an end. The people of Ghost Lane came to know that Abdul Aziz Byapari did indeed look for Abdul Karim to treat him to dalpuris, but he didn't go to his house and call him. Instead, he waited for him; it was as if Abdul Aziz Byapari simply cast the bait and then lay in wait, but he didn't have to wait very long. Three days later, on some Thursday evening, or it could have been a Wednesday as well, he encountered Abdul Karim and he was delighted. 'Why Miya, why don't I see you?' Abdul Aziz Byapari then perhaps thought that instead of getting directly to the real issue, he should take some time. And so, he decided to play with Abdul Karim a little bit, and he asked, 'So you didn't go to Mymensingh?' But that Thursday or Wednesday evening when they sat down with the packet of dalpuris, the play between Abdul Aziz Byapari and Abdul Karim was probably not one-sided: it was mutual. The people of the moholla saw, to their astonishment, that Abdul Karim was not a bad player either, because that day, in reply to Abdul Aziz Byapari's query, Abdul Karim gazed at the soft darkness of dusk, laughed and said, 'Are you asking me to go, then?' Hearing this, Abdul Aziz Byapari was taken aback, but he didn't lose his senses. He quickly changed tack and Abdul Karim was caught in that. In the face of Abdul Aziz Byapari's cross-examination, Abdul Karim had to elaborate on his proposed trip to Mymensingh and the story of Shefali. Abdul Karim said that, one afternoon, when he had gone to Mohakhali bus terminal with a friend, they had seen this young village girl there. The girl was alone and probably unwell. Right in front of them, the girl, who was sitting inside a bus, waiting for it to depart, stuck her head out of the window and vomited, and after that, when she got down from the bus to wash her face or to drink water, her legs were unsteady. And Abdul Karim saw that. So he held her by the arm and took her to a wooden bench and sat her down there. He brought water from an eating house and gave it to her, and then he learnt that the girl's name was Shefali. After that, he had a very unworldly conversation with her. In the face of Abdul Aziz Byapari's questions, he said that when he saw or realized that the girl was returning home alone and that she was unwell, he felt very worried for her. And he asked her, 'Will you be able to travel alone?' Perhaps the girl was amused to hear Abdul Karim say that. She retorted, 'Why do you say that? Why shouldn't I be able to travel alone? I've done it so many times!' Then, after that, until the bus left, the two of them got to know each other, and thus Abdul Karim learnt that one had to go via Mymensingh to reach Akua, and via Akua to Phulbaria.

There was so much rice, so much dal, so much sugar cane and jaggery to be found there. So much potato and beans and eggplant grew there, and all these things were sold at a very cheap price in the market in Phulbaria. The girl then probably told him at some point, 'Come and visit me for an outing,' and Abdul Karim noted down the girl's address on a sheet of paper and said, 'I've never been to Mymensingh. If you ask me to come, then I will one day. I'll come to meet you!' After hearing this much that day, the matter became clear to Abdul Aziz Byapari. And he was of the opinion that this was indeed a ruse on Abdul Karim's part, and maybe he was playing the ruse essentially on himself; maybe by talking about Shefali and an outing to Mymensingh, he was building up this single prop to add some action to his inactive life. Abdul Aziz Byapari then made his cruel decision. He probably thought that once the means to carrying out his artful device was closed, Abdul Karim would be rid of his secretiveness; and so he told him, 'You should go, bring back five kilos of dal for me, and if I see that I can sell it at a good price, I'll buy a greater quantity later.' But the people of the moholla said that, like Abdul Aziz Byapari, they too could not gauge Abdul Karim because he turned Abdul Aziz Byapari down, saying that he had given up the plan of bringing dal or potatoes or jaggery and doing that kind of business, and that he was going there now only for an outing. Maybe Abdul Aziz Byapari was not pleased to hear that, maybe he felt defeated or humiliated, and had nothing more to say. Giving a dalpuri to Abdul Karim, he said, 'It's all right, take it and eat it.' And Abdul Karim enjoyed eating the last dalpuri too.

The matter gathered an air of mystery, then, for the people of Ghost Lane. They were of the view that Abdul Karim was only trying to fool the people of the moholla as well as himself. Their suspicions did not leave them. As a result, Abdul Aziz Byapari once again bought dalpuris, or rather potato puris, and looked for Abdul Karim. After that, when he encountered him again on the street, he took him to his house. He told him, 'Come, since you won't bring me dal, come and have potato puris!' That day, Abdul Aziz Byapari told him, 'So you're going to Mymensingh just like that, for an outing, are you?' The people of the moholla say that Abdul Aziz Byapari probably understood the matter, and when Abdul Karim once again declined to bring back a sample quantity of five kilos of dal, he tried to keep the game going so that Abdul Karim wouldn't be able to escape. When Abdul Karim heard his query and nodded and said, 'Yes, I'll go just like that,' Abdul Aziz Byapari then said, 'Why don't you take my Dulal Miya with you? You can meet Shefali, and he'll take a look at what's available in the markets.' Abdul Aziz Byapari perhaps expected that Abdul Karim would not agree to this proposal of his because, after all this while, he probably thought that all this talk about Abdul Karim going to Mymensingh was still all fake and Shefali entirely imaginary. But it seemed that his thinking was incorrect yet again. Abdul Karim readily agreed to his proposal and said, 'That would be very good. The two of us can while away the time talking – there won't be any problem. There's a large tin shed in Shefali's house. We can stay there comfortably; the two of us will have a nice outing and return.'

The people of Ghost Lane narrate this story:

We then came to know about everything. Abdul Karim left for Mymensingh, and Abdul Aziz Byapari's elder son, Dulal Miya, accompanied him. All of us in Ghost Lane were pleased about this arrangement except for Ali Akbar and Babul Miya. Of course Abdul Karim's father, Khorshed Alam, wasn't pleased either. Be that as it may, we were happy because we thought that, since Dulal Miya was with him, we would get to know about everything in detail and Abdul Karim would not be able to make up lies and cheat us.

And so, Abdul Karim and Dulal Miya began their journey, a day or two after eating dalpuris for the last time at Abdul Aziz Byapari's house. It was a Tuesday, an auspicious day, and the two of them really set off very early in the morning. We didn't want to believe it, but they got into a rickshaw with kitbags on their shoulders and left the moholla, and once they had really left, we expected them to return after three or four days. We said, perhaps they may be away for as long as five or seven days – but they were back in the moholla the very same night. Later, we heard this account of their travels from Abdul Karim and Dulal Miya.

Dulal Miya said that, that morning, after reaching the Mohakhali bus terminal, they faced a problem right away, because they saw that there were two kinds of buses going to Phulbaria. If they wanted, they could take the Mymensingh bus and go to Mymensingh, and go to Phulbaria from there; or alternatively, they could catch the direct bus to Phulbaria. But we, the people of the moholla, could not understand the nature of the problem. We said, 'Is that any matter at all? You're going to Phulbaria, so you'll take the direct bus to Phulbaria.' But Dulal Miya said that in the directions that Shefali had given to Abdul Karim, it was specified thus: by bus from the Dhaka Mohakhali bus terminal to Mymensingh, then by the Phulbaria bus from the riverbank, in Mymensingh, to Phulbaria. When we heard that, we understood the nature of the problem, and Dulal Miya said that Abdul Karim decided to follow the instructions given by Shefali. So, they boarded the Mymensingh bus and reached Mymensingh at twelve noon. After that, changing buses at the riverbank, when they boarded a battered bus to Phulbaria, they felt terribly hungry. But because the bus was about to depart, they apparently gave up the idea of having lunch and bought and ate jhalmuri instead. Two hours after leaving Mymensingh, they reached the Phulbaria bus stand, and Dulal Miya said that their real difficulty began after that, because they couldn't find out anything. It seemed that, other than the girl's name,

Abdul Karim didn't have any particulars. But could one go around asking anyone about merely the name of a girl? Could one ask, 'Do you know Shefali? Which way is her house?' One couldn't, and so Dulal Miya was annoyed with Abdul Karim.

DM: 'I haven't seen an idiot like you in my entire bloody life!'

AK: 'Why? Why do you say that?'

DM: 'You don't know anything other than a name. How are you going to find this Shefali?'

AK: 'Why did you come? Did I ask you to come?'

DM: 'How was I to know what you had done? That you don't know anything but a name!'

But Dulal Miya said that Abdul Karim did not get agitated at what he said. He only said, 'Just see how I find the place!' They were sitting in a tea shop at the bus stand and drinking tea, maybe having a shingara or nimki as well, because Abdul Karim had explained to him that they would be able to eat soon, once they reached Shefali's house. Then, sitting at the tea shop, Dulal Miya saw for the first time the sheet of paper on which the address of Shefali's house had been written down. He told us, 'I've never seen such a bloody address in all my life!' Then, when we heard him, we thought that we too had never heard such a strange thing. But Dulal Miya could not narrate a lot of things properly, so we thought that we ought to see for ourselves the sheet of paper on which Abdul Karim had written Shefali's address. And so, we implored Abdul Aziz Byapari and told him, 'If we ask him, he won't listen to us, but you treat him to dalpuris, so tell him to show us the sheet of paper.' Abdul Aziz Byapari saw the reasonableness of our demand and told us that we should definitely be able to see that sheet of paper, and that he would arrange for it. Later, Abdul Aziz Byapari collected the sheet of paper, and we saw it. He then told us, 'The boy's not a bad sort. At first, he said he didn't have the paper, that he'd thrown it away. But then I said, "I'm your father's friend. Won't you listen to me?" He then came and gave me the paper. He said, "Take it. I'm giving this away to you!"' Then we, the people of Ghost Lane, saw the sheet of paper.

On a white sheet of paper, first the address was written:

Madam Shefali Begum
Phulbaria
Mymensingh

After that were the instructions on how to get there:

Dhaka Mohakhali bus terminal.
Mymensingh town, the riverbank.
From the riverbank – via Akua to Phulbaria market…
in front of the police station, on the opposite side, the eating house with a large koroi tree … in front of that

is the TNO office. When you stand facing the TNO office, the road on the left side – go straight past the low building which is the high school, and carry on straight … paddy fields, thorny bushes, red earth, a winding river on the left.

The river Ahaila / Akhaila / Akhaliya.

Cross the river and stand with the bridge behind you.

The direction in which the shadow falls in the afternoon – the opposite side of that.

If there's no shadow, the direction the soles of your feet feel comfortable walking in.

Walk along the bank of the river for a mile, you'll come to a pair of coconut trees.

Stand between the two trees and look in the direction of the village.

You'll see three tin sheds.

The road going beside the shed at the very left … take that road.

Paddy fields in all directions, you have to walk along the boundary ridges on the fields.

In the distance, more villages in all directions…

Walk in the direction in which the rice paddy in the fields tilt.

Or, if it's not the time of paddy, walk in the direction in which the wind blows.

Five homesteads will be visible. Three homesteads in front and two at the back.

The house at the back with the pomegranate tree.

Dulal Miya said, 'The bloody bitch says so much, but there's no father's name or village name.' But he said that, despite that, when he was sitting at the tea shop at the Phulbaria bus stand and saw this description of the address, he was amazed, and looking at him, Abdul Karim said, 'The address is all right, isn't it?' Dulal Miya told us that, at the time, he thought that the address was probably all right. Maybe if one looked from between the two coconut trees, Shefali Begum's village was visible. Maybe Shefali Begum would suddenly appear beneath the pomegranate tree, and looking at Abdul Karim's face she would say, 'You've come, you were able to find the place, come!' But he felt confused regarding the matter of the direction the paddy crop tilted towards, and about ascertaining the direction according to the shadow in the afternoon sun. He thought that he had never heard such strange directions before, but he realized that perhaps this was much better than not having anything. And so, in reply to Abdul Karim's query, he said, 'Yes, it's all right. Let's find the place now!'

They then set out once again from the Phulbaria bus stand. They took the metalled road and passed Aliya Madrasa. They arrived at the base of the ancient, tall and clustering koroi tree in front of the college. The TNO office building was in front of the tree; like travellers in olden times, they followed the directions written on the sheet of paper and advanced. As they stood facing the TNO office, along the boundary wall of the office, they saw a brick road laid in herringbone pattern going leftwards. With fields of ripe paddy on either side, they walked along this road and reached a crossroad. And on the right, across the vast field of golden paddy of late autumn tilting under the sunlight, they could see a white platform. They thought this might be the high school, but not being able to make anything out from so far, they thought they could ask someone, 'Brother, is that the school?' But not finding any person around, they read the sheet of paper again. It said: straight past the high school. And they realized that the road they had come along would continue going straight. They then went past the crossroad and came to a muddy road. After advancing along that road for a while, they saw that the colour of the earth here was red. Both sides of the road were covered with thickets like the hoods of serpents. They realized they were on the right track. And then, suddenly, they were done with the twists of this road and they arrived at the bank of the Akhaliya river. We learnt from Dulal Miya that they saw a narrow but deep creek in front of them. The bed of the river was almost dry then; a thin stream of water continued to flow with great difficulty. Dulal Miya told us that, seeing the river, his enthusiasm increased, because he said, 'A river was such a thing that, when one saw it, one always thought that one had reached somewhere!' We learnt that a wide bridge made of posts and planks of the gojari tree, arched slightly like the back of an able-bodied lover in coitus, hung over the river, touching the red earth on the two banks. We learnt that in the afternoon, or late afternoon, Dulal Miya, and behind him, Abdul Karim, climbed up to the bridge over the Akhaliya river. Dulal Miya said that after reaching the other side, when they stood at the bank, or at the edge of the bridge, they saw that their shadows did not want to shed their attachment to the body and wander far. They lay at their feet like pet dogs. Dulal Miya said that, when it was not possible to proceed by looking at their shadows, they decided to follow the second instruction. Abdul Karim then realized that if one had to find out which way to walk by what felt comfortable to the soles of one's feet, one had to remove one's shoes. He said to Dulal Miya, 'Wait, I'm taking mine off, you don't have to take yours off.' Dulal Miya told us that it was while he was removing his shoes that a problem arose. Abdul Karim was leaning against the wooden railing of the bridge, slightly bent, with his right foot raised, and he was trying to untie his shoelace, but by pulling the wrong end, he made a knot instead. After that, as a result of pulling erratically, it became even more knotted up. He then rested on his knee, with one foot on the ground, and pulled at the lace for a while. He tried to undo the knot with his nails, and when, after a lot of toil, he was finally able to do so, that was when the problem arose. He raised his head and looked at Dulal Miya. Dulal Miya told us, 'I thought that he was perhaps stretching his neck.' But we found out from Dulal Miya that that wasn't what the matter was. What Abdul Karim said, looking skywards, made Dulal Miya feel bewildered at first, and after that he lost his temper because, resting on one foot on the wooden surface of the bridge over the Akhaliya river and looking at Dulal Miya's face, Abdul Karim said, 'Come Dulaiya, let's go back.'

DM: 'What are you saying!'

AK: 'Come, let's go back.'

DM: 'Why?'

AK: 'Just like that. Let's go.'

DM: 'You're saying that now! Why did you come at all?'

AK: 'I came. Now let's go.'

DM: 'Why did you bring me along?'

AK: 'Why did you come?'

We heard from Dulal Miya that Abdul Karim then tied his shoelace again and stood up, and disregarding all of Dulal Miya's protestations, he began walking in the other direction. In fact, they probably never crossed the Akhaliya river at all. And Dulal Miya was compelled to follow him. Dulal Miya mentioned visiting the market before going home so that he could find out about the prices of various things, but Abdul Karim did not pay any heed. Something happened to him on the bridge over the river. He said that they would first go to the bus stand and find out about the return bus, because they had to catch the last bus to Dhaka. But if there was time after that, they could go around the market. But that day, they were unable to go around the

Phulbaria market. Maybe the shopkeepers or the people in the market waited with all the dal, all the rice, potatoes and jaggery, but Abdul Karim and Dulal Miya did not have the time. When they reached the TNO office, they saw a bus a short distance away, in front of the college. The helper of the bus was shouting out, 'Dhaka, Dhaka! Last bus, last bus! About to leave, about to leave!' Dulal Miya said that they had no option but to run and catch that bus.

The people of Ghost Lane later said that they knew Abdul Karim was bound to do something like this, and after that, they again forgot all about Abdul Karim. But in the moholla, Abdul Aziz Byapari could not give up his habit of eating dalpuris. He sometimes went and bought dalpuris, or rather potato puris, and when he encountered Abdul Karim, he sometimes asked him to come over and eat them: 'Come and have dalpuris.' And then Abdul Karim sat in the living room of his house and ate the puris, and remarked, 'The bastards make dalpuri with potato!'

(1999)

The History of Our Cottage Industry

WE RECALL THE INDUSTRIALIZATION OF our moholla, South Moishundi; when the days began to get hot, it was Chaitra, and in Baisakh or Jaishta, the watermelon vendors arrived with their watermelons and we began eating them, and thus we became conscious of watermelons; we would notice that these vendors were inclined to set up their makeshift shops beside a wall in a narrow part of the street of the moholla and lay out the round watermelons in small heaps on the ground, but we couldn't figure out why they sat there, and so rickshaws, push- and bullock-carts, baby-taxis, dogs, goats and humans created a snarl when they arrived there; the population of flies in South Moishundi increased, fat bluebottles and thin black flies came and sat on our noses, and so we would get annoyed; we berated them, 'Why do you bring watermelons in this time of flies!' When Babul Miya or Dulal, perhaps Babul Miya was the one, came out into the street with a football in his hand, the small boys who had been making an uproar on the road would follow him towards Graduates High School; silence would descend upon the moholla and we would realize what torment we had been in for so long, and then amidst the silence we would hear the sound of the lathe machines; we then remembered the history of our moholla and learnt in detail about watermelons; we would take a watermelon in the cup of our hands and try to guess how much it weighed, and looking vacantly towards the sky, try to master the skill of figuring out the correlation between the weight of a watermelon and the quality of its inner substance; we would place our palm very delicately on its shiny skin, which resembled a bald head, and try to intuit whether the fruit was fresh and its juiciness was intact; we would ask the watermelon vendor, 'Are flies born during the time of watermelons, or is it that watermelons fruit during the time of flies?' The boys of the moholla would then return because they felt like playing gollachut on the street of the moholla, and as a result we would no longer hear the deep muffled sound of the furnace of the glass factory; we would cut the watermelons into slices during this recess and enrich our knowledge about watermelons, the ones with the skin coloured deep green had a whitish inside, sometimes pink, but basically whitish, while the ones which were of a lighter colour, or with a skin like printed fabric, would be red as blood inside, and we would then ask the vendor, 'Why are there two kinds of watermelons?' Because we were confronted with the dilemma of choosing between two kinds of watermelons, something our fathers weren't, since in those days, there was only one kind of watermelon; our fathers said that, when the days got hot and the watermelon vendors arrived with watermelons, the flies in the moholla would increase, and they would shout at the vendors, like we did, 'Why do you miyas bring watermelons in the time of flies!' Then Haji Abdur Rashid fetched sand for the construction work on his lozenge factory and unloaded it on the street in front of the temple, and the boys of the moholla would scale the wall of the temple to the roof and jump down into the heap of sand below; the hullabaloo would shatter our afternoon nap and we would learn a lot about watermelons; we would then cut the watermelons with one kind of knife or another from the kitchen and eat it, while the boys on the street would become tired and put aside the ball and return home; but we would fail to note that along with the watermelons we had swallowed a lot of seeds as well, and because of that, or on account of having eaten too much watermelon, our stomachs would start rumbling; we would go to the watermelon vendors and exclaim, 'Why do the watermelons have seeds!' The sound of the lathe machines in the moholla would then cease, and we would turn melancholy, because it then occurred to us that we would perhaps be deprived of something glorious in the moholla simply on account of watermelon seeds; we came to know that they, that is to say our fathers, used to eat white pyramid-shaped slices of watermelon with deep green skin, and they would swallow the shiny black seeds too, and so the history of our moholla became clear to us; they told us things that we did not know, and reiterated things we already knew; when Haji Abdur Rashid felt a twinge in his stomach, he went and lay in bed and began to ponder over why there were so many kinds of mangoes but only one kind of watermelon, and lying in a darkened room at that time, he realized that he ought to install a lathe machine for his son, Abdul Jalil; and in this way, when we lay down to rest after eating watermelon, we would recall the history of the manufacture of nuts and bolts in our moholla, and we would then remember the only poet, the only lover, the only woman to have fled her home, and the only incident of suicide in the moholla; after Haji Abdul Rashid swallowed watermelon seeds and had a stomach ache, in the throes of the ache he had a vision: he saw the future potential of lathe workshops in the moholla, and he thought that he needed the house standing on the one-and-a-half kattha plot of land that belonged to the old childless widow, Rahima Bibi; and as we rested in bed, we thought about our stomach aches and we lamented, 'What else would we eat if can't eat watermelons in this hot summer!' Our knowledge regarding watermelons grew because the heady scent of its juice attracted a swarm of flies and the flies got into our nostrils; we sneezed and we discovered the erotic, physical pleasure of sneezing; we could identify three significant things in our lives, namely, lathe machines, watermelons and the pleasure of emitting a sneeze that rose from the stem of the brain; we remembered how Shefali Akhtar grew up in the moholla, and we were in anguish the day she went missing or ran away from home; we recalled that this was the final straw that broke Abdul Gafoor; we imagined that we heard the sound of him falling apart, like that of a bell metal water pot falling from the crook of a village girl's arm, and we were neither happy nor sad about this; we felt that this tragedy was inevitable, because it happened during our adolescence; after having swallowed watermelon seeds, while Haji Abdur Rashid reclined in the semi-darkness of his bedroom where the plaster on the walls was peeling, pressing his stomach with his hand, he had the dream and then sent for his youngest son, Abdul Jalil, and we came to know how, after swallowing the watermelon seeds, a vision of the future of our moholla and that of the country had flashed before Haji Abdur Rashid's eyes, and subsequently, when we ourselves fell ill after swallowing watermelon seeds, we became anxious because we heard the sound of the lathe machines in the moholla coming to a stop, and we were worried that perhaps Alamgir Hossain, the Chairman of the South Moishundi branch of the Machine Tools Factory Owners' Association, too might fall ill, and thus not be to able include the name of our moholla in the speech that the Deputy Prime Minister and Industries Minister was scheduled to deliver the following Friday in the Dholaikhal locality, but we were yet to know about watermelons; we thought that it was only our fathers who knew happiness, because their lives had been simple, and they were not faced with the dilemma of choosing between two kinds of watermelons; although we consumed red Japanese watermelons, we couldn't be certain that they were indeed red inside, and so we swallowed watermelon seeds, and as Haji Abdur Rashid lay in bed, he sent for his youngest son, Abdul Jalil, and when he arrived, he told him about his plan of installing lathe machines in the moholla, but he could not take possession of Rahima Bibi's house which abutted his lozenge factory, and we could not figure out why this old woman conducted herself in this way; then one day, Abdul Gafoor arrived from Dohar or Nawabganj accompanied by his three children and presented himself, and we learnt that he, Abdul Gafoor, was Rahima Bibi's younger sister's son, and that she had gifted her plot of land and the house on it to him by signing a deed to that effect; this incident could have changed the history of our moholla's industrialization, but at the time we thought that the twinge we felt in our stomachs was really harsh and acute, and then Haji Abdur Rashid got back his inspiration to implement his dream; when we learnt about this, we became terribly excited, because we figured out that very soon sand would be brought by bullock cart and piled in front of the temple, and we waited for this to happen; and then when we saw Shefali, we remembered that shefali was the name of a flower, and seeing the small and frail figure of Abdul Gafoor, we thought that he wouldn't look bad as the owner of a shop selling motor parts or electrical appliances, but perhaps the flies had annoyed him, and as a result we observed that he became indifferent towards us and began working as a teacher in the Narinda Primary School, and that was when we spotted his sons, Azizul Haque, the elder one, and Aminul Haque, the younger one; we would bite off a piece of watermelon and press it with our tongue against the palate, and even within the pleasure we felt while eating watermelons during the days of summer and heatwave, we couldn't forget about Shefali's treachery, we couldn't identify the man she had fled with, and it occurred to us that, although we lived in the same moholla, she had deceived us because perhaps she had come to despise watermelons like her father; but then we heard about Alamgir Hossain, and came to know that the respite of lying in bed that he got on account of his stomach ache proved to be a big blessing for us; we then remembered Shefali, and when we, the people of South Moishundi, remembered her, we would also remember Jharna Basak, and we felt a kind of unspecified grief; and when sand was brought and unloaded in front of the temple for Haji Abdur Rashid's construction work, Babul Miya and his gang of boys were occupied all morning playing in the sand; we returned home after that, and our mothers came rushing at us, shouting, 'Hai Allah! Haven't you gone to school yet?' We snatched our untidy notebooks and textbooks with torn pages and ran off; here, in Graduates High School, we encountered Azizul Haque and Aminul Haque, and a kind of proximity was established with them in one regard when, as our Physical Training teacher, Nani Basak, pulled our ears as we stood in line, he also pulled Azizul Haque's and Aminul Haque's ears; we then returned home from school, but our grief for Shefali Akhtar persisted for a long time, we didn't know it, but it was there; we called her a flower, 'Hello Shefali Flower,' we would say, she would come walking in the turquoise blue school uniform of Bangla Bazar School, stand in front of us and smile, and ask, 'Is shefali a flower?' We fell into confusion, we could remember that we had not seen a flowering tree in the moholla for a long time, and we wondered, is shefali a tree and not a flower? We then corrected ourselves and said, 'Hello Shefali Tree,' and then she presented us with the first enigma of our lives, because she smiled once again and asked, 'Is shefali a tree?' We then became doubly confused, and we found out that, even though Haji Abdur Rashid had not got hold of the bit of property belonging to Rahima Bibi, he had not given up his plan of installing lathe machines in the moholla; he prepared his plans while lying in bed after eating watermelons or swallowing watermelon seeds, and we became even more aware of watermelons because we observed how closely this fruit was related to the leisure time in our lives; as Alamgir Hossain of the Machine Tool Factory Owners' Association was laid up in bed after eating watermelons or swallowing watermelon seeds, he remembered Haji Abdur Rashid having been confined to bed with a stomach ache after swallowing watermelon seeds, and as he lay in bed, he composed the speech in his mind, or perhaps jotted it down, but we came to know that the mention of Haji Abdur Rashid swallowing watermelon seeds could not be included in the speech prepared for the Deputy Prime Minister; after the Jumma congregation on Friday, many people went to the Dholaikhal locality and observed the Deputy Prime Minister, in his white punjabi and kishti-cap, peep into the rows of tiny, shanty-like lathe machine workshops, and following that, they heard him deliver his long-awaited speech, and in this speech he also mentioned the name of our moholla, South Moishundi; Alamgir Hossain then contacted his friend, the Public Relations Officer of the Deputy Prime Minister, via whom he had inserted the name of our moholla in the speech, and collected a copy of the full text of the speech, and in one of the sentences of the speech we saw the name of our moholla, South Moishundi, mentioned thus, 'We have to value and praise the silent efforts being undertaken in small lathe workshops by the people of Dholaikhal, South Moishundi and other localities,' we soon found photocopies of the text of the speech hanging on the walls of all the lathe workshops in the moholla, and for our convenience the name 'South Moishundi' had been underlined with a red marker; we felt happy and proud, but we also remembered something we were deprived of; we did not have Abdul Gafoor with us in the moholla then to show him our success, we remembered that, after he arrived in our moholla, he swore at us, calling us 'greedy watermelon-gobblers', but in the end we survived, because watermelon kept our heads and tummies cool, and on a confused and lonely afternoon he hanged himself from the iron roof beam in his house; we were not surprised when we got the news because, after all, we knew about watermelons; we then went out to the street and saw that the police jeep had got stuck in the narrow street owing to the snarl caused by the watermelon vendors, and after all these years, we understood why the watermelon vendors chose to open shop in that narrow spot; it was difficult for the police to enter the moholla that street led to, and even before they could reach we got the news of their coming, and so we could be prepared; we asked a question to the policemen who had got stuck, the question came to our minds all of a sudden because, as the watermelon vendor cut open a watermelon just then, revealing its bright red inside, the brightness of its colour seemed incredible to us, and we asked the policeman, 'Say, bhai, do you think watermelons can be adulterated?' The policeman from the Sutrapur Police Station sitting inside the immobilized vehicle didn't reply, he glared at us, and we then returned to our houses, each of us carrying a big, pumpkin-like watermelon, and then we in the moholla heard an expression of exceptional intelligence and taste by our womenfolk; when we bought watermelons, the vendor would cut and pull out a square piece and show us the richness of its red colour, and after we had examined it, he would say, 'It's just like butter,' and put the piece back in its place, and when we brought these watermelons home, our wives at first took the cut piece out again and we heard them exclaiming, 'It's so red, it's like I have pulled my heart out of my chest!' When we heard that, we were amazed at first, and after that, different kinds of reactions went through our minds, we thought: why didn't we think of this before, and where did these women get this idea from? Would such a simile regarding a watermelon be found in the poems of Azizul Haque? And do our wives read his poetry? We thought that perhaps they did, but at the same time we wondered, did our wives understand Azizul Haque's poetry when they read it? We didn't know, but we felt dejected, because when we came to know about Jharna Basak, we felt angry with our teacher, Nani Basak; after all, we had completed our schooling in Graduates High School, replete with the ear-pulling and caning imparted by his hand, and then begun working in lathe or glass workshops or shops selling spare parts for old cars or electrical appliances for our livelihoods, but were still unaware of the fact that Nani Basak had a daughter, and we felt assailed by the sense of having wasted our lives when Jharna Basak became a heroine in the cinema and we discovered her; we went to Rupmahal cinema hall and saw her either in the film *Chanda* or in *Talash*, or in both; seeing her, we became more melancholy, because we realized how exceptionally beautiful she was, but she didn't belong to us; we thought that with her having become a film heroine we had lost her; she had been so close by, perhaps somewhere in Twin Bridge or Banagram or Padmanidhi lane, or somewhere else, in some old and dilapidated house, only we never knew; we decided that we would call Nani Basak teacher one day and ask him whether Jharna Basak was really his daughter; but we didn't find time for that, we left school and our grief over Jharna Basak gradually waned, but we did not forget about her; when we then heard that Azizul Haque had started writing poetry, we wondered: what does he write poems about? Because we had never come across a single poem of his; however, we had no doubt that we would come across some poem like 'Our little stream loops ahead' or 'Morning has dawned, open the door', or perhaps some love poem involving Jharna Basak, because after putting up with all the torture by Nani Basak, did Azizul Haque have any option but to be stricken with grief over Jharna Basak? We didn't think so, but by the time Azizul Haque became insane and was taken to the mental asylum in Pabna, we were able to get only a single poem of his and we could not comprehend its meaning; however, we had learnt something regarding watermelons, so we asked the policemen, 'Would you like to have some watermelon?' They rebuffed us, 'Dhut,' and we laughed, because we always felt like laughing when we saw the police; we realized that watermelons were like eggs, they might go bad but they couldn't be adulterated; but in the course of time, this matter pushed us into another kind of confusion: after producing one and a half maunds of nuts and bolts, ten maunds of bread-biscuits-lozenges and seven gross of drinking glasses in the moholla each day, we found out in the late afternoon or evening one day, that watermelons could be adulterated, that red-coloured, sweetened water was injected into whitish watermelons as a result of which the watermelon turned red and sweet, and when we heard about this we were both surprised and angry, we wondered whether any values at all would remain to be cherished in life! We then heard the melody of a flute wafting through the moholla, our wives stood at the windows listening eagerly, we observed them, and we remembered that even this most innocent fruit, the watermelon, was being adulterated; we then cut the watermelons into slices, but looking at their red insides we were unable to fathom whether the colour was real or fake; thanks to watermelons, the problem of knowing too much became clear to us, knowledge destroyed the peace of mind we had enjoyed so long, and we said, 'Bloody women are after all only women, even watermelons can be fake!' But then, after a while, we saw Shefali; we were standing in line in front of a wall and pissing, a leg of our shorts rolled up, and after that when we turned around, we saw that Shefali was returning from school; we boys saw the sapling of a plant in her hand and immediately recognized it, we didn't know how we did, but we did, and we screamed out, 'Hello, Shefali Flowering Plant!' We observed that as Shefali went by, she turned her tired face and looked, and looking at her face we couldn't figure out who or what we had called 'Shefali Flowering Plant', whether it was the plant sapling, or Shefali, and then, after that, it occurred to us that we had found the solution to our earlier dilemma regarding Shefali: she was neither a flower nor a plant, Shefali was Shefali Flowering Tree; when we were convinced about this, we found out about Mamun who lived in the house on No. 25: he had done something great, we learnt that he had gone up to the watermelon vendor and asked him, 'Miya, why do you come with adulterated watermelons?' But the watermelon vendor couldn't understand him, and when we heard about it, at first we thought that the watermelon vendor had really not been able to understand him, watermelon vendors were idiots after all, because unless that was the case they wouldn't be selling watermelons, they too would buy and eat them like us; but later, it occurred to us that it was the watermelon vendor who was actually cunning, he forsook eating watermelons and thus saved money, and when Mamun asked him, he deliberately pretended not to understand, saying, 'What are you saying?' But when Mamun explained the matter to him once again, he laughed, and we were convinced about his cunning; he cut out a small slice of watermelon and rubbed it on the lower end of the white shirt Mamun was wearing, it made a red stain, and Mamun declared with a triumphant air, 'Where did this colour come from, Miya? And you say you don't inject colour!' But things weren't over yet, the watermelon vendor then scraped off a pinch of moss from the wall nearby and rubbed it on Mamun's shirt, and now there was a green stain beside the red one on the white shirt, and he asked, 'Well, now?' There was nothing Mamun could say; when we heard about this incident, we tested it ourselves, and we also had nothing to say, and so our wives would cut the watermelon in small, square pieces and bring it in a bowl, we picked up the pieces and put them into our mouths and the pieces of watermelon kept melting inside our mouths like candy floss, as did the womenfolk in our hands; holding the watermelon bowl in one hand and a breast of our young wives in the other, we realized the significance of round objects in the world; then one day, we fled from school and went to Balaka cinema hall to watch the English film *And When She Was Good*, we remember Azizul Haque was also with us; we couldn't understand the English dialogue of this film, but spotting a watermelon in a scene of the film, all of us, with the exception of Azizul Haque, were delighted; the heroine in the film was trying to obtain a job as a hairdresser, and was practising shaving men by using a watermelon as a dummy on which she applied the lather; although our fathers swore at us for watching films with kissing scenes, we understood that that there were many things to learn in life; all of us, with the exception of Azizul Haque, completed school, and our beards and moustaches went on sprouting, and when we kept nicking our cheeks and chins, the experience of watching the English film proved useful for us, we realized the importance of practice when it came to shaving one's beard, and so we went and bought watermelons, and they served two purposes: practising shaving, and eating, and we applied lather on the surface of the watermelon and cleared it with a razor without scratching its skin, and thus we became adept at shaving; and Azizul Haque was the only one in the moholla who was unshaved, and his hair grew long and reached his shoulders, all because there was a deep and strong contempt for watermelons in his very blood; we heard that when his father, Abdul Gafoor, called the moholla folk 'greedy watermelon gobblers', the people in turn had called them 'a tribe of madcaps', and when Azizul Haque was studying in Salimullah College, his hair came down in twisted locks, and we remembered Kazi Nazrul Islam or Rabindranath and remarked, 'He's got a poet's look,' and we found that our surmise was indeed true, because we learnt that Azizul Haque wrote poetry; but we could not comprehend his poetry, one day we came across a poem by him in some literary journal, and we then tried to read it, the poem was like this: there were three dots in front / on the right and left, and / in the centre / or / there was a line / running from right to left, or / from left to right / or there was a sentence like a line / because there was no meaning then / because the sentence was a line then / and the line was a dot, or / there was meaning then / the line was a sentence then / and the sentence was life / because there were dreams then / the sentence was words then / but there were no dreams then / we were asleep amidst the oppression of awakening / the bud of love wasn't there within our sleep / because the sentence was a line then / the line was three dots / on earth / on water / and in the sky / because there was no meaning then / and your words / were different words; when we failed to comprehend any meaning in Azizul Haque's poem, we bought watermelons and cut and ate them and remarked, 'He's mad!' After that, when he emerged on the street one day without a lungi, we took him to the lunatic asylum and left him there; the moholla was then suffused with fragrance, and returning home from school, we dropped our books and rushed towards Kafiluddin Byapari's new biscuit factory; there, we found that the workers were making biscuits from kneaded flour on a long, high table and putting them on metal trays, while below, on the floor, a group of people were sitting on the spread-out bed sheets, waiting, and then the moulovi arrived, and we recited the milad, 'Ya Nabi Salamalaika', the song of praise of the Holy Prophet, and when the recitation concluded, the workers opened the four hut-like doors of the oven, inserted a long wooden ladle that looked like the oar of a boat and brought out a tray with the first biscuits manufactured in this factory, and Kafiluddin and his sons filled small paper packets with these biscuits and put them into our hands; in the same way, after the milad was recited, we got a share of the first lozenges manufactured in Haji Abdur Rashid's lozenge factory, but after the lathe machine was installed, a 440-volt, 1-2 horsepower motor was installed, and a crowd of us went to see Abdul Jalil's workshop, and once again, after the recitation of the milad, we ate jilapis; and amidst the noise and sweet fragrance in the moholla, we remembered Putul, the lame girl, and we said to Kafiluddin Byapari's son, 'Putul was unable to come, give us some biscuits for her,' but we couldn't deliver the packet of biscuits intended for Putul Begum, because after getting caught up in various hassles, we ate it up ourselves, and we then scented a floral fragrance and our wives said, 'It's the smell of shefali flowers'; surpassing the sweet aroma spread by the biscuit and lozenge factories, this fragrance came wafting, and our wives then fell into confusion, was it the shefali flower or hasnahana? We hadn't seen any flowers in the moholla in a long time, but hearing mention of the hasnahana, we remembered that during winter the powerful fragrance of the hasnahana attracted snakes, but we hadn't seen any snakes in the moholla in a long time either; we then asked for jilapis for Aslam Byapari's lame elder daughter, Putul Begum, and dangling our legs as we sat at the temple hang-out, we ate them ourselves, and then we learnt about an incident from our wives and waited for Putul on the street of the moholla, but she didn't come, and so we went to Aslam Byapari's house, which was joined to the boundary wall of Abdul Gafoor's house, and that afternoon we saw Putul standing at one end of their outer veranda and looking over the wall towards Abdul Gafoor's house; when she turned to look at us, the grace of her beautiful, fair-skinned face and the black mole on her upper lip perturbed us, but as we looked downwards, we saw her disabled leg dangling in her shalwar; we figured that Aminul Haque, who was across the wall, could only see the girl's face, he couldn't see the lower part with the leg resting on a staff, and that's how the incident occurred; we were assailed by so many complications pertaining to watermelons, the moholla was divided along the lines of men and women, and the cessation of watermelon consumption, which was the sole source of delight in our lives, commenced, because our wives refused to touch them; we realized yet again that nothing was pure, and we learnt that our wives heard this tale from Alamgir Hossain's wife: Alamgir Hossain had gone to Bogura to attend a meeting or convention of the factory owners' association, and somewhere on the way, although he was unable to say exactly where, somewhere near Bera or Ullapara or Sherpur, seeing vine-like plants growing on straw laid out on the earth in a vast field, he recognized them, because large, egg-like, white watermelons lay all over the field, and then he witnessed this scene: a man, probably a peasant, squatting with his back to the road and his backside uncovered, was defecating in the watermelon field; we were sad to hear this news, we became melancholy, but it wasn't possible for us to give up our addiction to watermelons, we bought watermelons as we returned home, and our wives vomited when they saw the fruit, and so when we sat at the temple hang-out we became annoyed; after repeated urges to urinate, and standing in front of a wall thrice to urinate through the opening of our shorts, we had to sit in silence, because with the road having become a slimy bog on account of the rain, we couldn't use it as a playground, and then the rear wheel of a green-coloured lorry carrying bricks for the construction of Abdur Rashid's lathe workshop got stuck in a pothole in the muddy slime in front of Ali Akbar's house, and we immediately left the temple veranda and flocked around the lorry like the watermelon flies to watch the spectacle; but we couldn't forget about the peasant, so we went once again to the watermelon vendor, and going up to him, we asked, 'Why are the village folk so filthy? The bastards expose their arses,' and we picked up the watermelon cut into cubes from the bowl and put it into our mouths, but our wives didn't eat it, and it occurred to us that we didn't like eating it all alone, and then we had a feeling or realization: by trying to eat watermelons all by ourselves, we had become aware of the importance of our wives in our lives; the watermelon vendor then rescued us from this predicament of ours, he said, 'Wash it with soap before eating it,' and we brought home a cake of Bangla soap each, and then, when we heard the flute's melody, we remembered having met Putul; it occurred to us that when the teacher Abdul Gafoor's younger son first arrived from the village, he had brought a flute along with him, but his flute was different, we had never heard anyone in the moholla playing such a flute until then, and before Aminul Haque arrived in the neighbourhood, we used to play the flute by blowing at its base, but seeing his flute we were at a loss, since this was like a tube with both ends open, there was no arrangement to blow at the base, the blow-hole to play the flute was at one end, on the surface of the tube; when we tried to play this flute and were unsuccessful, the lame Putul probably heard it and her curiosity grew, because we thought that lame folk were like that, that because they themselves were unable to walk, their minds wandered through distant alleys; we then realized how fortunate we were, because like Putul's, our legs too could have become ineffective like dry twigs from polio, but that hadn't happened, and then hearing about this good fortune of ours, our wives once again agreed to eat watermelons with us, so we sent our servants and bought shavings of ice, and when we mixed the ice with the pieces of watermelon in the bowl and then put them into our mouths and looked at our wives, they pressed the buttons on the two-in-one radios and said, 'There's Amin bhai's programme on the radio today,' and then we heard a prolonged wail of the flute, which made us terribly restless, so we went once again to the watermelon vendor and asked whether watermelons were really the eggs of plants, but he replied that one didn't get watermelons from watermelon plants but horses, but again, nobody hatched horses from watermelons either, because there were mares to produce baby horses; when we heard about horse's eggs, we understood that on some day, Aminul Haque had stopped playing the flute and looked across the wall of their house, and he spotted an egg-like face over it; we learnt about all this in detail, or perhaps we didn't hear about it in detail but only learnt a bit about it: as he gazed at Putul's face, Aminul kept edging closer to the wall, and one day he looked over to the other side, and that day he discovered that the woman was lame, but there was no way for him to turn back then, because the number of people in the moholla grew, work began in the lathe-machine workshops, and Babul Miya and his companions screamed as they played cops-and-robbers on the street of the moholla and caused us headaches, we bought and swallowed Codopyrin tablets for the headaches, but the pain didn't ease, then Yakub Ali, the cloth merchant from Patuatuli, installed the fourth lathe machine of the moholla, and the machine was brought by lorry, packed in a large wooden crate, and lowered, but it proved to be difficult to carry through the doorway of Byapari saheb's house on No. 64, we then got the news, and applying Salonpas patches on both our temples, we went to Yakub Byapari's house and took a look at the machine and volunteered to help the workers who had been hired to push the thing in; when four lathe machines began functioning in our moholla, we heard the noise they made and we remembered Haji Mohammad Abdur Rashid Byapari; we felt sad, thinking of how we hadn't been able to insert his name and the story of his having swallowed watermelon seeds into the Deputy Prime Minister's speech, and when we asked that a copy of the full text of the speech be given to each of us, Alamgir Hossain got it photocopied at his expense and gave it to us, and we read it several times and fell asleep; even in our sleep, we could feel the headache and smell the menthol in the Salonpas patch; we then saw her, turning her tired face over her shoulder, she looked at us, and then we knew the real thing about watermelons and realized how deeply we were connected to them; after we ate all the biscuits and jilapis meant for Putul while we sat in the temple veranda, we heard about her meeting Aminul Haque by looking across the top of the boundary wall and we went to her house and said, 'So you're having a love affair!' We came to know that actually there were two people who had fallen in love with Aminul Haque, and then we discovered a racket: the supply of watermelons reduced and their price kept rising, and finally one day, we got the news that the watermelon vendor had come to the moholla with only three watermelons; hearing that, we became furious, we went up to him, struck his shoulder and knocked him on his head and said, 'Are you're playing the fool with us?' But the supply of watermelons didn't increase; the watermelon vendor cut the three fruit into slices and laid them on a gamchha spread out on the ground, we bought a slice each and ate it standing on the street, we remembered the famine, our lives turned sorrowful, there was only a breast of our wives in one of our hands, the other was empty, we were deprived of the pleasure of our wives' company; we then caught hold of the watermelon vendor once again, and he told us that watermelons from Rajshahi, Bogura and Chattogram had failed to arrive because of the transport strike, and so we needed to know why there was a transport strike; we went to Dr Wajed's clinic in Twin Bridge and found that day's *Ittefaq* there and learnt that a transport strike was on because the prices of truck tyres, tubes and spare parts had risen drastically; we then thought that there needed to be a speedy resolution of this crisis, so we went to the people in the moholla who ran spare-parts shops and learnt the two reasons for the rise in the prices of spare parts: first, those who produced these parts locally had tripled their prices, and second, the duties that were levied on the import of motor parts had been increased by twenty per cent and now amounted to forty-five per cent; we in the moholla had, by then, started using modern home appliances like grinders and blenders and so on, and our wives had learnt to make watermelon juice using them, and when we sipped it, it occurred to us that there was no end to the qualities of the watermelon, and that's why we looked for Alamgir Hossain and told him, 'Please do something for us, the price of watermelons has risen, watermelons that sold for ten taka earlier now sell for thirty taka, how will we survive?' He then told us that prices of the raw materials needed in his lathe machine operations had risen, taxes had been levied, and besides, the prices of daily requirements like rice, dal, watermelons and so on had risen too, and so what could he do? Hearing him, we understood how the price of watermelons rose, how the watermelon raised its price by itself through a racket, and we discovered the position of South Moishundi in this racket, but we could find no way to bring down the price of watermelons, the price stabilized at twenty-five taka, and so the prices of the biscuits, lozenges, and nuts and bolts manufactured by us also rose; how a wonderful thing like a watermelon had made our lives difficult! But our experience with regard to watermelons expanded, because the powerful, sweet fragrance of hasnahana and the plaintive melody of the flute in our moholla came wafting through the air, and later, when we thought about it, we realized how beneficial and profitable eating watermelons was, it wasn't just that it kept both mind and body cool, it also brought a sense of purpose in life, or else man lost his way in emptiness; we then gazed at the face of Putul Begum, who was trapped within a sound mind and disabled body, and hearing us, her face turned melancholy, we felt bad looking at her face, that's why we continued to sit near the truck that had got stuck in the puddle to watch the spectacle, and we came to know about all the work that needed to be done in order to pull a truck out of a puddle, and sensing then that something was visible through the bottoms of our shorts, we stood up; the truck driver's helper then fixed a jack under the rear axle and turned its handle, thus raising the wheel, and then, after carefully inserting pieces of broken bricks under the wheel, the driver fired the engine and pressed the accelerator, and the vehicle swung out of the pothole and emerged; we then returned home dejectedly, and our wives got annoyed because of the odour of grease from the lathe machines on our hands, 'It's awful,' they said, and we looked at our hands, we turned them this way and that, and it occurred to us that we wouldn't be able to survive if we didn't have hands, it wasn't just that we worked with our hands and survived, it was also easy to protect one's hands, they hung down at a safe distance, they didn't have to bear their own weight, while one's legs had to do so, it was difficult to protect one's legs, they fell into potholes and broke, dogs and snakes bit them, and it was because he had legs that Aminul Haque died; after hearing about that, we went to the watermelon vendor, and when we held a watermelon in our palms with the ten fingers of our two hands spread like lines of longitude, and gazing blankly at the sky tried to grasp the matter, it then occurred to us that there was a relation between snakes and women; we then asked the watermelon vendor a lot of complicated questions regarding watermelons: about why watermelons didn't grow all year long, and we thought that this needed to be solved; then, the first fridge in the moholla arrived at Ali Akbar Byapari's house, and a group of us went to see the fridge and drank cold water and heard a litany of its praises, and it occurred to us that perhaps it would be possible for us to eat watermelons all year long, but that didn't happen, our crisis persisted and this anguish never left us, and so we always felt dizzy; we then went to watch the night show of a movie at Nishat cinema hall, *Naginir Prem*, about the love of female snakes, and we learnt that a lot of snakes were women and a lot of women were snakes; and then we asked the policemen whether or not watermelons could be adulterated, because we thought that if watermelons could be adulterated, then why couldn't women be snakes and snakes be women, but the policemen didn't reply to our query, they collected Abdul Gafoor's dead body from his deserted house and took it away, and we demolished this house that had belonged to Rahima Bibi and built a mosque there; because female snakes always fell in love with men, female snakes had love affairs, and when they fell in love they became terrifying; we realized that Aminul Haque had not seen this movie, because we thought that was the rule, that the person in whose life something happens wouldn't know about it, wouldn't see anything, or else before something happened everyone would know everything about it, and so whatever had to transpire would not; we found out that half a woman and a full snake appeared in Aminul Haquc's life, we could understand that both of them had been drawn by the fragrance of a flower and the melody of a flute, and it occurred to us that this was natural, because it was not feasible to stock twelve months of watermelon rations in the fridge, and so we had to wait once again for Haji Abdur Rashid to be unwell, and like always, this time too he didn't disappoint us, and one day we got news of his being unwell and confined to bed and we thought that something would happen now, and something did happen: when he got annoyed lying in bed, he felt like having watermelon, but it was not the season for watermelons then, his five sons and three sons-in-law went all around Thatari Bazar, Raysha Bazar, Badamtali and Shyam Bazar and returned empty-handed, all the fridges in the mohalla were searched, but watermelon was simply not available; we were terribly sad then, and that was when Shefali, meaning Shefali Akhtar, planted shefali and hasnahana plants and we got the fragrance of the flowers, the power of the fragrance overwhelmed and frightened us because we could understand that too much of anything wasn't good, and so there was no way for Aminul Haque to turn back, he discovered the split existence of the woman on the other side of the wall standing amidst the melody of the flute and the fragrance of flowers, and then, one day, when Aminul Haque stretched his hand and touched Putul's face, he realized that Putul was silently crying; when we heard about all this, we could understand why she was crying, and we could hear Haji Abdur Rashid's words, his condition worsened, he wanted to have watermelon on the second day too, but since watermelons were unavailable, we told him about the seasonal character of watermelons; he already knew this, but hearing it in his bedridden condition, it seemed as if that was the first time he became aware of the fact, he became melancholy, and he called his sons to his bedside; he thought that when humans themselves weren't permanent, there was no way watermelons could be permanent, because both humans and watermelons were perishable; we then became aware of the relation between humans and matter, and when Aminul Haque's finger touched the wet mole on Putul's face, he thought or perhaps he sensed that tears were the melting heart flowing down, perhaps he unwittingly preferred half a woman to a full snake; he threw his flute near the hasnahana thicket and crossed over the wall and held this woman to his breast in the darkness; we later went, once again, to Nishat or Mukul or Shabistan cinema hall and saw a movie, *Behula*; in this movie, the eponymous heroine saves the hero

Lakkhindar even after he is bitten by a snake, and to us Putul Begum seemed to be like Behula, but she could not save Aminul Haque, perhaps his first kiss turned out to be his final kiss, because at dawn the next day, the dead body of the flautist of our moholla, Aminul Haque, was found lying near the hasnahana thicket, and we found out that he had died of snakebite; we later learnt that a female snake was madly in love with him, and female snakes don't know how to share love, so when Aminul Haque crossed over the wall and went to Putul, it lay in wait near the hasnahana thicket; we understood that this love of the female serpent was perhaps a one-sided affair, and we learnt how fierce one-sided love could be, and when, even on the fifth day, people returned empty-handed because watermelons were unavailable, Haji Abdur Rashid was anguished and began weeping, and then he gazed at his sons' faces, wiped his tears and said, 'I'm not going to survive,' and he really didn't survive; but his death opened up another new horizon in our moholla as the Haji Food Products Company was established in South Moishundi entirely for the purpose of canning watermelons; we heard from Haji Raisuddin, the eldest son of the company's proprietor, Haji Abdur Rashid, about his father's instructions, and we realized that even as Haji Abdur Rashid lay dying, his thinking faculties were clear, and since watermelons had been unavailable for five successive days when he wanted to eat them, he understood the depth of the crisis and said to his eldest son, Raisuddin, 'Set up a watermelon factory,' and then he passed away; we returned after burying him at the Postogola burial ground and knew that now we would get watermelons all year long, and we would not have to be dependent on peasants or nature; Haji Raisuddin then purchased a small plot of land lying vacant at the southern end of our moholla, and the construction work on the Haji Food Products Company's factory began at that site; we then went to Haji Raisuddin's house, and he explained his plans to us in detail, and we learnt that the watermelons would be cut, sorted, cleaned and then canned in sterile conditions in the factory, and that fifteen to twenty people from our moholla would get jobs there; when bricks and sand were once again piled up in the moholla, the local boys jumped up and down in the sand, and we were unable to forget about Haji Abdur Rashid, and we screamed out, 'Hello Shefali Flowering Plant,' but she was not to be found any longer, we had lost her,

(1995)

The Fig-Eating Folk

A MYSTERIOUS SMILE SEEMED TO be pasted on his face. The bottom of the right leg of his trousers was fastened with a bicycle clip, he had a pair of white canvas shoes on his feet, his white, full-sleeved shirt was tucked inside a pair of grey trousers, he had a worn-out, battered cloth hat on his head; and when he lifted his head in a slightly theatrical pose, one could see the vague smile on his face. Standing in this position, he inserted his left hand into his trouser pocket, raised his right arm sideways, like the branch of a tree, to the level of his shoulder, and in the evening light at Victoria Park, the people standing around him on the green grass saw that he held a dry, grey-coloured bone in his raised hand. 'What is this?' he asked, and looked successively at the faces of the people standing in front of him, among whom were boys as well as adults. Gazing at the hint of a smile on his face and the deep pool of light in his eyes, the people remained silent, the same kind of a hint of a smile quivering on their lips; they probably thought that there was some deeper question lurking behind his question, the answer to which they didn't know, or that the question itself was a trick question, and being adults they ought not to be trapped in such a trick; they realized that if what was obviously a bone was held up in the clear light of day and they were asked 'what is this', the matter became somewhat mysterious. Then the man once again waved the six-inch-long, slightly curved bone and said, 'Tell me, tell me what this is, look at it properly, look at it properly and tell me,' and when, even after that, the people standing there, facing him, remained silent, it seemed that the man intentionally wanted to mislead the people slightly, as if, unless that happened, the matter would not be complete; he said, 'Tell me, what is this? Tell me' – and after that he himself said, 'This is a bone, you see, here, below the throat, this is a bone from the collar.' After that, it was as if the boys and men standing around him felt like they had been freed. When the fact that the bone was really a piece of bone was declared, they laughed remembering their doubts thus far and slanted their heads and said, 'Yes, this is a bone'; and then they sensed that the man standing in front of them was waiting for just this moment, because, at once, keeping the smile on his face intact and making the light in his eyes deeper and giving them darting glances, he said, 'No, this is not a bone,' and saying so, he straightened his torso from its exaggerated backwards-leaning position and removed his left hand from his trouser pocket. After that, the smile on his face steadily transformed, and in its place a blank or perhaps a slightly sad expression became manifest. Moving his hatted head to the left and right, he said, 'This is no bone, this is a maiden, a woman, her name is Preetilata,' and saying that, the man again inserted his left hand into the pocket of his trousers and leaning backwards again, flashed a radiant smile. Waving the piece of bone held in his right hand a few times, he said, 'This is my lover, my wife, and if you people wait patiently, you'll be able to see Preetilata for yourself at the end of the show, she is a very beautiful maiden, I tell you the truth.' The man then began to laugh, and when the boys and men standing around him joined in the laughter, he feigned seriousness and asked the people not to laugh, 'Don't laugh, listen to me, is this a bone, or is it Preetilata? Is this Preetilata, or is it a bone?' Saying so, he laughed once again at his own words and said, 'All of you who are standing here, how many are you?' He counted and found that in that circle of people there were eleven who were fully men, by way of age, and he asked them, 'What's your name? Altaf Hossain; yours? Jasimuddin Ahmad; yours? Abdul Jalil; yours? Idris Ali; yours? Jyotibhushan Das; yours? Abdul Jabbar; yours? Abdul Gafoor; yours? Shahidul Huq; yours? Humayun Kabir; yours? Sharful Alam; and yours? Iliyas Ahmed.' After hearing the names of the eleven men, the man laughed and said, 'People have so many names and abodes,' and as he said that, it seemed he did give the matter importance, but at the same time, one got the sense that he was only joking. After having heard the names of the eleven people just the one time, he repeated them all out again, unfalteringly, and coming to the end, he said in a very jocular, unctuous tone, 'Are you really you? Or are you too only bone?' And then, in full view of the people standing in a circle around him, he placed on the grass the piece of bone he had displayed so long, spread a faded cotton sheet lengthwise over it, and said, 'Preetilata is sleeping here, or a piece of bone is sleeping here. In a little while she will rise and greet you.' The man then took out another bone of the same size and appearance from his black, poplin sling bag, and holding it aloft, he said, 'This is Abdul.' He laughed a bit, and then spoke again, 'My name is Mohabbat Ali the magician. I, Mohabbat Ali, and Abdul here, are present before you now and are at your service.' Mohabbat Ali the magician then took the piece of bone and drew a circle in the air, twice, and shutting his eyes he muttered various things, after that he burst into laughter and pinched the nose of a boy standing on his right, and at once, inside the boy's nostrils, quivering like a silver hilsa fish, was a half-taka coin. He threw the coin on the brown sheet spread on the grass, and expressed astonishment at the fact that boys kept money inside their noses when all of them had pockets on their shirts. When he said that, everyone tittered, and he went around the entire circle and pinched the noses of all the boys and went on taking out half-taka coins. Tiring after this play, Mohabbat Ali declared that frivolousness was actually not just an attitude common to children, and that adults too were frivolous by habit; and hearing him, the people standing in the circle became extremely excited, because they sensed that Mohabbat Ali would now change the direction of the attack and the game; they gazed with a nervous smile pasted on their faces and they warmed to the man. Mohabbat Ali removed the hat on his head and flung it on the sheet below, and then his shiny, completely bald head was visible to the audience; he bent forward and showed the people the middle of his head and rubbed the palm of his right hand on his bald pate, which looked like a bare, well-mopped courtyard; he laughed loudly to himself in an affected manner, and at the same time hastily straightened his body and said, 'Didn't I hear something?' The audience then once again saw that hint of a smile on Mohabbat Ali's lips and the slow flickering of dense light in his eyes, and they laughed nervously and waited. Mohabbat Ali seemed to be trying to hear something with his ears trained somewhere, after that he walked ahead and placed his hand on the bulging paunch of a fat man standing in the middle of the circle; the audience waited impatiently as Mohabbat Ali stroked the paunch twice and gently poked it, and at once everyone heard a funny sound, like the sound of bus horns in olden times, then when Mohabbat Ali went on poking the paunch, a *waon-waon* sound kept emerging and the audience present at Victoria Park laughed until they became restless. Then Mohabbat Ali again stood with his right arm held aloft and drew a circle in the air in front of him and stared blankly at the waiting people for a while, as if that too was part of the act, and after that, when he thought that the sequence of silence had gone on long enough, then, without moving the slightest bit and without making any sound whatsoever, he laughed like a circus clown, as if he had a stitch in his side, and the very next moment it was like a frozen, still picture suddenly melted, and Mohabbat Ali picked up the battered hat from the ground and set it on his head, and after a long and noisy spell of coughing, he declared that he was actually a fruit seller, and it was in order to gather people to buy his fruits that he showed all these magic tricks. Then he asked the fourteen boys and the eleven adults present there what their favourite fruit was, and the fruit that they would like to eat right now if they could get it. Of the twenty-five individuals present there, comprising boys as well as adults, thirteen wanted to eat grapes, seven wanted apples and four said pomegranate, the remaining man, who appeared to be middle-aged, said that he wanted to have a plum. Mohabbat Ali then looked at the people with wide eyes and pretended to be embarrassed for a while, after that he held the piece of bone named Abdul high in the air and began to have a conversation with it so that the people present could hear, and then, fixing his gaze on the audience, he said that he, and as he put it, his friend Abdul could not offer them grapes, apples and so on. He told them that, in fact, he sold only one kind of fruit, and the name of the fruit was fig. Flashing his habitual smile, he said, 'It's called a fig; actually its name is country-fig, the fruit grows in the forests and jungles of this country.' He said that he had a palatial house in Forashganj, right on the bank of the

Budiganga river, and he lived there with his wife, Preetilata, and Abdul too lived with them there. Behind the palace was an orchard spread over five square miles. 'It's my orchard,' he said, 'the three of us developed it together.' And he said that the orchard had only fig trees, bunches of yellow-coloured, round, ripe figs hung down from the branches, and the three of them survived eating only those figs, they didn't eat anything else; they sold the leftover fruit and used the money to buy clothes and suchlike, and they also bought kerosene for lighting the lamps because there was no electricity in their palace. Then the magician, Mohabbat Ali, took out another sheet of cloth from his sling bag and spread it on the ground and placed a square tin box, painted black, on top of it. The black box was a foot long in length, width and depth, and one side of it was open, with a hinged lid made of tin over it. Opening the lid, he held the box high in his hands and showed its empty interior to everyone and asked, 'Is there anything inside?' The boys present there screamed out, 'No, there's nothing,' and then Mohabbat Ali shut and locked the lid of the tin box and laid it on the sheet on the ground, and moving the piece of bone over the box in a circular fashion, he shut his eyes and muttered something for a minute, after that he opened his eyes, put the bone on the lid of the tin box and stood up. He told the people standing motionlessly around him that inside the box in front of him was the cream of dreams, and that in a little while he would serve it to them. Looking at the disbelief writ large on the faces of the people standing in front of him, he laughed and said that he would give a fig each, free, to all the twenty-five people present there to taste, and after that, if any of the adults wanted more, the price for half a dozen figs would be two taka. Following that announcement, Mohabbat Ali began his next item; he straightened his hat, pulled up its brim a bit, unrolled the sleeves of his shirt then folded them back again mindfully, and with his two feet struck the green grass with small blows as if he were dusting off his canvas shoes, and after that he picked up the piece of bone from the top of the tin box with utmost caution, and like before, drew a circle in the air and muttered for a while. And in this way, when he thought that the impatience of the people present there had reached its limit, he kneeled down and gave a small, intimate kiss to the piece of bone and put it inside his black sling bag and placed the palm of his right hand flat on the lid of the black tin box. He looked fixedly at the box for a while, as if he were trying to look into it from outside, and once he seemed certain about what was inside the locked box, he first unlocked it and after that he pulled open the lid with a tug and revealed the inside; at once, all the members of the audience present there cried out in joy and couldn't stop clapping; through the open end of the box was visible a branch with leaves that were long like donkey's ears, and green and rough. When the magician then laid down the open end of the box on the sheet of cloth he had spread out on the ground, the branch fell on the cloth and the people present there saw through the leaves several more small boughs, all full of yellow-coloured fruit. Mohabbat Ali laid his hat upside down on the cloth and began plucking the figs and depositing them inside the hat. When all the fruit had been plucked, Mohabbat Ali's hat looked like a wide-brimmed fruit bowl and the figs seemed about to overflow the brim. Mohabbat Ali then emptied the contents of the hat on the cloth and counted the figs as he put each one back again into the cavity of the hat, after which he stood up and said, 'Ninety-nine in all.' He then divided the people present there into two groups. On one side stood the boys, and on the other side the adults; after that he began the distribution and sale of his fruit. At first, the fourteen boys came one by one and picked up a fig each, and all of them then made a face and threw the figs on the ground. When it was the turn of the adults, they suspected there was a trick somewhere in this too and that as soon as they set foot in the trap of the deception everyone would burst out laughing. Nonetheless, once Mohabbat Ali invited them, the first man approached timidly, picked up a fig and put it into his mouth, and then when he began chewing it with great caution, the other people present there began to laugh; but the man did not pay any heed to that, he ate up the fig. When the others were beside themselves with laughter at what the man had done, Mohabbat Ali clapped his hands and shouted out, 'How was it?' Responding to this query, the fig-eating man said that he liked it, he liked it very much and he wanted to eat some more. Mohabbat Ali then put six figs in a small polythene packet and handed it to the man, and taking two taka from him, he put it into a small tin box inside the black sling bag. That day, or that evening, things took a different turn just after this; Altaf Hossain, Jasimuddin, Abdul Jalil, Idris Ali, Jyotibhushan, Abdul Jabbar, Abdul Gafoor, Humayun Kabir, Shahidul Huq, Iliyas Ahmed – all of them took six ripe figs packed in small polythene packets and stood in front of the magician, Mohabbat Ali, and one could sense a kind of lustre on their faces, but they were silent. Mohabbat Ali put the twenty-two taka he had collected inside the box in his sling bag, picked up the cloth spread on the ground and stood up straight, and in the lacklustre light of late afternoon he gazed at the faces of the eleven new fig consumers, and the meaning of what he then said to the gathering in front of him was difficult for them to give due consideration to; he said that he remembered the names of all those he ever sold figs to for his whole life; that's why, he said, they ought to consume the fruit slowly, so that some figs remained until the end of their days. After that, laughing heartily and expansively, he said, 'Come now, come and see the last trick'; and following that announcement, he clapped his hands loudly a few times and shouted out, 'Come, dear Preetilata, come my sweetheart, come, let's go home.' Then the people who were now standing around in a disorderly fashion, remembered Preetilata, they realized that, after having bought the figs, they had broken the circle and were now facing Mohabbat Ali the magician while the forgotten Preetilata lay behind them. Once they heard Mohabbat Ali calling out to Preetilata, they looked back, and beneath the brown-coloured sheet spread on the ground, where so far there had been only a piece of bone, the figure of a sleeping person could now be discerned. When Mohabbat Ali once again clapped his hands and shouted out, the figure beneath the sheet moved a little bit, and when Mohabbat Ali did the same thing for a third time, the figure sat up and removed the sheet with a single shove, and on the dust-laden grass of Victoria Park there appeared a young woman, as radiant as the full moon; and then, as if in a flash of lightning, the eleven men standing there realized this was Preetilata, this was the maiden in flesh and blood who had risen from the magician's walking-stick-shaped bone; they became extremely glum, and in front of their gloomy eyes, Mohabbat Ali tucked the black cloth sling bag into the carrier at the back of his cycle, and with the salwar-kameez-clad Preetilata sitting on the rod in front, he cycled away, ringing the bell, *trring-trring*; he went past Muslim High School and then towards Bangla Bazar before going out of sight. A week after this incident, Mohabbat Ali was once again to be found on the expanse of green grass at Victoria Park, and that day, at the end of a show full of various kinds of tricks in front of a rapt and astonished audience, when he began to distribute the magical figs, he was able to identify two individuals standing in the adults queue; 'You've bought figs earlier,' he said, and he separated those two from the queue and sold the figs to the other seven at two taka for a packet of six. Then he looked at the two old fig-eaters. 'Is your name Abdul Gafoor?' The man nodded. 'And are you Shahidul Huq?' The other man too shook his head in acknowledgement. Then Mohabbat Ali the magician told them that they would now have to pay a price of four taka for six figs. Abdul Gafoor and Shahidul Huq agreed to it, and Mohabbat Ali once again advised them not to consume the six figs in a hurry and went off on his cycle with Preetilata, who had risen from a bone of the clavicle that had been covered with a sheet. After that, one or another of the old fig-eaters like Altaf Hossain, Sharful Alam, Abdul Jalil, Iliyas Ahmed, etc. was to be found in Mohabbat Ali's magic show assemblies, and six months later, the sound of Mohabbat Ali the magician's tabor could be heard at the small traffic island in front of the main gate of the Christian burial ground at the intersection of Narinda Road and Tipu Sultan Road, and that day, when he began distributing figs at the end of his show, Abdul Gafoor could be spotted among the people standing in queue; he was standing in the queue to buy figs for the sixth time. When he had bought the figs for the fifth time, the price for six figs had been thirty-two taka, and this day, after giving him six figs in a polythene packet, when Mohabbat Ali demanded sixty-four taka as the price of the figs, Abdul Gafoor emitted an inaudible groan and returned home without buying any. After that, Abdul Gafoor was regularly spotted at Mohabbat Ali's magic shows, but he didn't buy any figs because of the exorbitant price, he just sat nearby and watched the magician selling his figs. It was thus that he discovered the other old fig-eaters, namely Abdul Jalil, Sharful Alam, Shahidul Huq and Idris Ali, and he saw that, like him, they too sat on one side and silently observed the magician's activities. They didn't get up to buy figs. These five old fig-eaters, who had eaten up their fruit quickly and could not buy any more now because of the exorbitant price, became acquainted with each other, and one day, at the end of the magic show, they surrounded Mohabbat Ali and pleaded with him that they were each eager to buy a plant of his figs, and for that they were prepared to pay a thousand taka each. Mohabbat Ali laughed when he heard that and went away shaking his head. But these five fig-eaters encountered each other regularly, and after having failed time and again to convince the magician, Mohabbat Ali, to sell them his fig plants, one day they decided to go to his house, and so one Saturday morning, after they had gone past Shyam Bazar, as soon as they looked southwards, they saw a very tall palatial building; they saw that right on the riverbank, as if on the river itself, there was an immense building with a golden dome that seemed to rise to the very sky. When the five fig-eaters went through the main entrance of the palace, which was emblazoned with the figure of a lion, they observed that the entrance, the grounds in front, and the stairs and veranda of the palace were all unguarded; they could not see any fig orchard, but they guessed that the orchard, which spanned five square miles, probably lay behind the palace, even though they could not see any path on the side leading to the rear. Then, walking across a terrace adorned with a row of circular pillars, they stepped into a room, and at once, the desolation there seemed to envelop them in fear; they saw large, ornately upholstered sofas lying all askew in the immense room. In that situation, they did not have the courage to advance any further; piercing the silence, they called out, 'Mohabbat Ali, where are you?' Then they spotted a door behind curtains, beside a cupboard near the rear wall of the room. A voice answered from behind the door, 'Come inside,' and the five fig-eaters recognized the voice, it was Mohabbat Ali's. They hesitated for a moment, and then moved the curtain aside and went in and saw that Mohabbat Ali was lying on a high cot, on a bed made of white feathers. Seeing them, Mohabbat Ali got down from the bed and inquired, 'Why have you people come to my house!' He told them that there were no fig plants for sale, and that they ought to go back, 'Please go away, don't disturb us.' When the five fig-eaters heard Mohabbat Ali say that, they looked all around but they could not see anyone else there, and then Mohabbat Ali said that the three of them had been resting after tending to the fig trees in the morning, and soon they had to practise their magic tricks. The five fig-eaters then saw a bone lying on the feather bed and another on a round, one-legged table in one corner of the room. They guessed that the one on the bed was Preetilata and the one named Abdul was on the table; although they had seen Preetilata rise up from the bone, they had not seen Abdul other than in the form of the bone. They realized that there was only one person in physical existence in the vast palace, and that was the magician, Mohabbat Ali. They requested him once again to give each of them a fig plant; they said that they could not survive by eating only a few figs, and now so much money was needed to buy the figs that they could obtain them only through hard toil; and they could not bear such hard toil any more, that's why, they said, 'Please give us a plant each, we'll pay you money.' Mohabbat Ali became very annoyed then, and suddenly grew enraged; he screamed out that the fig plants were not for sale and he asked them to leave the palace at once. Observing the magician's furious countenance, the trespassing fig-eaters fled in fear to the room outside, and just as they were about to exit this room, Abdul Gafoor opened the door of a cupboard placed by the wall and they saw various things stored on different shelves in it. They saw the black cloth there, a bundle of rope, the tin box, an iron rod, a skull, two large knives, a fig branch with dry leaves, and a spear with a short shaft; and then, in that mysterious environment of semi-darkness inside the room, the five fig-eaters lost all sense of the consequence of their actions. Abdul Gafoor picked up the knife, and following his lead, the others too picked up the spear and iron rod. When the five of them then re-entered the inner room, they found Mohabbat Ali lying on his back on the feather bed. They smashed his skull with merciless blows of the iron rod to his head, and then, striking him with the knives and the spear, they severed his head from his body. Leaving the magician, Mohabbat Ali, dead on the bed, they entered the interior of the palace and advanced towards the fig orchard at the back, and in this way, as they went through one room after another, they suddenly heard a soft yet definite sound, and they stopped running, they stood still, and saw that the building was splitting into two like an eggshell, with a soft, crackling sound. They stood dumbfounded in this split shell for a few moments, and then they ran in the opposite direction in order to get out, and when they left the building and reached near the lion entrance, they seemed to come back to their senses, and then, looking back, they could not see any trace of the gold-domed building, they couldn't see any grounds or even the lion entrance, they found themselves beside a sawmill on the bank of the Budiganga river, by the water; at first they thought that whatever had happened so far was a dream, but then they saw the iron rod and knives in their hands and their clothes all bloody. They hastily flung the weapons in their hands into the river and washed off the blood on their clothes, and they felt a great sense of terror as well as a kind of languor, their eyes and faces became flushed, and their bodies were trembling too. In a state of semi-consciousness, driven entirely by an instinctive force of willpower, the five fig-eaters made their way to Lakshmi Bazar, or to the alley in Padmanidhi Lane, to Narinda or Dayaganj, Kalta Bazar or Rokonpur, or Kagjitola or Shahsahab Lane or Banagram, and stood in front of their respective homes. That Saturday afternoon, leaving the world behind with bloodshot eyes and trembling bodies, they entered their rooms to lie down on their beds, and because of high temperature and physical convulsions, their folks covered them up with sheets. After that, although their folks were unable to say exactly how many minutes or how many hours later, but after a while, they entered the room and looked towards the bed and did not see the figure of any person under the sheet. At the time, they thought the person had probably gone to the bathroom, but they could not find him in the bathroom; and then this person, the one who had not so long ago got into the habit of eating country-figs, could not be found anywhere in the entire house. The folks at home then lifted up the sheet spread on the bed, and in five homes in Lakshmi Bazar or Narinda, Dayaganj or Banagram, they saw a grey-coloured piece of bone lying on the bed. And now, the people of all these localities talk about those fig-eating folk, they talk about the agony and the ecstasy of fig-eating, and they talk about the outcome of being unmindful of consequences.

(1992)

The Breeze of the Dolu River

THE DOLU RIVER WAS BRIMMING, or perhaps there wasn't that much water, but nonetheless a moist breeze wafted in from that direction, and accompanying the breeze was the smell of shit from the clump of bamboo at the riverbank. Ahmad Taimur Ali Choudhury lay suspended like a bundle on a low easy chair by the side of the road in front of his house. Perhaps he had fallen asleep as he lay in the sun, or perhaps, despite the smell of dry shit carried by the morning breeze of the Dolu river, his eyes had shut on their own in pleasure. He lifted his right leg over his left knee, and as a result his lungi gaped, exposing his ancient, brown-coloured balls which looked like a large palmyra fruit.

As the people of Satkania, those who were going to the market, or returning from there to Boyaliapara or Satipara, walked past the mosque, they observed Taimur Ali lying asleep on his easy chair with his lungi gaping, and perhaps they were struck by how big his balls were, or perhaps they didn't notice anything at all, perhaps they thought there was no point in seeing the same sight every day, perhaps they only gazed at his slanted face as he lay huddled on the canvas sheet of the easy chair, perhaps there were one or two blue or black flies sitting on his face, licking the drool leaking from the corner of his mouth; after that, when it became too hot in the sun, he left the easy chair and headed towards his house where his wife, the elderly Somorto Banu, had prepared breakfast and was waiting for him.

When Taimur Ali got off the easy chair and stood up, it was evident that he was lame, because when he walked he had a pronounced limp; perhaps some scoundrelly students of the Satkania Model High School sometimes shouted out to him, calling him 'Taimur the Lame'. Although the elderly Taimur Ali's even older Ma, Golenur Begum, definitely knew the history behind the lameness, if she was asked about the subject, she was at a loss, or pretended to be. When she was queried, she first tried to rise from her prone state in the dark room and sit atop her dirty quilt, and then when she couldn't rise, she lay atilt on the bed, and she held up a shrivelled hand in front of her eyes, which looked like that of a mummy whose skin was wrapped around its bones, waved it in the air and said in an irritated tone, 'Hey, are you asking about my Taimur, my boy? He's there, take a look, he's at home.'

After that, when she was told that no one was looking for her son Taimur, and that actually she was being asked how he became lame, was Golenur Begum still unable to hear that? Because she replied, 'But we were in Burma, I can't remember whether it was in Akiya or Pegu. I was two years old when my boy Taimur's dad came there and married me.'

Since that seemed an impossible age for marriage, she was told that, and eventually, after counting her fingers and the lines on her fingers, she was willing to concede that she was nine or ten then; they had crossed the mountains and the sea and had travelled by ship and sampan, and had arrived at the dock on the Shonkho river in Dohazari; perhaps the railway station was nearby then, but there was no bridge over the river. She said that she didn't remember anything after that, 'I've forgotten, my son!' Consequently, the third time she was asked how Taimur Ali became lame, she fervently tried to explain that her son was certainly not lame when he was born, and that he became lame later. And then, because she was exhausted from all that agitation or from talking, she stopped moving her hand about, put it down beside her and shut her eyes, and then she said, 'It was in his fate, his fate!'

Perhaps it was that, and it was his fate that was to blame; the wheel of Ahmad Taimur Ali Choudhury's fate was set in motion when he was twenty-seven or twenty-eight.

When he got up, after having napped on the canvas easy chair with his lungi gaping, one of his four sons, or the servant boy, or his son-in-law, or one of his grandchildren, or the driver of his personal motor car was sitting in the outer room and reading the two-day-old newspaper, or chatting, and seeing him, he asked, 'Will you be going to Chittagong? The car's ready, you can go if you want.'

'Why should I go to town?'

'What? Didn't you say that you were going to meet the DC or the SDO?

'I won't go today. I don't feel good today!'

He didn't explain why he didn't feel good today, or perhaps he remembered that he hadn't yet had his breakfast, and so, instead of going to the city of Chittagong to meet the DC or the SDO, he went inside the house, where Somorto Banu was waiting alone for him with his breakfast; because when he was at home, the responsibility of feeding Taimur Ali was entirely Somorto Banu's, and even a fly was forbidden to be in the room then. Taimur Ali sat on the cot with his legs folded, and ate freshly made rotis with a curry of papaya or eggplant or potol, or with sugar or jaggery; Somorto Banu remained standing, or she sat on the edge of the cot and observed him eating, and after that, she brought two glasses of water from the table in one corner of the room. Taimur Ali, who had grown old now, looked at the two glasses and said, 'You aren't planning to poison me today, are you?' Hearing that, Somorto Banu glared at him in reprimand, and she told him that she was her father's daughter after all, that her father's name was Jasimuddin, alias Jaissa Karati, and her mother was Ongmeching of Arakan, and so she was certainly true to her word; she had said that she would poison Taimur Ali and kill him, and she would definitely do that – so he ought to count his lucky stars every day for having survived so long! Taimur Ali then surrendered once again to this game, or to fate; he selected one of the two glasses of water in Somorto Banu's hands and drank the water, and on this day too he didn't die; Somorto Banu stood observing him, and after that she took the other glass to the courtyard outside and emptied it; and thus did the other people of the house come to know that Taimur Ali had finished his breakfast.

It would seem, then, that at least Golenur Begum perhaps knew what this was all about; but if she was asked, she would only say, 'I can't tell you.' Perhaps she didn't know, or perhaps she knew that this was a game, and that they played this game in accordance with the terms of a pact with Somorto Banu; perhaps in the course of time Taimur Ali tired of this, but Somorto Banu didn't spare him. After youth and middle age, the days of old age advanced, the ring Somorto Banu wore on the middle finger of her right hand became embedded in her flesh, or perhaps it became loose after she got old – nevertheless, Taimur Ali spent his days playing the game of dying, or not dying, from drinking the poisoned liquid Somorto Banu prepared by dipping her diamond ring in water. Taimur Ali had got involved with Somorto Banu, the daughter of Jaissa Karati and the Mog maiden Ongmeching, in the course of breaking his leg, or even before that, and the involvement went ahead unhindered, and so Taimur Ali agreed to his second pact with Somorto Banu. Perhaps he hadn't initially thought that the game of two glasses of water would turn so grave, perhaps he had thought that all these conditions and suchlike could be rendered futile through cunning and deception, like he had done before; or perhaps he had thought that maybe Somorto Banu wasn't telling the truth, that she was bluffing like she had done earlier, and that actually there was no poison or anything like that in the glass of water. He was assailed by such a suspicion several times during his life, and then it occurred to him that Somorto Banu had frightened him falsely just for fun. But Somorto Banu did not pay any heed to his suspicions; she continued the game throughout Taimur Ali's life, and on two occasions she proved her ability to poison and kill. The first time was on their wedding night itself, when she killed a cat, although it was Taimur Ali who ought to have done that, since he was the man; on the day of the wedding, once the moulovi of the mosque left after having them recite the kalema, Taimur Ali asked Somorto Banu in jest whether she would poison him that very day. But it seems Somorto Banu didn't take that joke lightly, because that night, when Taimur Ali was about to enter the nuptial chamber, he found that the room was locked from inside; after he banged on the door, Somorto Banu opened the door a bit and said that if the groom wished to enter the room, he must do so carrying two cats. Hearing that bizarre demand, everyone at home was annoyed, but since she was a new bride, people set out in search of cats and brought back a pair from the house of Akhtar Chacha, the barber, in Boyaliapara. That day, clad in an achkan and pyjamas, Taimur Ali entered the nuptial chamber holding a cat under each arm, and he saw that there were two small bowls of kheer, or payesh, and two brass or bell metal glasses with water on a table in a corner of the room. Perhaps he thought that this food and drink had been kept for him, for when he was exhausted, but when he entered the room, Somorto Banu placed one bowl of kheer each before the two cats. After they had eaten the kheer, one contented cat licked its lips and miaowed, while the other one jumped and fell spreadeagled on the floor, dead. Perhaps Taimur Ali got scared on seeing the fate of the unfortunate cat, and he quickly turned that fear into rage; he opened the door and flung the dead cat into the courtyard, and those who knew the old story of the cat being killed perhaps derived a sense of delight in thinking that Taimur Ali had killed a cat on his nuptial night! Although it was Somorto Banu who had killed the cat, looking at Taimur Ali's face right then, one would think that it was he who had killed it; he was almost emitting steam in fury, and that day, in the face of this monstrous combination of arousal and fury, Somorto Banu swayed like a blade of grass stricken by a storm. After that, when Taimur Ali went towards the table in order to drink water, he realized that there were two glasses filled with water. His excitement then abated, and he accepted the game; he lifted up one glass and drank from it, and Somorto Banu opened the window and threw out the water in the other glass. That was how it began, and there seemed to be no end to it after that; perhaps Taimur Ali once again began suspecting the matter to be a bluff, and then after many years, Somorto Banu killed a cat or a dog or a goat again and thus frightened Taimur Ali.

A long time went by after that, and Taimur Ali got old and began lying on the easy chair and falling asleep; then one day, when it became hot, he got up and went inside the house to have breakfast. Perhaps on this day he didn't feel like having rotis with a curry of potatoes or snake gourd or ash gourd, he wanted to have them with sugar; and so Somorto Banu left the room to fetch sugar. As old Taimur Ali sat there, he noticed that there were two glasses of water on the table in the corner of the room, and that's when it happened; perhaps it was the first time that the dangerous idea of investigating Somorto Banu's trick entered his head, or perhaps he was just very thirsty and did it unthinkingly – he got down from the cot and drank all the water from both the glasses.

This wheel had begun turning long ago, although when Taimur Ali returned from Burma it didn't seem like he was the kind of man to fall into such a trap. But one evening in the month of Agrahan or Poush, when the paddy had been harvested, as he went looking for a second mynah, he met Somorto Banu for the first time and thus fell into this predicament.

Ten years before spotting a mynah and losing his way, Taimur Ali broke his father Mowla Baksh Choudhury's wooden safe and disappeared; perhaps he boarded a sampan or ship and went to Akyab, and from Akyab to Rangoon or Pegu, and from there he perhaps went by train to Mandalay. God knows what he was doing there – he was doing well; but one day, he brushed off and cast aside his past and returned to his village. Satkania was still a village then, or a bit larger than a village even; perhaps leopards swam across the Dolu river and came and sat on a tree then, and perhaps at night herds of wild elephants descended from the forested Charamba hills. On getting back Taimur, her only surviving son, his mother was overjoyed, perhaps his dad was too, but the neighbours were not, because he created all kinds of crises with the young and almost young women of their households; the Husnearas and Manowaras and Roshanaras cried in secret, and their mothers bit the dirty, rag-like anchals of their saris and carried a grimace on their faces, and they went to Mowla Baksh and shed tears; two or four or ten drops of the distraught women's hot tears fell on the earth and made a mark, but there was nothing Mowla Baksh could do; fully aware of his advantageous position as the boy's dad, he said, 'I don't know. What can I do!'

Then one day, the misfortune of spotting a mynah descended upon Taimur Ali's life.

Perhaps he was alone then, or perhaps he was accompanied by his friend Noore Alam, or Yusuf, or both of them; perhaps they were going somewhere by the road along the bank of the Dolu river and beside the bamboo clump, and then in some place at the far end of Boyaliapara they saw a brown mynah bird on the grass that had grown on the sloping edge of the road, pecking at something with its head down. Seeing a single mynah, they felt bad, but they were certain that there must be another one nearby; they continued walking and looked this way and that for the bird. And then, as they were looking for the second bird, they saw a girl sitting far away on the grass at the riverbank, and a bare-bodied youth wearing a lungi standing near her.

Taimur Ali could not recognize the girl; at first he thought that it must be someone like Husneara or Manowara or Roshanara, or perhaps it was Jamila or Kamila or Alfun, and so he asked, 'Hey Yusuf, who's that girl?'

Noore Alam, or Yusuf, recognized Somorto, aka Somorto Banu, the fifteen-year-old, buxom daughter of Jasimuddin, aka Jaissa Karati, so in response to Taimur Ali's query, they replied, 'That's Somorto, Jaissa Karati's daughter, Somorto Banu.'

'I don't think I've seen her before.'

Perhaps Taimur Ali had not met Somorto Banu or her dad before he left for Burma, because Abu Bakr Choudhury's son, Jaissa Karati, had left by then, going first to Burma, and then returning to the country and taking up work as a sawyer in timberyards in Chittagong, and living with his Arakanese wife Ongmeching and his daughter Somorto on the bank of the Matamuhuri river. Then one day, Ongmeching ate a pufferfish and died – but why Somorto and Jaissa Karati didn't die too was a mystery; but as she was dying, she asked the little girl Somorto to come to her and whispered into her ear, and from the knot at the end of her topcloth she took out a ring and put it on the middle finger of her girl's right hand, and on the ring, a white, glass-like crystal sparkled. After Ongmeching died, Jaissa Karati returned to his own village, and now, having received his share of the family property, he built a house on the bank of the Dolu river where he lived with his daughter. No one in Satkania had seen the Arakanese maiden Ongmeching, or perhaps one or two people had and had forgotten about it. She was a beautiful woman and a sorceress, and after her death, Jaissa Karati didn't marry again; he went to Somodorpara or to Kanchona or to Mirjakhil across the river, and took on work in timberyards, and at night during the rainy season, when the sound of Ongmeching's voice came wafting in with the murmur of the brimming waters, he sat on the bank and talked to her.

Ongmeching forbade Jasimuddin from marrying again; she declared, 'If you marry, I won't live, I'll die; and my girl won't survive either, she'll die too!' And so, in order to keep the dead Ongmeching alive, he remained unmarried, and the motherless Somorto grew big, strong, beautiful and buxom, and her glass ring was stuck tight under the knuckle on the middle finger of her right hand. Taimur Ali encountered her then, while he was looking for the second mynah, and he said to Yusuf or Noore Alam, 'Call the girl here.'

Taimur Ali did not know about Somorto Banu's ring then; she told him later that the crystal on the ring on her finger was not glass, but diamond. Her grandfather, that is Ongmeching's father, Achori Mog, came across it when he was working in a tin or copper or silver mine in Burma, and bringing it home, he made a ring with it and gave it to his daughter, and later it was found to be diamond – diamond was poisonous, and she told Taimur Ali she would poison and kill him. At first, Taimur Ali didn't believe what Somorto Banu said; he laughed and said, 'And who will kill me? You? Are you mad!' But later, it was proved that Somorto Banu wasn't mad, what she said was probably true, the crystal on her ring was perhaps really a diamond, and perhaps this diamond was poisonous; but there was nothing Taimur Ali could do. He tried to forcibly remove the ring from Somorto Banu's finger and failed; after that, he called Goursundar the blacksmith from the marketplace, and Goursundar found that the iron base of the ring had adhered so firmly to the skin on Somorto Banu's finger that there was no way of cutting it off.

Taimur Ali said no more on the subject, and then it seemed that perhaps Golenur Begum knew about the matter; when she was asked about it, she tried to sit up on her bed once again and failed, so she continued to lie down and said, 'Are you asking me about my daughter-in-law, my son? Her mother was a Mog. We too lived in Burma, but we weren't Mog.' When she was then asked about the diamond ring, she said that she did not know anything about it, but it was clear that she wasn't happy about Somorto Banu.

All this began after the spotting of a single mynah; and that day, following Taimur Ali's instruction, Yusuf or Noore Alam descended from the road, walked through the paddy field and went and called Somorto Banu, and on account of being a poor man's daughter, because the saheb was calling her, without asking any questions, she went and stood before him and said, 'Why did you call me?'

'Hey, don't you recognize me?'

'I don't. Tell me who you are.'

'Can I employ you to work in my house?'

'I don't work.'

'Why?'

'I won't!'

Taimur Ali got angry, and that anger descended upon Somorto Banu's male companion; when he inquired about the youth – 'Who's that man standing there?' – Somorto Banu replied obliquely, 'Why do you want to know that? His name's Surat Jamal, Jamaillya.'

Taimur Ali couldn't figure out the matter. He asked, 'Who's this Surat Jamal? Is he your brother?'

'No, why do you ask?'

'What are you people doing here?'

'What are we doing? We aren't doing anything!'

'What do you mean you aren't doing anything? Weren't you making love in broad daylight?'

'I don't want to hear such talk.'

That day, Taimur Ali went away without saying anything more; Surat Jamal worked with Jaissa Karati in the timberyard in Somodorpara or in Kanchona or in Mirjakhil, and flirted with Somorto Banu whenever he got the opportunity; perhaps Taimur Ali, like a fool, told his father Mowla Baksh about this, and when he heard that, he didn't know what he ought to do. 'What can I do?' he said.

After that, Somorto Banu was constantly on Taimur Ali's mind, but wooing her was difficult; for one, she was the sorceress Ongmeching's precocious daughter, and besides, there was the matter of Surat Jamal, and so it seemed hopeless – when he thought about Surat Jamal's success, he felt ravaged inside, and so he reflected upon the matter. He did four things then:

1. he cleared the bamboo clump on the bank of the Dolu river, beside the police jetty, and set up a timber mart;
2. he employed Jaissa Karati as a sawyer in this timber mart;
3. he sent Surat Jamal to Alikdam to manage their two-hundred-bigha estate there and build a hut where he would live;
4. and after that, he went with Jaissa Karati one morning to Loharpara to buy trees, and then on the pretext of being short of money or something else, he left Jaissa Karati behind with the timber merchants and returned to Satkania in the evening.

Perhaps, notwithstanding her precociousness, Somorto Banu could not clearly discern the motive behind all these tasks and efforts undertaken by Taimur Ali, and so he drew in his net, but perhaps he himself got caught in it; or perhaps Somorto Banu saw through the whole thing, albeit a little late, and got ready for battle. After returning alone from Loharpara, Taimur Ali went to Jaissa Karati's house, and drawing Somorto Banu out of their hut, he told her that Jasimuddin would return the next day, or the day after. Then, when he said, 'I'll come tonight,' there was no reason for the fifteen-year-old, adolescent girl to not understand what he meant, and she remembered the poison ring; she then gazed at the river and observed in the dim light of evening that a blueish-greyish mist had gathered over the water. She realized that she had very little time, and so she said, 'No, I won't be in tonight. Come tomorrow.' Taimur Ali was amazed to hear that; he gazed at the face of this girl dressed in a thami and a blouse, with no ornaments on her, and he reflected and then asked, 'Why tomorrow? Are you planning to run away tonight?'

In reply, Somorto Banu said that she wouldn't run away at night, and Taimur Ali once again gazed at her face, and it occurred to him that this maiden he had found instead of the second mynah was as verdant, deep and mysterious as the jungles of the Arakan; Somorto Banu said she wouldn't run away at night, but what if she did? He said, 'Where will you run away to? My name's Taimur Ali, I'll find you for sure.'

The next day, when Taimur Ali came to Jaissa Karati's house, he figured out Somorto Banu's cunning; because he saw that having got a day's time, Somorto Banu had fenced the four sides of their small homestead with bamboo wattle and thorny branches of jujube. Taimur Ali could find no way to enter the house. When Somorto Banu became aware of his presence, she asked, 'So you've come?' And when he in turn reminded her that she herself had asked him to come today, Somorto Banu then presented to Taimur Ali her proposal for the first pact. She told him that if he looked, he would find three ways to enter the homestead, and that in one of the three, a hole had been dug and a rabbit-trap had been laid, and Taimur Ali had to avoid that trap and enter; if he was unable to do so, and in case he fell into the hole with the trap, he would have to go back and never come this way again.

Perhaps Taimur Ali was amused; he agreed at once and then went around the homestead looking for the hole to enter by. He went around a few times in the darkness, but he could not spot any hole or niche; he thought that Somorto Banu was close by, but when he said, 'Are you playing a trick on me?' there was no response from her. And so Taimur Ali's anger and frustration grew, but after that, he did find three openings in the thorny fence: there was a niche just beside the path that came through the field and ascended to the homestead, the second was on the rear side of the homestead, and the third one was to the right of the house, facing the river; all three openings were so small and low that he thought only dogs and jackals could enter through them, and it was almost impossible for any person to do so. Nonetheless, having spotted the three openings as specified by Somorto Banu, he began to believe her, and he thought that the task before him was to find the one which did not have a trap, or easier still, to find the path which had the trap and to move ahead through any of the safe ways. He sat down on the grass near the main road leading to the homestead and rested for a while, then said, 'Wait, I'm coming.' After that, he undertook an analysis of the two levels of the special game of hunter-and-prey – perhaps he had learnt all this while living in Rangoon, Pegu or Mandalay. His analysis was as follows:

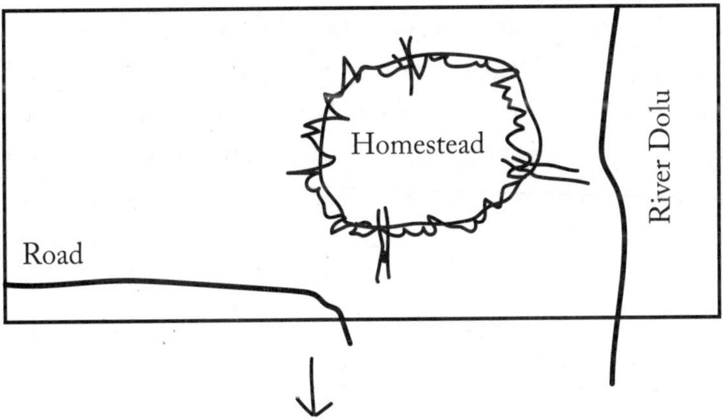

Path	Analysis - 1	Analysis - 2	Decision
Path no.1, in front of the homestead.	The path is straightforward, and in the front, and so it would seem that the trap has been laid on this path, but because it would seem to be like that, perhaps it's not here but elsewhere.	Because the prey would think that there's no trap on this path, and that it's elsewhere, the hunter too would know that, and so perhaps it is on this path.	
Path no. 2, at the rear of the homestead.	The path is concealed, one has to take a turn at a distance, it would seem that the trap could not be here, and so for that reason it could be here.	Because it would seem that the trap is here, it is not here.	The path at the rear of the homestead is safe.
Path no. 3, to the right of the homestead, towards the river.	Although the path isn't in the front, it is used to go to the river, even if not right away, it is visible from the commonly used road during the day, and so it would seem that the trap could be on this path, it could not be there as well.	The status of paths no. 1 and 3 are the same. The trap is either on path no. 1 or on path no. 3. Because it would seem that the trap is not on path no. 1, it is actually on path no. 1 and not on path no. 3.	

When Golenur Begum blamed Taimur Ali's fate, it seems that she wasn't entirely wrong; because as soon as Taimur Ali moved the fence of bamboo wattle and thorny jujube branches at the rear of Jaissa Karati's homestead and tried to crawl in, the cover of earth that had been spread loosely at the base of the fence and patted down broke, and he fell headlong into a pit. He was cursed by fate, but it could have been worse; Taimur Ali landed in a gap between the sharp, spear-like bamboo slices embedded in the bottom of the pit with which Somorto had cruelly prepared the deathtrap; he survived, but because he fell in an awkward position, the kneecap on his left leg was dislocated. Perhaps he was unconscious for a few moments after falling into the pit, and then he clambered up to the homestead, clawing all the way, went close to the hut and banged his fist against the fence – he had either forgotten about Somorto Banu's pact, or disregarded it. Perhaps Somorto was sleeping in the room inside because she was certain Taimur Ali would fall into the pit; but she woke up at the sound of the banging on the fence, and opening the screen window, she saw Taimur Ali standing at the door. That night, Ongmeching's daughter, Somorto Banu, couldn't protect herself, and Ahmad Taimur Ali Choudhury's lameness commenced that night.

When Golenur Begum was asked again about his lame leg, she once again pretended not to know. But when she was told that she wasn't being asked how Taimur Ali broke his leg, only where exactly and how badly it was broken, she then said, 'He suffered a lot, my son, but it didn't heal fully.'

When Taimur Ali crawled out of the pit and stood before Somorto Banu that night, he forgot about his broken leg, and then that same night or the following morning, when he emerged through the gap in the thorny fence, he perhaps became aware of the pain in his leg and found that he was unable to stand or walk on account of his injury, and his left knee was badly swollen. Perhaps Golenur Begum and Mowla Baksh were not aware of everything, or perhaps they knew, they couldn't have been unaware; but whether or not Somorto Banu wept silently like Husneara and Manowara and Roshanara wasn't possible to know because she lived behind a thorny fence, and because she didn't have a mother, no one came to Mowla Baksh and shed even a tear. Somorto Banu's father, Jaissa Karati, stayed in Lohagara for two days, but he returned to Satkania without meeting Taimur Ali or spending any time waiting, because he was worried about his motherless daughter, Somorto Banu; and when he arrived, he saw that the hut was surrounded on all sides with thorny jujube branches and there was no way to get inside. He then called out to Somorto Banu, and when she came out of the hut, he crawled through the gap in the thorny fence and entered the homestead.

After that, Somorto Banu was no longer seen outside the homestead with the thorny fence, but Taimur Ali's broken leg became infected and swelled up, and after being in torment with pain and fever, he was taken by bullock cart to Shyamapada, the kobiraj in Gachhbariya village in Dohazari, who fixed broken bones. Shyamapada housed Taimur Ali in the outer room of his hut and treated him for ten or twenty or thirty days; at first, he applied a poultice of hollyhock seed, burst the infected swelling on Taimur Ali's knee and drained the pus; he then pressed the kneecap down into its proper place, and washed the wound with water in which kalmegh leaves had been boiled; bushy lippia was ground into paste and applied all around the wound. Finally, after tying it with a clean rag, he prepared a potion by boiling or grinding the bark of the arjun tree, seeds of the Persian lilac and mimosa roots, and made him have that twice a day. With the daily attention and application of the ointment of bushy lippia, and regular doses of the medicine prepared by Shyamapada, the wound on Taimur Ali's leg healed.

Perhaps Golenur Begum knew about all this; she said that after spotting a single mynah, Taimur Ali survived a major calamity and then returned from Dohazari with two bottles of bitter potion, and he drank this medicine every morning and evening from a bell metal glass. He was down with this hardship for a long time, for one month or two months or six months; someone or the other went to Shyamapada and brought fresh stocks of the medicine. And thus, he was able to stand up again, but because the injury was a serious one and the treatment had been delayed, or for whatever reason, he became lame, or a hobbler or shuffler!

Then one day, Somorto Banu arrived at Mowla Baksh's house; if Golenur Begum was asked, it would seem that she knew nothing about this, although she knew – Taimur Ali had started hobbling around a little bit, that was when Somorto Banu arrived. There was no news of her all these days, but after Taimur Ali's lameness became certain, she arrived and presented herself one day, and she met Taimur Ali, because it was to meet him that she had come, and she asked him, 'How are you? I thought I'd look you up.'

Taimur Ali then observed that Somorto Banu's eyes sparkled and a suppressed smile played on her lips, and he said, 'You cheated me!'

It was observed that, when it came to cheating, their complaints were mutual; hearing Taimur Ali, Somorto Banu said that it was Taimur Ali who hadn't kept his word and that she knew he wouldn't keep his word. Perhaps Golenur Begum could have been asked once again about all these matters, although it was pointless; the upshot of whatever Golenur Begum said about all this was that it was spotting a mynah that was Taimur Ali's misfortune and that he gradually got caught in this snare. Of course, Taimur Ali was certain that Somorto Banu had cheated him, and he was determined to break her leg; but hearing her now, perhaps his anger subsided, and he asked her, 'What are you going to do now?'

What Somorto Banu said in response to this question made the situation even more complicated; she said that she would go to Alikdom now. Although Taimur Ali knew exactly where in Alikdom Somorto Banu wanted to go, he still asked her, 'Where's Alikdom?'

'Don't you know where?'

At first, Taimur Ali thought that this didn't concern him, but he could sense that he was burning to ashes inside on account of Surat Jamal; perhaps this was jealousy, perhaps hatred as well. Of course, Golenur Begum contended that she knew nothing about all this; she said, 'It's all fate, my son!' But after that, she said that everything was a snare laid by Somorto Banu, and that this was an example of how a stupid daughter of a Mog trapped the most able-bodied and worthy man in the village; before literally falling into the pit of the trap laid by Somorto Banu, Taimur Ali was caught in her magic web the moment he encountered her on the banks of the Dolu river, because Somorto was Ongmeching's daughter, and she too had a Mog name, Elaching. Taimur Ali fell into this girl's clutches; Somorto Banu, or Elaching, had planned and carried out everything; and Golenur Begum said, 'The girl's not a good sort!'

And so, another name of Somorto Banu's was revealed, Elaching, but perhaps the other things Golenur Begum said weren't correct, perhaps Elaching wasn't a bad girl then, because all this began with spotting a single mynah, and perhaps Somorto Banu, or Elaching, had not wanted to trap Taimur Ali in a magic web. Or perhaps she had, it's difficult to say; perhaps Golenur Begum was right. Instead of fleeing, she put up with Taimur Ali's doings, but again, by imposing conditions, she kept his life tied up and spun him around randomly. Taimur Ali became lame after making the first pact, and by making the second pact he hung all his life like a spider dangling at the end of a long, invisible, silken thread, and finally he died without making head or tail of it. One day, during breakfast, when he found the eggplant or papaya or potol or some other kind of vegetable curry tasteless and Elaching went to fetch some sugar, he drank all the water in the two glasses. Elaching then came with the sugar and saw Taimur Ali lying stretched out on his back on the cot, beside the breakfast that was laid; his eyes were shut and his hands were folded on his chest, which was heaving like a pair of bellows, and his forehead and nose were glistening with perspiration – seeing that, Elaching understood the matter.

It seemed Taimur Ali had broken the terms of the second pact too; even if the matter of making a pact for the purpose of breaking it did not eventually produce good results, he had found Elaching, and she had gifted him twelve children as well as the trap of the supernatural pact. Although Taimur Ali held Elaching to be entirely responsible for his lameness, it was to go to Alikdom that she had thereafter got ready; but once again his lust, jealousy and perhaps rage overwhelmed him. The evening of the day Elaching came to see Taimur Ali's broken leg, or the following day, he went to Jaissa Karati's riverside hut and saw that the homestead was surrounded by a thorny fence like before and one had to crawl inside. Perhaps he was afraid to go in that day, or perhaps he couldn't crawl in because of his broken leg; standing below the homestead, he called out to Elaching.

When Taimur Ali cried out, 'Where will you run away to, Elaching, you daughter of a Mog' – Elaching sat silently inside the hut, she didn't speak.

When Taimur Ali said, 'Tell me honestly why you're going to Alikdom, you're not to go there' – Elaching still didn't respond.

When Taimur Ali said, 'I won't spare you, girl' – one didn't hear Elaching say anything.

When Taimur Ali said, 'There's something I have to tell you, come out' – Elaching continued to sit inside.

Taimur Ali got angry again, and he said, 'Hey girl, can't you hear' – even after that, it was as if Elaching didn't hear anything.

Perhaps Taimur Ali became even angrier then. He screamed out loudly, 'You'll never be free of me,' and after that, when he said, 'I'm not going to spare you, I'll marry you' – Elaching then emerged from her hut and came and stood near the thorny fence at the edge of the homestead. Once again, it seemed that perhaps Golenur Begum was right, because seeing Elaching then, it seemed she had been ready and waiting for Taimur Ali; or perhaps that was not correct, but she looked very neat and tidy, she was wearing a bright, yellow-coloured thami and a red cotton blouse above that – her bumblebee-black hair was left loose down her back. Taimur Ali, who had returned from Akyab, Rangoon and Mandalay, looked at her through the thorny fence; perhaps this was a magical moment, and he emerged from his lust or jealousy or rage, and perhaps gazed at Somorto Banu or Elaching; perhaps he thought, this girl's going to Surat Jamal! That day, Elaching accepted her fate, either right then or a bit later, and showed Taimur Ali the diamond ring on her finger and stated the conditions of her second pact. Perhaps Taimur Ali didn't properly hear everything she said, or perhaps he did hear it but the matter of falling into Elaching's trap and breaking his leg had escaped his memory, and so, perhaps he thought this was a joke or a children's game and said, 'I agree.'

In effect, although Elaching killed cats on more than one occasion, perhaps Taimur Ali did not believe the stuff about the diamond ring, especially when this game went on for almost forty years and he never failed to recognize the correct glass even once, and his doubt became a kind of belief – he thought that it must be some kind of pressure tactic; after all, Elaching had lied earlier and perhaps was lying even now. But the day Taimur Ali lay flat on his bed after drinking the two glasses of water – because of his suspicion, or eventually tiring of the matter, or perhaps simply because he was thirsty – and Elaching returned with a bowl of sugar and saw him, she understood; she then rushed out and told everyone at home. After that, Dr Mojahar from the dispensary next to the police station was called, but by then, the heaving of Taimur Ali's chest had stopped, and after examining him, Dr Mojahar declared him dead. Dr Mojahar wrote out a death certificate too, in which he wrote that Taimur Ali died suddenly of severe cardiac failure, and so the question of whether the story of Elaching's ring was true or not remained unsolved even after Taimur Ali's death. But once forty days had passed since Taimur Ali's death, Elaching called her youngest son, Miraj Ali Choudhury, and told him, 'I'm going to stay in Alikdom; drop me at Alikdom and come back.'

Her sons then built a proper room in their house in Alikdom, which was midway between the bus stand and the marketplace, and arranged for her to be dropped there by motor car, accompanied by a maidservant. As she was leaving, Elaching took off the ring that now hung loosely on her aged, withered finger and gave it to Miraj Ali, and she said, 'Keep it, it's a diamond.' After that, she, that is Elaching, aka Somorto Banu, the daughter of Ongmeching of Arakan, set off for Alikdom.

Elaching's diamond ring remained with Miraj Ali, and then one day, accompanied by his two friends Humayun Kabir and Golam Ferdous Kasem, Miraj Ali Choudhury went to SB Jewellers in Hazari Lane, near Cinema Palace Hall, in the city of Chittagong. The proprietor of SB Jewellers, Jyotibhushan Das, a seasoned businessman in the gold and silver trade, was sitting in the shop right then;

Miraj Ali and his friends asked him whether he would buy a diamond ring. Although Jyotibhushan had seen diamonds in his professional life, he had never bought or sold them, but perhaps he could recognize a diamond; he couldn't believe that anyone would come to this narrow alley, Hazari Lane, to sell a diamond, yet he said, 'Why won't I buy it,' and then Miraj Ali took out the ring, wrapped in white tissue paper, from his trouser pocket and showed it to the man. Like a seasoned jeweller, Jyotibhushan examined the ring from different angles; he held it against the light to see the degree to which it dispersed light, he placed it under a round magnifying glass with a handle and examined the stone to see how smooth its edges were, he looked for whether there were any fine cracks there, and then he made a scratch on the glass top of the showcase and declared, 'This isn't diamond, it's glass.'

Miraj Ali lost face in front of his friends. Nevertheless, they tried in a couple of other places, perhaps in Andarkilla or in Bipani Bitan, and then, although it was ascertained that it was not diamond but glass, he nevertheless felt an attachment to the ring and so he put this diamond or glass ring of Elaching's into his pocket and returned to Satkania.

(2003)

(Translated with assistance from Sarbani Chakravarty)

The Woodcutter and the Ravens

ELDERLY RESIDENTS OF DHAKA CAN remember that a long time ago the city became devoid of crows, and that was when this event or series of events took place, over a period of five years or so, and it all began in a village called Boikunthopur. The town of Sirajganj lay on the west bank of the Jamuna river, and six miles west of Sirajganj was a small village, and the name of that village was Boikunthopur. A canal flowed on the south-western side of the village; when it was dry, the boys in the village played football there, and during the rainy season, when the water was waist-deep, people crossed it on rafts made from banana trunks. Some fifty feet from the bank of the canal, on a fallow plot ringed by trees and plants, a woodcutter lived in a shanty, his name was Akalu, that was his only name, and his wife, Tepi, lived with him, Tepi too had just the one name. Akalu was a poor landless man, Tepi's father too had been landless; the plot of land on which they had built the shanty they lived in was the property of Miyas in the village, they were only there with their permission. They had a room to live in on that plot, and a thatched space to cook in; there was no toilet, for that they used the dense bamboo clump on the eastern side of the plot. Both Akalu and Tepi were dark-skinned, and both of them were slight of build, but they were young then and they were very fond of each other. Akalu thought that his wife was not a bad sort, she was only a bit soft in the head; she muttered to herself, and at night, after she fell asleep, her teeth chattered. Because of that, Akalu obtained various kinds of amulets and hung them on different parts of Tepi's body; a number of amulets were slung on Tepi's neck to stop her from talking to herself; there were two squarish amulets tied on her arms to stop her teeth chattering at night; and another amulet, which couldn't be seen, was on Tepi's hip, so that she would bear a child quickly. But no child came to her womb, and she kept on talking to herself. Then one day, towards the end of the month of Asharh or the beginning of Shrabon, Akalu woke up early at dawn and decided that he would not go out in search of work, he would just sleep with his wife all day, and so he went back to sleep. After that, when sunlight came into the shanty through the cracks in the sponge-wood matting on the wall, he woke up again and he heard a soft sound from the rear of the house; Tepi was walking around barefoot, muttering, Oh my precious gem, oh dear, did an insect get you? Wait, I'll bring some ash; when Tepi came indoors to collect ash from the clay oven, Akalu called out to her, Tepi, what's happened to you, who is your precious gem?

Tepi returned to her senses then, she laughed and said, Come and see.

Akalu got up, and Tepi took him and showed him the little finger-like gourd that had come up on the cucumber creeper at the window, with a white flower at its head. Akalu stood there and looked, while Tepi searched for insects and killed them, and sprinkled ash on the leaves of the plant. Two ravens then came flying over the trees, one went and sat on a branch of the mango tree that was a little distance away, the other one sat on the thatched roof of their hut; after that they began to caw, *caw-caw*, and Tepi's attention drifted from the cucumber to the crows.

Where did such large crows come to this village from? Akalu thought about that and said, I think they've come from Sirajganj, they've come to your house to feast today. Tepi was very amused by what Akalu said, and she began to talk to the crow, Oh dear, really? Have you really come flying from so far away? Are you very hungry? Do you want to drink water? Wait.

Tepi brought water in an earthen bowl and kept it at one end of the courtyard and then went over to the other end; she said, There, drink.

But the crows did not come down to drink water, they continued to caw, and that annoyed Tepi; she said, What are you saying? Go away, be off; when she feigned throwing a stone, the crow sitting on the roof of the hut flew away and went and sat near the other crow on the branch of the mango tree. Tepi then forgot about the crows and went the other way, while Akalu went and squatted beside the door of the shanty; and then Jabbar Ali, from the Pangasi market, came along the path through the wooded clump and presented himself; he told Akalu that the contractor from the town of Sirajganj who had bought the high school's large banyan tree was looking for a woodcutter. But Akalu said that he didn't feel like going, he wanted to spend the day walking around the trees and woods with Tepi.

Tepi's attention now drifted back to the crows; she said, What are you saying, huh?

The crows cawed, and Tepi cried out, In the name of Allah, what's this they say – *cut-it, cut-it*; saying that, Tepi went into the room and brought out the axe. Akalu didn't want to go, but Tepi forced him to. Some woodcutter of Sirajganj had by now already cut, sawn and carted away the wood from the century-old banyan tree which had taken root on one side of the playground in the Pangasi High School, so when the contractor's man went with Akalu to the tree, he saw that all that remained on the field were eight large nodes and the roots beneath the earth.

Cut these so they can be used for fuelwood.

That will be fifty taka.

Rubbish! Are you crazy? There isn't even fifty taka worth of wood there. I'll give you ten taka.

Akalu did not agree to that, but he finally agreed to do it for twenty taka, and when he began cutting the wood, he realized that he had been cheated. The nodes of the tree could not be hewn easily, and after working hard from morning to evening for three days, he was only able to cut seven nodes; he felt terribly dejected thinking about the fact that Tepi had forced him to do the work. On the morning of the fourth day, Akalu began cutting the last remaining node of the tree, and then clouds appeared in the sky and it began to rain. But Akalu did not stop working; he kept cutting off layer after layer from three sides of the node, and this remnant of the tree gradually became small and semi-circular. Then Akalu suddenly got annoyed at the downpour and rained down a series of blows with his axe; in his fury, a gurgling sound emanated from his throat, and the blade of his axe penetrated the small, circular node. Akalu realized there was a hollow inside the node, and after that, when without further thought he cut some more, he could see a khaki-coloured cloth inside the hollow. He became cautious then; he looked closely and saw that on the side of the node which adhered to the earth, the hollow had a mouth that was covered with mud. He removed the mud at the mouth of the hollow with his axe, and pulled out a bulging cloth bag resembling an infant's pillow, and under the pouring rain, he wrapped the bag with his gamchha, and returning cautiously to his house, he called out to Tepi from the door.

Take it.

What is it?

I don't know. Be quiet, don't say anything at all.

They then opened the cloth bag and took out a polythene bag from inside that and saw that it was full of currency notes. When Akalu opened the mouth of the polythene bag and emptied it out on the bed laid on the floor mat, Tepi was speechless in astonishment.

Isn't it money? Where did you find so much money?

Inside the hollow of the tree.

In the name of Allah, that's why the crow said, *cut-it*; aren't the crows great?

Yes.

If they come again, I'll make payesh and treat them.

Do that.

Akalu counted the money and found that there were ten bundles of one-hundred-taka notes; and Tepi asked him, How much money is here? Akalu kept calculating, but he could not work it out; he said, These are one-hundred-taka notes, there are a hundred of them in a bundle, and there are ten bundles.

How much money is that?

A lot, Akalu said.

Then they put the money back in the bag like before, dug up the floor and buried it there, and at night, lying on the kantha spread over the floor mat, Tepi grazed her nose on Akalu's chin and talked to him. First, they tried to guess where the money had come from and were certain that this was money hidden by robbers; after that, they thought about possible ways to spend the money. Tepi said, Buy this plot of land, but Akalu said, If we take out this money, it's dangerous; they became worried then, and Akalu put his arms around Tepi and said, First thing tomorrow, I'll go to Sirajganj and talk to a lawyer.

The next morning, wrapping the chira and jaggery given to him by Tepi in his gamchha, Akalu made his way to the courthouse in Sirajganj, and he asked a man selling paan and cigarettes, I say, brother, can one get a lawyer here?

Yes, there are so many lawyers in town. Why do you need a lawyer?

It's just that I need some advice.

What advice?

Oh, I was simply asking. Let's say you find one hundred taka lying on the road. Now, does that money belong to you? Can you spend that money?

When the cigarette seller of that mofussil town heard what Akalu said, the hair on his head stood on end.

Did you find money?

No, I was asking just like that.

How much did you find?

Two hundred taka, Akalu said.

Rubbish, you bloody peasant, you're telling lies.

No, no, actually I found one thousand taka. Now I need some advice from a lawyer.

I'll take you to a lawyer, but you have to give me a share of the money.

I'll give you that, said Akalu.

Give me half.

All right, I'll give it.

The cigarette seller took Akalu to the residence of a lawyer in the eastern part of the city, behind Mumtaz Cinema Hall. The lawyer saheb, who wore a black coat and held a bulging bag under his arm, was about to leave; they arrived just then, and the cigarette seller said, Sir, I've come to you because my cousin needs some advice.

The lawyer furrowed his brow and looked at Akalu, and he said, If you need advice, that costs money too, do you know that?

Yes, I have money, Akalu said.

How much do you have?

Twenty taka.

But my rate is thirty taka.

Then the cigarette seller agreed to pay the remaining ten taka and they entered the lawyer's chamber and sat down. When Akalu explained why he needed advice, the lawyer saheb was completely dumbfounded.

How much money did you find?

One thousand, or was it … yes, one thousand.

Rubbish, you thieving fellow, you're telling lies.

No, actually I found one-hundred-taka notes.

The lawyer's eyes gleamed; he asked, How many one-hundred-taka notes are there in a bundle?

A hundred.

How many bundles?

At first, Akalu said, Two; after that, he said, No, five of them.

Hmm, the lawyer suddenly exhaled loudly, he stood up and went and shut the door, and then he said, I can't give you such advice for thirty taka.

Then?

You have to give me half.

All right, I'll give it, said Akalu.

In that case, you have to give me half of the remaining half, the cigarette seller said.

All right, I'll give it.

Then let's go to your house now, the lawyer said, pay me my money first and then I'll give you the advice. The three of them arrived at Akalu's plot in Boikunthopur in the afternoon. Tepi was not at home then, and when Akalu took out the money, the lawyer saheb counted the bundles and smiled, exposing his teeth; after that, he kept five bundles for himself, and returned five bundles to Akalu. The man who sold cigarettes took away three bundles from Akalu's hands, and then, looking at the remaining two bundles in Akalu's hands, the lawyer saheb said, Don't take out this money before a year, that's my advice to you; once a year's passed, take out small amounts and spend it, because as soon as people see that you have a lot of money, they'll suspect you and you'll land in jail.

After the lawyer and the cigarette seller left, Tepi returned; and when she heard about everything from Akalu, she fell into despondency. She said, Why did you pay so much money for that rotten advice?

I still have two bundles, Akalu said, even the two bundles is a lot of money.

When he said that, Tepi's dejection vanished, her dark-skinned face broke into a radiant smile, and in the evening, she again started talking to the trees, the birds and the breeze. At night, after they had eaten and gone to bed, five people with gamchhas covering their faces barged in and woke them up; they tied them tightly with rope to the mango tree in the grounds, and then they dug up the floor of the room and took away the money. Akalu and Tepi remained tied to the mango tree all night, and because cloth had been stuffed into their mouths, they could not make any sound; but after biting through the cloth all night, come morning, Tepi tore the cloth and began screaming, but Akalu was unable to remove the cloth in his mouth. After she'd been screaming continuously for three hours, Quddus Moulovi from the village, who had come to tether his goats at the bank of the canal, heard her screams, and when he saw Akalu and Tepi tied to the tree, he screamed louder than Tepi and ran towards the village. Seeing Quddus Moulovi's crazy behaviour, the people of the village rushed to Akalu's plot and found Akalu and Tepi. After they untied and freed them, they were shocked to see the floor of their room.

The village folk concluded that robbers had come, and they asked, What did you have here?

Akalu replied, Who knows, I don't know. Then, when the people of the village were about to take him to the police station, Akalu got an unbearable pain in his stomach and the pain persisted until evening. He clutched his stomach with both hands and lay in the dirt; after that, when it was evening and darkness had descended, he rose from the dust of the courtyard, and Tepi asked him glumly, Did the robbers do something to your stomach?

Nothing's happened to me, Akalu replied, but Tepi, we can't stay here any more. The police will come tomorrow after they hear about the robbers, and once the police arrive, they'll find out about the money; and that means jail. Tonight's the last night; we'll leave at dawn tomorrow and go to Sirajganj, we'll catch the launch there and cross the river, and then we'll go to Dhaka. Get ready, we'll set off at the break of dawn.

The next morning, the people of the village arrived and saw that Akalu wasn't there, his wife, Tepi, wasn't there either, the house was completely bare. Meanwhile, Akalu and Tepi sat on a bench inside the hold of the launch and crossed the Jamuna, and after the crossing they took a bus from Bhooyapur, and at three in the afternoon, they got off at Dhaka's Gulistan. At that time, Chandu, a rickshaw puller from Dayaganj, was waiting for a passenger near the bus stand; when Akalu got down from the Bhooyapur bus, Chandu was stunned to see him. Hey friend, you? Chandu shouted out, but Akalu did not see or hear him amidst the jostling of the crowd; he just held his wife's hand and walked on. When Chandu realized that shouting was of no avail, he left his rickshaw, walked up to Akalu, and grabbed his torn shirt at the shoulder.

You bloody fellow, didn't you see me?

Akalu was frightened, his face seemed to shrivel, and without letting go of Tepi's hand, he said, Excuse me, boss?

Now Chandu was really surprised, and he said in an anguished tone, Hey bloody Zainal, can't you recognize me, my friend? Do you really not recognize me? I'm Chandu, my friend, I'm Chandu!

Akalu gulped, and Tepi just stood there, her eyes shut in fear.

Hey, I'm Chandu, Chandu; aren't you Zainal? Can't you recognize me, my friend!

Akalu grasped the situation now; gulping once again, he said, My name is Akalu, boss; and this is my wife, Tepi.

Chandu's teeth flashed in a smile; he said, So she's your wife? What did you say her name was?

Tepi.

Hey Tepi! Hey, my dear friend, you have a very sweet name. My wife's name is Haowa Bibi!

Akalu and Tepi remained silent; then Chandu said, Where did you run off to, my friend? It's been so many years since you ran away, and now you're back! But I looked so much for you, how I looked; people said, Zainal's dead, but I didn't listen to them, I said, No, Zainal is not dead! Where did you run off to, my friend?

Akalu said fearfully, My name is Akalu.

Chandu didn't pay any heed to what Akalu was saying; he said, You're Zainal, I know. Where are you going now?

Akalu was still afraid, but he told the truth when he replied that he didn't know where he would go. Then Chandu said to him, Come along with me. When I'm around, can't you ask me, man? Where on earth will you go! Hey man, is Chandu dead or what!

Akalu's suspicions didn't leave him, and all the while Tepi looked on through the gap of her ghomta. Akalu said, Actually I'm Akalu, I've come from Sirajganj.

Chandu then stared at him gravely and said, Your earlier name was better. You've changed it from Zainal to Akalu. Akalu, ha ha, what a funny name!

Akalu got annoyed now; he said, Akalu's fine. And your name is Chandu! *Chandu!*

Listening to Akalu and Chandu, Tepi was about to laugh; she tugged at Akalu's arm and said, Come, let's go with brother.

And so Akalu and Tepi began to live in the basti in Dayaganj, in the shanty next to the one Chandu and Haowa Bibi lived in. The people of the basti who learnt about Akalu from Chandu knew his name to be Zainal, and those who heard it directly from him, knew his name to be Akalu; only Tepi's name was correct. Chandu took Akalu to the field in Dhupkhola and taught him to ride the cycle rickshaw, and then he got him a rickshaw from a mahajan in Dayaganj. Akalu was very happy, but Tepi was cheerless and Akalu could not figure out why. Then one night, while lying on the kantha spread out on the floor mat, Akalu asked her, What's happened to you, Tepi?

Nuzzling against Akalu's chin, Tepi said, I feel strange inside my stomach!

How does it feel?

It feels like there's a stone inside.

The next day, Akalu told Chandu, Brother Chandu, my wife, Tepi, is very unwell. She's got a stone in her stomach.

Chandu thought over the matter, All right, let's take my dear friend to the doctor; and so, they took Tepi to a doctor in the hospital. The doctor had her blood and urine tested, had an X-ray image of her stomach taken, but nothing was found; Tepi became even more depressed as a result; she said, It feels like I'm carrying a load weighing a maund in my stomach, but the doctor says it's nothing. I won't survive. After I die, get married again. Akalu was very unhappy about Tepi's condition; that night, he held his wife close to him and wept, and the next morning, he woke up very early and saw that Tepi was no longer in his arms. He then went outside and began to search for her, and he saw her on the empty field across the railway line; Tepi was walking around slowly in the empty field, she did not notice Akalu. Then, a raven came flying and sat on top of a bamboo pole fixed to the ground on one side of the field; it looked this way and that a few times, and began cawing, *caw-caw*. Tepi saw the crow, and at once began to speak.

Oh dear, aren't you that crow? Where have you come from? From Sirajganj? Oh dear, you're that crow from my village!

The crow tilted its head as if listening to Tepi, and Tepi said, Oh dear, how far you have flown! Are you very tired? But why are you alone, tell me why you're alone?

The crow stared silently, and Tepi began to cry, It's dead, oh dear, it's dead, isn't it?

Akalu then advanced towards her, and Tepi hugged him and lamented, but Akalu did not feel any sympathy, he got annoyed; he said, This bloody crow is a bastard, I'm going to kill the bastard. But Tepi did not let him chuck a stone at the crow; she ran to her shanty and brought a silver pan with water for the crow to drink, but the crow simply stared, it did not drink the water. When Akalu noticed that people had gathered around to watch his wife's antics, he brought Tepi home. The people in the basti said Tepi was soft in the head, but after a long time, Tepi once again wandered around in the nooks and corners of the house and beside the tap outside, muttering to herself, and hearing that, Akalu's heart was filled with joy. Three days later, Akalu was taking a passenger from Dayaganj to Jatrabari when, seeing a bus headed for Gulistan approaching, the passenger got off the rickshaw and, in the blink of an eye, jumped into the moving bus. Even before Akalu could shout about his fare, he saw that the man's wallet had slipped out of his back pocket and fallen to the ground, and the man didn't even realize it.

He then quickly picked up the wallet and hid it under his vest; after that, he moved away, he took out the wallet and counted the money, there were seventy-one taka in the wallet. At that moment, he remembered the money he had found in the hollow of the tree, and he became fearful. He took out his fare of one taka from the wallet and stuffed it in the waist fold of his lungi, and with the remaining seventy taka in the wallet, he went and presented himself at the Mandira police station. There were three policemen present in the police station then, and Akalu went and stood in front of the duty officer and said, Sir, I found a wallet with money, sir.

The duty officer furrowed his brows and looked in his direction.

What's your name, boy?

Akalu.

The duty officer counted the money in the wallet.

How much money was there in the wallet?

Seventy-one taka … no, seventy taka.

Tell me exactly how much money was there in the wallet!

Akalu was frightened, It was seventy-one taka, I took my fare of a taka.

Saying, You bastard, thief, the duty officer got up and hit him on his backside, thighs and shoulder with a thick and knobbly stick for half a minute. Akalu wept loudly as he was beaten, Sir, I'm not a thief, sir, I did not steal any money.

The other two policemen observed this all the while; the duty officer returned to his chair and sat down, he said, Take out the money you've got.

Akalu took out six taka from the fold of his lungi and placed it on the table. The duty officer said, Hmm … it's too difficult to divide seventy-seven taka. If the bastard had ninety taka it would have been convenient. He then asked Akalu, Don't you have any more money?

No sir, I swear on Allah sir.

If you had one more taka it could have been divided. Don't you have even one taka? Bloody son of a pig!

Akalu began weeping again, and the duty officer finally said after much thought, The bloody son of a bastard cunningly brought the money so that it can't be divided into three. But I won't spare you, you bastard! Bring another thirteen taka by afternoon, and if you don't do that, I'll find you and break your leg, you bastard.

Akalu wept, he swore on the Prophet of Allah that he would definitely bring the money. The policeman then noted down the number of his rickshaw and let him go. That day, after depositing his rickshaw when it was past 2 p.m., Akalu returned home and sat gravely; Tepi chattered about this and that, but Akalu did not break his silence; Tepi's face then darkened with fear and she began to weep loudly, Come here, everyone, look, something's happened to this man! Hearing Tepi screeching, the neighbours came running, Chandu and Haowa Bibi came too; they saw that Akalu was sitting silently at the foot of the door of the shanty. Akalu did not speak, and after everyone else left, he said to Chandu, My friend, I'm in great danger.

Tepi had stopped crying and had been silent so far; now, on hearing Akalu, she began weeping loudly once again. Chandu said, Don't fear, my friend, as long as Chandu's here, you have nothing to fear. Tell me what's happened to you.

The raven is after me, I won't survive.

A raven!

Yes, a raven. It came to my village once and drove me out of there. It's arrived in Dhaka now; I almost got thrown into the lock-up today.

After Chandu heard what Akalu said, he sat speechless for the rest of the day; then, when it was evening, he said, Don't fear, I'll take you to an astrologer baba. He'll give you a stone that will ward off every kind of harm and difficulty.

Chandu's words brought back Akalu's and Tepi's courage, and Akalu once again heard Tepi muttering to herself. When it was past evening, Akalu went with Chandu to the astrologer, and Akalu sat with the palm of his right hand outstretched in a dimly lit room in a lane in Nazira Bazar, and the middle-aged astrologer studied the palm of his hand for a long time, all the while scribbling and drawing something on a piece of paper. After that, the astrologer said a lot of things to Akalu, most of which he could not understand; but when the astrologer told him that Saturn was watching over him, he broke into tears, Brother astrologer, please save me. Chandu and the astrologer consoled him; the astrologer said, Don't be afraid, I'll give you a blue stone. Wear it on your hand, and inshallah, all your difficulties will be averted and you will progress in life.

What's the blue stone?

It's a blue-coloured stone. There's a land with a blue river, that's King Solomon's land. Merchants bring this stone from there and sell it in a lane in Patuatuli. I have it too, I'll give you one.

Akalu asked, What will it cost?

The price of the stone is fifty taka, and the ring costs ten taka. It will be sixty taka in all. Akalu was stunned. The price of a small stone was fifty taka! When he told Chandu that he had only twenty taka, Chandu lent him thirty more, and with the fifty taka he bought a stone that was light blue in colour; he didn't buy a ring, he said, I'll make do by tying it to my arm with cloth. Then, suddenly, all the electric lights of Nazira Bazar went out. Akalu and Chandu sat for a while in the darkness in the tiny room of the astrologer, and then they emerged from the room in darkness. On returning home, Akalu gave the stone to Tepi, who put it in the corner of her sari's anchal and knotted it. The next morning, Tepi made a belt with some old cloth and inserted the stone inside it and sewed it up, like a pillow, and Akalu tied this belt made by Tepi around the wrist on his right hand and set out with his rickshaw. That day, Akalu earned twenty-seven taka by the time it was 2 p.m., and when he returned home and gave that to Tepi, she hummed with joy and astonishment and said, Twenty and seven taka in a single day!

Akalu too said joyfully, Just wait, just see what's to come! This stone is from the blue river, it's come from King Solomon's land. Now I am going to fill your house with King Solomon's money; all you have to do is eat and hum.

The next day, Akalu earned thirty-two taka. In order to make Akalu happy, Tepi dressed in freshly washed clothes in the evening and oiled and plaited her hair. But the day after, the police arrived at the basti and arrested Akalu from his shanty on the charge of stealing jewellery from the glass case of Bhaskar, the astrologer, when the electricity went off two days ago. The police went looking for Chandu, but as soon as he got wind of it, he fled. Even before Akalu and Tepi could really understand anything, the police took Akalu away and put him in the lock-up in Sutrapur police station. When the police refused to listen to anything he said, and instead gave him a terrible hiding two or three times, Akalu realized the situation he was in; he knew that it was certain that he would go to jail now, and then, after sitting quietly for a long time, he told the duty officer that he too had been involved in the theft together with Chandu, and that it was his wife, Tepi, who had hatched the plan for them. His confession worked; the duty officer sent two constables to fetch Tepi. When the police left after bringing the terrified and pale Tepi at around 10 p.m., unlocking the iron door of the lock-up and pushing her inside, Akalu held her close to his thrashed body and slept on the floor of the lock-up. The next day, the police took them to court, and they were sentenced to a year and a half's imprisonment. Although there were separate wards in the jailhouse, they spent the day standing on either side of the iron fence in the jail compound and talking to each other. After fourteen months went by in this way, one day, high up on the wall on the western side of the cell which Akalu occupied together with eleven other prisoners, inside the vent to allow light to enter the room, he saw the shadow of some twigs, and very soon after that, he saw that a black-coloured bird was sitting on the twigs, and at once Akalu realized what it was. That very day, after a lot of entreaties and solicitation, he met the jailer saheb, and requesting him to transfer him to another cell, he said, Save me, sir, this crow will be the death of me. After he heard everything that Akalu had to say, the elderly jailer was of the view that all this was just a story, he could not figure out what Akalu's real motive was for wanting to change his cell, so he turned down his appeal; as a result, subsequent events took a turn in accordance with Akalu's belief. A few days later, Akalu came down with a fever and was lying down during the daytime, having spread a sheet on the floor of the cell, when, in his drowsy state, he thought the shadow of the outspread wing of a bird was silently crossing over him. Akalu opened his feverish eyelids once and looked; he did not see anything. After that, when evening was about to descend, as the light inside the cell waned, he sat up, and then he felt something hard, like a piece of stone, beneath his thigh, so he made to move it away with his hand, and when he brought it in front of him he saw that the thing that had been pressed beneath his body was a ring. It was an extraordinarily beautiful gold ring with a large and finely cut gemstone on it; the stone dispersed bright light even in the hazy darkness of the room. Akalu threw the ring on the floor and covered his face with his hands, and possibly some distressed sound escaped from his mouth, because just then, another inhabitant of that cell, the petty thief, Abul Hossain, entered and asked, What's happened to you?

Akalu kept one hand over his face, and with the other, he pointed towards the ring lying on the floor; Abul Hossain then advanced and picked up the ring. He was dumbfounded.

Where did this come from?

A crow dropped it.

What are you going to do with it now?

You can take it.

Abul forbade Akalu from telling anyone else about the ring and concealed it among his personal items. Ten days later, Abul's wife was caught trying to smuggle the ring outside, and when Abul was summoned by the jailer, he kept trembling and said that Akalu had given him the ring. Akalu was then summoned, and when the guard found him and brought him, he told the jailer that it had fallen on him from the crow's nest while he was sleeping.

Whose ring is it?

I can't tell you that, sir.

Bastard, you're lying!

No, sir, this was dropped by the crow. You please take it, sir.

The jailer saheb then thought for a while, and then he put the ring into a drawer on his desk and let Akalu go; Akalu then returned and saw that Tepi was sitting gloomily at a distance, under a kodui tree, and muttering to herself. Four months later, the two of them were released.

The same jailer called them to his office.

Where will you go now?

We have nowhere to go, sir.

The jailer saheb then took them in his own official jeep and brought them to Noyatola, on the eastern side of Mogbazar; here, they entered a walled compound in the middle of a vast tract of vacant land spreading out in all directions. Akalu and Tepi saw that there was a palm tree in the middle of the compound, and under the palm, a shanty; and the jailer unlocked the door of the shanty and said, This place belongs to me. There was a man who used to guard it, he's gone away; now you can stay here. So Tepi once again set up her household inside the shanty; Akalu worked as a day labourer, Tepi took up work as a part-time maidservant in a house near the dargah of Shah Noorie. After a few months went by in this manner, one day, when Akalu returned home in the evening, he found Tepi sitting silently beside the door of the hut.

What's happened to you?

The crow's arrived.

Looking up then, Akalu saw the raven sitting on a branch of the palm tree, with its head drooping down, and then Akalu and Tepi observed, to their astonishment and horror, that the number of crows spending the night on the branches of the palm tree kept increasing by the day. Very soon, there was not enough space for the crows on the palm tree and on the roof of their hut. Then, Akalu and Tepi finally accepted the inevitable; with the money the two of them earned from work, Akalu purchased long lengths of borak bamboo and laid beams and cross beams overhead, spanning their entire compound, with fifty-one rows and thirteen columns, thus forming six hundred and sixty-three frames. The people of the moholla did not notice this at first, or even if they did, they did not attach any significance to it; at first, they merely thought that the bamboo platform had been built for some construction work. But gradually they became aware of the increased presence of crows in the locality, and after a time they saw that, like fruits hanging from the leafless branch of a tree, black crows had filled up Akalu's bamboo structure. When some of them asked Akalu and his wife about the crows, they did not say anything clearly, and when Akalu returned home at dusk after work as a day labourer, and Tepi after work as a maidservant, swarms and swarms of crows accompanied them and returned to their open bamboo frames. Even though the number of crows increased, the people of the moholla were indifferent at first, but the next Joishto, when the crow chicks that had been born here began to fly, and Akalu dismantled the crows' nests and sold eighteen-and-a-half maunds of scrap, comprising cycle spokes, metal wire, pieces of steel and so on, the people of the moholla became aware of the matter. They were amazed at the business acumen of the rustic man and his wife, and this sense of astonishment on their part turned into a kind of desire and envy when they came to know that, one day, Tepi had invited Nimphol Dasi, the woman who swept the streets of the locality, to her house and fed her fried crows' eggs, and that when she was leaving, Tepi took out from the hollow of a bamboo post in the shanty a pair of gold earrings retrieved from a crow's nest and gave it to her. Many people of the Noyatola–Mogbazar locality then gave up keeping pigeons and vacated their pigeon coops and the high bamboo platforms in their compounds in favour of black crows. But even after trying continuously for six months, their efforts towards raising crows remained futile, so then one evening, they assembled in front of the gate in the wall of the compound where Akalu lived and called him out, and they told him, You gave gold earrings to the sweeper, you have to give the same to us too.

I didn't give it, Akalu said, my wife did.

Call your wife.

She's cooking.

Why do you eat crows' eggs?

We eat them because we like them. Would you all like to try some?

No, we don't want crows' eggs, give us what you gave to the sweeper.

All right, I'll give it to you, said Akalu, but I don't have it now. If I find it again later, I'll give it to you. Please go now.

After the people of the moholla left, Tepi cracked and peeled the shells of the blue-coloured eggs that had been boiled in a pot and gave them to Akalu to eat.

Tepi inquired, Why had the people come?

You gave a pair of earrings to the sweeper, now they want it too. We've got to give the same to them.

Where will we find so many earrings now?

You've got us into trouble by giving the earrings to the sweeper. Don't ever give anything to anyone again.

Over the next six months, the people of the moholla became embarrassed and enraged after returning empty-handed time and again; for thirteen days at a stretch, they flung jackfruit rinds on Akalu when he was returning home, and after that, for the next five days, they threw putrid cow dung. When the people of the moholla saw that Akalu did not react to their harassment, they became very crestfallen, and then one day, they set dogs upon Tepi when she was walking homewards, almost shadow-like; and after that day, they did not see Akalu and his wife on the streets of the moholla. They waited uneasily for a few days, and after that, one day, a few of them went and gathered in front of Akalu's residence; standing in front of the shut gate in the wall, they got the smell of crows' eggs being fried and saw that, although it was only noon, the frames were full of crows. Three people then tried to force the gate open from outside, but when they were unable to open it and tried to climb over the wall, then, from among the hitherto silently gazing crows, seven ordinary crows and three ravens, ten birds in all, casually left their bamboo frames and flew towards them. The people of the moholla were already furious at not getting any of the jewellery brought by the crows, and now, after being pecked at by the crows, their rage knew no bounds. When the three people who had climbed over the wall lay injured following the crows' attack, the others moved back and then surrounded the walls of the compound where Akalu lived. In this way, they watched over the place all day and night; they waited under the assumption that, if Akalu and Tepi were human, they would have to emerge one day. But when night descended at the end of the twenty-sixth day of the blockade, and clouds gathered in the sky and it rained continuously, and then the rain stopped and two more days went by, many of the blockaders then realized the truth that Akalu and his wife could survive quite well on crows' eggs and water from their hand pump, they did not need to come out into the external world any more; and then these people wound up the blockade and returned home. But all those whose wives had seen the gold earrings on the ears of Nimphol, the sweeper, returned once again, very soon after, to the task of blockading, and at the end of the thirtieth day of the blockade, when it was quite late at night, they laid dry grass and leaves all around Akalu's compound and set them on fire. It was only when the hut surrounded by walls was engulfed by the smoke and heat from the fire that the crows began leaving the bamboo frames, and then the people of the moholla who were keeping watch beside the fire said that thousands, nay, hundreds of thousands of crows flew away, and after the night passed, in the first light of dawn, these people saw that the collection of frames built like a fortress, as well as the branches of the palm tree, were all completely bare. Carrying a staff or spear or iron rod in one hand and a jute sack in the other, the people at once broke open the gate in the wall and entered Akalu's compound. Stepping over the heaps of crow dung, they entered the shanty under the palm tree and saw that there was no sign of anyone there; but on one side of the room, on the clay oven, there were nine boiled crows' eggs in an aluminium pan. These people from the moholla cut the joints on every bamboo stem of the matted walls of the hut and examined them, they dug up the earth on the floor and sifted through it, but they found nothing. Then they became certain that this apparently simple and illiterate village man and his wife were very clever and cunning, because despite their vigilant watch they were able to escape with all the valuables brought by the crows. But some of them were still confused, and they said that it was impossible for the couple to slip through and escape a continuous watch like the one they had maintained; and then some other people said that the nine blue-coloured boiled eggs that were found in an aluminium pan of water in Akalu's shanty were very recently boiled, they were probably boiled the very night the crows flew away; because they realized after dipping their hands into the water in the pan on the stove that it had been recently boiled, and when they took the boiled crows' eggs in the water into their hands, they were certain they felt a slight warmth. The bewilderment of the people of Noyatola regarding Akalu's and Tepi's slipping past the blockade became even more acute when the story spread in the moholla that, actually, when the crows left their bamboo frames and flew away, they carried Akalu and Tepi in their beaks. The people of the moholla said that, on the night when the crows in the bamboo frames at Akalu's residence flew away after being unable to bear the heat and smoke from the fire, that same night, some people were lying on the deck after tying their boat on the bank of the Rampura lake. When the boatmen were lying on their backs on the deck of the boat and puffing at bidis and chatting among themselves, they saw an immense swarm of birds fly past, the sound of their flapping wings resembling that of countless hands clapping. They saw that almost the entire sky, in all directions, was shrouded by these flying birds; as they lay and gazed at this scene, after a while they saw that, in one or two places, the birds were crowded together like ants; but after that, they realized that, actually, in one place there weren't too many birds, rather, they were carrying something in their beaks that floated through the emptiness. At first, they thought it was two sheets of cloth, but after that, a bit later, in the hazy light of the sky, they saw the forms of two people gradually becoming clear within that mass of flying birds. The black birds flew over the Rampura lake and into the mist of the Dhaleshwari range.

After this incident, the city of Dhaka became devoid of crows, and Dhaka's elderly folk can now remember that, in those days, incidents of cakes of soap vanishing from beside the tap stopped completely; but at the same time, mounds of un-scavenged garbage kept piling up on the streets, and the sky over the city became monotonously void of birds. Many days went by in this way, and after that, some crows arrived in the city from nearby mofussil areas, and these mofussil crows gave birth to a new generation of crows, and thus, once again, filled the city's sky.

(1992)

The Thorn

IT WAS LEARNT THAT THE people of Ghost Lane went through a prolonged crisis; after Bangladesh became independent, the second period of military rule commenced during the 1980s, and around this time, when Abdul Ali pulled down his old hair-cutting salon located at that precise spot on the western end of Ghost Lane where it trifurcates and goes towards Twin Bridge Lane, Padmanidhi Lane and Rankin Street, and replaced it with a new and modern one, giving it the name 'Your Choice Salon', people from Rankin Street and Banagram to Twin Bridge Lane, and from Padmanidhi Lane, Shahsaheb Lane and Narinda arrived at Abdul Ali's new salon to get a haircut, and they then learnt about this problem of the people of Ghost Lane. Subsequently, the people of all these mohollas said that the people of Bhojohori Saha Street, that is, Ghost Lane, suspected that they were caught in some kind of time warp. Because one day, when with spades in hand, they dug the earth to seal off a well inside the compound of Abdul Aziz Byapari's house, they discovered that the framework of time had broken down as far as their lives were concerned, and that the present had entered the past, or that the past had become attached to the present. In that state of bewilderment, they carried out the task of digging up earth and filling the well, because they thought that if they didn't do it, Abdul Aziz Byapari's new tenant, Subodhchandra, would fall into this well in the past, the present or the future. The people of the nearby mohollas learnt about this dilemma of the Ghost Lane folk regarding Subodhchandra when they got a haircut or a shave at Your Choice Salon, and they said that the day a tenant arrived at Abdul Aziz Byapari's house, the people of Ghost Lane heard about it, and after that when they became aware that the tenant's name was Subodhchandra Das and his wife's Swapna, they then said that they already knew this, because they had realized from their experience that the wives of Subodhchandras were always named Swapna. Towards the end of the 1980s, the people of Bhojohori Saha Street, or Ghost Lane, had been severely oppressed by a heatwave and the foul stench of rotting animal and bird carcasses, and they had been extremely perturbed to hear about the arrival of Subodh and Swapna in the moholla; they were annoyed too, because with the arrival of Subodh and Swapna, a kind of helplessness and sense of guilt arose in their busy and disorderly lives. Unsettled by the heat and the foul stench, they spat and exclaimed, 'Where does this bastard keep returning from!'

The moholla folk then hoped that this was some other Subodh, and some other Swapna, but that hope was soon dashed. They found out that those in the moholla who went to meet Subodh and Swapna didn't really recognize them, but even though they felt relieved then, it was as if they knew the fact of the matter in their heart of hearts; they sipped the tea prepared by Swapna and stared at Subodhchandra's face and asked him, 'Why did you come as a tenant to this house?' The people of Ghost Lane contend that when the dark-skinned and gaunt Subodhchandra heard that, he was silent, and his wife's dark-skinned yet radiant face turned pale; they perhaps thought that the people of the moholla didn't like them. Observing their crestfallen faces, these moholla folk turned silent, and after that they asked, 'Isn't Poranchandra your brother?' Aziz Byapari's new tenant, Subodhchandra, was astonished to hear them say that, and he felt ill at ease; when he nodded gently and admitted that he had a younger brother by the name of Poranchandra who lived in a village near Sirajganj town, it occurred to the people sitting in front of him with teacups in their hands that they weren't surprised, and then when those in the moholla who were middle-aged or elderly heard this, they said that they already knew about the matter, because Subodh's younger brother's name was always Poran. When the people of the moholla heard all this, a kind of anxiety became noticeable in their demeanour, and when they remembered that even after piped water arrived in the moholla the well inside the compound of Abdul Aziz Byapari's house had continued to exist like before, their anxiety turned into fear, and some of them remarked to Aziz Byapari one day, 'Subodhchandra's come to your house once again as a tenant!'

'So what can I do?'

'The bloody chap's wife's name is also bloody Swapna!'

'Yes.'

'Do you know his younger brother's name?'

'No.'

'Poran.'

'Is that so!'

'You still have your well. Let's hope this fucker doesn't fall into the well now!'

'Oh, don't worry.'

The moholla folk didn't feel reassured by Aziz Byapari's words, because they couldn't forget that many years ago, deceived by these very assurances from Aziz Byapari, they had carried out the most shameful and despicable act of their lives. They could not remember clearly now which year it was when they learnt, one day, that a new tenant had arrived in Abdul Aziz Byapari's house, and that this tenant's name was Subodhchandra, and with him was his wife, Swapna. They then went to Aziz Byapari's house to inquire about the matter, and these moholla folk had the tea and nimokpara prepared by Swapna, and they observed that a tulsi sapling had been planted beside the courtyard wall of Aziz Byapari's house, in a slightly isolated spot, and they surmised that it was Subodhchandra's wife who had done this. The moholla folk had felt terribly upset as they gazed at this tulsi sapling, and when they remarked to Aziz Byapari that they hoped Subodhchandra and his wife didn't fall into the well again, Aziz Byapari had then replied, 'Oh, don't worry,' and the people of the moholla had been deceived by this assurance of his, and subsequently, they had said that, as a result of this, during the Liberation War, that incident in their lives happened. The people of the moholla remembered that in the month of March in 1971, when the situation in the country turned grave, among all of them it was Aziz Byapari's tenant, Subodhchandra, who was most perturbed, and when he thought to send his wife to her village house in Satkhira, the moholla folk realized how apprehensive he was; but they then simultaneously remembered the nimokpara and tea prepared by the dusky, sweet-natured Swapna, they couldn't forget about having had all that, and so they wanted to assure them, and said, 'Aren't we there? Are we dead or what!' But on Friday morning, the day after having stayed awake all through the night of the 25th of March amidst the shelling by the Pakistani Army, when the western sky turned red with the blazing flames of the fire engulfing Nayabazar, the people of Ghost Lane had no clue about whether they themselves would survive! Yet, even in that predicament, they subsequently remembered, they had been worried about Subodhchandra and his wife, and two days later, when many people in the moholla, including Aziz Byapari, fled to Jinjira, they took Subodhchandra and his wife along, and after that when they returned to the moholla following the sudden military counter-operation on Jinjira, Subodh and Swapna too returned with them. Subodhchandra had no option then but to remain in this moholla, because he had neither any place to flee to nor the time, since his village house was very far away, and he had felt strengthened by the assurances of the people of Ghost Lane; in fact, like the moholla folk, he too had been deluded and hadn't realized that, after the 25th of March in 1971, even the Muslims of the moholla were uncertain about whether they could protect themselves. When the people of the moholla returned from Jinjira and encountered Subodhchandra, then despite their own state of acute insecurity, they looked at his haggard face and inquired, 'Are you doing all right?' But no one in the moholla was doing all right then, and when Subodhchandra heard them and smiled cheerlessly, the moholla folk realized their mistake, and they said, 'Why are you afraid? Whatever happens to us will happen to you. If we survive, so will you.' At that time, though the people of the moholla couldn't remember how many days later that was, but only after having gradually become accustomed to the terror did they realize how disoriented they had been at the time; because some time during that period, their wives told them that Subodhchandra's wife had wiped off the sindoor on her forehead and removed the conch-shell bangles from her wrists, and that the two of them were memorizing the kalema; when they heard that, it seemed to them that they had returned to their senses, and they could remember that on the 27th of March, while curfew was on, when they slunk through lanes and alleys and reached Sowarighat and crossed the river, the only Hindus with them then were Subodhchandra and his wife Swapna. And they remembered that Swapna did not have sindoor on her forehead or the conch-shell bangles on her wrists, but at that moment, it seems they didn't notice it; later, after hearing about this from their wives, they recalled it, and they felt a kind of shame then, and they became dejected. Then, when they themselves were unable to ensure their own safety, they went to Subodhchandra's premises in Abdul Aziz Byapari's house and fell silent as they gazed at Swapna's face, and then for the third time they said, 'Don't be afraid, there's no point being afraid, after all we're there!' But the people of the moholla later realized that they had been entirely wrong. Subsequently, the moholla folk gradually remembered all this and their hearts were bestrewn with shame, because they could not forget that not only had they failed to protect Subodhchandra and his wife even after all their assurances, in truth they had abandoned them. The people of the moholla remembered that, until moments before this final incident occurred, they had repeatedly emboldened Subodhchandra and his wife, and the moholla folk once again failed to remember exactly when, but they recalled that with the situation turning even more dire and survival becoming even more uncertain after Moulana Abubakr from their adjacent moholla became Chairman of the Peace Committee and the razakars arrived, they once again heard from their wives about Subodh and Swapna reciting the kalema, and they again landed up at their residence in Aziz Byapari's house. The people of the moholla later said that, after entering their residence that day, they found Subodhchandra lying on his back with his eyes shut; they then observed his wife Swapna slouching as she read a book near the cot, sitting on a low wicker stool. Seeing the people of the moholla, Subodhchandra sat up and Swapna shut her book, and then seeing the title of the book, *Namaz Made Easy*, the moholla folk realized that their wives weren't wrong; they then gazed at the silent husband-and-wife duo and observed sadness in their faces, and they didn't know how to begin a conversation; they too were then immersed silently in the sadness of Subodh and Swapna, and after that they said, 'What's happened to you?'

'No, nothing's happened!'

'Why did you buy this book?'

'Oh, I'm just flipping through it.'

'Are you memorizing the kalema?'

'Yes.'

'Let's see if you can tell us how many kalemas there are.'

'Four.'

'Let's hear you recite the Kalema Taiyeba.'

Hearing the moholla folk say that, it seemed Subodhchandra and his wife became upset; in the dim light of that small room, they raised their melancholy faces and stared in silence at the moholla folk, and then the moholla folk realized their error and became perturbed; they then thought that they could no longer say, 'After all, we're there,' and in that situation, they said, 'Allah's our hope.' The people of the moholla then saw that even learning the kalema failed to suffice for Subodhchandra; soldiers entered Ghost Lane one day, and as terror and panic swept through the entire moholla, Subodhchandra and his wife were killed. The people of the moholla couldn't get over their mortification over the incident, and after the Liberation War, when a general amnesty was declared, Moulana Abubakr and his razakar disciples returned to this locality, and they found out that Moulana Abubakr had said that Subodhchandra and his wife died because of the unnecessary panic and stupidity of the people of Ghost Lane. Moulana Abubakr held that, after all the Hindus left their homes and fled from the various mohollas of Dhaka, the Pakistani army was looking for a Hindu for the sake of publishing a picture in the newspapers, but they weren't able to find one; he then learnt about that, and he recalled that he had heard there was a Hindu family in Ghost Lane. He contended that army men arrived in Ghost Lane twice to look for Subodhchandra for that reason, but the stupid folk of Ghost Lane hid Subodhchandra and his wife the first time, and the next time they pushed them into the well, thus killing them. In silence, the people of Ghost Lane heard about what Moulana Abubakr said, and it wasn't very difficult for them to deduce why he said all that; they asserted that no one had forgotten about 1971, Moulana Abubakr hadn't forgotten about the people of the moholla, just as the people of the moholla hadn't forgotten the specifics of his conduct. The moholla folk retorted, 'The son of a swine is telling lies,' but at the same time they couldn't get over the incident of throwing Subodhchandra into the well. Subsequently, though they couldn't clearly remember the exact date, they said that soldiers arrived for the first time in Ghost Lane in May or June, but since the people knew that the army could show up at any moment, on any day, they were prepared for that. That day, on getting the news of the soldiers' arrival, they put up green flags with the white crescent moon and star on their roofs and waited, and right then, those whose houses abutted the main road heard the sound of heavy boots, and those among them who peeped out saw Pakistani soldiers in khaki uniforms with Chinese rifles on their shoulders, accompanied by the long-robed Moulana Abubakr of the nearby locality of South Moishundi. The soldiers tramped through the moholla silently that day, without saying anything to anyone, and later, the moholla folk said that there was a young Pathan lieutenant with the soldiers, and upon entering the moholla he was overjoyed to see green flags flying from the roofs of all the houses, and he exclaimed to the robed Moulana Abubakr, '*Yeh log toh sab Pakistani hain.* All these people are Pakistanis.' Moulana Abubakr knew that the Pakistani army officer was wrong, but owing to the language barrier, it was not possible for him to explain to the Pathan lieutenant the complicated matter of why, despite hoisting the flag of Pakistan, the people of Ghost Lane were not Pakistanis, and so he walked along in silence beside the Pakistani soldiers with a sense of despondency. The people of the moholla say that Moulana Abubakr then explained to the Pathan lieutenant that all these people were Hindu, he said, '*Yeh sab Hindu hain.*' The Pathan lieutenant returned to his senses when he heard that, and the Pakistani soldiers went and banged on the door of the house on No. 64. Hearing the sound of military boots and the banging, the owner of the house, Haji Mohammad Abdul Karim, opened the door and stood in the doorway, and the people of the moholla say that Moulana Abubakr then faced another kind of dilemma, because when the Pakistani lieutenant observed the white beard of Haji Karim, who was clad in a white punjabi and had a skull cap on, he fell into confusion once again and asked, '*Yeh aadmi Hindu hai?* Is this man a Hindu?' Moulana Abubakr was then able to explain in his broken Urdu mixed with Bangla that not all of them were Hindu, but he was certain that there were Hindus in this moholla. After that, the people of the moholla were tested in regard to their religious identity; the soldiers lined up the forty-one adult males of Ghost Lane on the main road, and observed that all of them had skull caps on their heads; the people of the moholla later said that Subodhchandra was also standing in that line wearing a white cap, and that day, his having memorized the kalema worked. The Pakistani soldiers made the men recite the kalema one by one and then let them go; Subodhchandra too passed the test successfully and returned to his silent and terrified wife at home, and after that, when no one remained on the main road, the Pathan lieutenant became furious and Moulana Abubakr fell into confusion, because he had learnt that there was definitely a Hindu in this moholla; he gazed silently at the lieutenant's livid face. That day, the Pakistani soldiers left the moholla. The people of the moholla later said that, after the soldiers left the first time, they thought they had survived, but this notion of theirs was wrong, because they later saw for themselves that there was no way of surviving in this country in 1971, and then, on the day the soldiers arrived again in the moholla, they threw Subodhchandra into the well, but they were unable to protect themselves either, and they bore this shame all their lives. The people of the moholla say that, although the Pakistani lieutenant was fooled by the kalema recitations, Moulana Abubakr continued to be suspicious, and on account of not being able to identify the Hindu family among all the others in Ghost Lane, he was left with a kind of unease as well as a sense of anger against the people of the lane. But because the situation in the country was changing rapidly, circumstances became very complicated for Moulana Abubakr; the people of the moholla then heard the name of the Mukti Bahini, or Bangladesh Liberation Forces, for the first time, and learnt that five youths from the moholla had joined the Mukti Bahini. When Moulana Abubakr heard about this, he forgot about finding a Hindu person, and instead he sent his razakars to identify the five families whose boys had joined the Mukti Bahini. So, one Thursday evening, four razakars wearing khaki uniforms and canvas shoes marched through Ghost Lane to the accompaniment of their 'left-right' call, and the people of the moholla say that these razakars had no clue as to how they would find the freedom fighters in this country where they were surrounded by enemies. After marching through the moholla for a long while, they banged on three doors, and when the people in each of those houses opened the door and stood at the doorway, the razakars asked them about the freedom fighters, and when the residents said that they knew nothing in that regard, the razakars became dejected and presented themselves before Moulana Abubakr with crestfallen faces. That day, as Moulana Abubakr gazed at the razakars who were silently awaiting his instructions, he understood the matter and growled in a low voice, 'Couldn't you find them?' And hearing him, the razakars standing in his courtyard shook their heads.

'Whom did you ask?'

'We asked in three houses.'

'What did you ask? Whether they knew who the freedom fighters were?'

When the razakars were silent, Moulana Abubakr swore at them, 'Idiots, is that how you get information? Stupid goats!' And the moholla folk say that, on the same night, they learnt that the razakars had come to the moholla to find the freedom fighters, and they became perturbed because of that. They say that, seeing the razakars marching left-right once again the next day with lathis in their hands, they locked the gates outside their residences and sat inside in silence; but they say that the razakars fell into another trap that day. Because they had been scolded by Moulana Abubakr, this time the razakars didn't knock on anyone's door and instead walked up and down the lane, keeping an eye on the one or two people who came out on to the street. The people of the moholla later said that, this time, by trying to be too clever, the razakars fell victim to a new blunder; that day, like seasoned detectives, they observed the people walking along the street, but they couldn't pick on any one, and that was when Kulsum, a young maidservant, emerged from the house on No. 38 and went towards the provision store. When she was returning from the store after making her purchases, she spotted the razakars loitering near the moholla's mosque, and the razakars spotted her too; the people of the moholla say that this encounter invited disaster. They say that, on account of being a maidservant, Kulsum was a somewhat independent woman, and she was of an age at which she was bubbly and flirty, and so she failed to recognize the inner desire of men, or the razakars, and she began engaging playfully with them, and as a result, the first person to be killed in Ghost Lane during the Liberation War in 1971 was the vivacious, young, ever-giggling maidservant Kulsum, who worked in the house of Ali Akbar Miya on No. 38. The people of the moholla say that Kulsum went and stood near the mosque, right in front of the razakars, with one hand on her hip, and exclaimed loudly, 'Why do you do so much left-right, don't you get fed up?' Hearing that, the razakars halted; more than her fresh body, it was the warmth within the liquefaction of her voice that startled them; and it occurred to their commander, Abdul Jabbar, who carried a .303 rifle on his shoulder, that they had finally found the key person in this unfriendly moholla, so they surrounded Kulsum and asked her, 'What's your name?'

'Kulsum.'

The razakars then called Kulsum to a shaded, somewhat concealed spot beside the mosque, and inquired, 'Where do you work?'

'Right here, in Ali Akbar's house. Why?'

The people of the moholla say that, until this point in the conversation with the razakars, notwithstanding Kulsum's unnecessary giggling, everything seemed normal, but they say that just after this she went the wrong way, and although there was a rifle on one man's shoulder, she forgot that these people weren't just men, they were razakars too, and that even if she could play with men, it was dangerous to play with razakars. The people of the moholla, who later heard about all this, say that when Kulsum's giggles ceased, Abdul Jabbar said in a grave yet soft and quiet voice, 'Do you know about the Mukti Bahini?'

Hearing that, mischief entered the mind of this uneducated, immature and somewhat independent woman;

she set aside her skittish manner, stared at him gravely and replied, 'I've heard the name.'

'How many people from this mohalla are in it?'

'I know the names of two people.'

'Who are they?'

The people of the mohalla say that a coy snigger once again bloomed on Kulsum's face, and biting a corner of her anchal with her teeth she replied, 'I've heard that Rahim Bux's son, Sohrab, joined the Mukti Bahini; that's the house next to the house next to that of the family of seven brothers. And Zahiruddin's son, Ajmal, from the lane behind the temple, also joined.' The people of the mohalla say that after releasing Kulsum that day, the razakars rushed back to Moulana Abubakr, and after he heard the details, a hint of a smile spread over his face, he raised his right arm upwards and waved it a bit and muttered to himself, 'I've got you!' After that, following that day's Jumma prayers, in the afternoon, he sent the razakars to fetch Zahiruddin and Rahim Bux. The mohalla folk learnt about everything later, and they say that when the razakars entered No. 25, behind the temple, in search of Zahiruddin, the people in the house said, 'But he's not at home, he's gone out.' Hearing that, the razakars remained silent, and after that, when Zahiruddin returned, they asked him to meet Moulana Abubakr and exited the house, and then went to Rahim Bux's place. The people of the mohalla say that when Rahim Bux opened the door and stood in the doorway, seeing the greying hair on his head and his bulging paunch, the razakars thought that they had apprehended the correct person, and they said, 'Moulana Abubakr is calling you.'

'Why?'

'I can't tell you why. He's called you, that's all.'

When Rahim Bux arrived at Moulana Abubakr's house, he was sitting on a chair in the veranda outside, waiting for him, and seeing Rahim Bux entering his compound with the razakars, he stood up and asked Rahim Bux, who was surrounded by the razakars, 'What's your name again?'

'Rahim Bux. Did you call me?'

The people of the moholla say that Moulana Abubakr began to enjoy the matter, and so he decided not to reply directly to Rahim Bux's query but to catch him like an angler who toys with a fish before reeling it in; but he was floored right at the outset, because when he asked, 'How many children do you have?' Rahim Bux replied, 'Allah didn't grant me any.'

'What did you say? I couldn't follow you!'

'I don't have any children, Allah didn't grant me any. Why do you ask?'

The people of the moholla recount that Moulana Abubakr and his band of razakars were terribly embarrassed by Rahim Bux's reply, but despite that, they couldn't figure out the true nature of the wily Kulsum's mischief until they met Zahiruddin. After detaining Rahim Bux for some more time, Moulana Abubakr let him go, and then, gazing at the razakars standing with glum faces in the courtyard of his house, he reined in his anger and said quietly, 'Goats! Idiots!' After having stood there, downcast, when it occurred to the razakars that this elderly man by the name of Rahim Bux might be a cunning fellow and might have been lying, their disgrace reached its zenith, because they saw a teenage boy entering Moulana Abubakr's compound. The boy went up to Moulana Abubakr, who was standing in the veranda, and asked, 'I heard you called me?'

The people of the moholla say that this time Moulana Abubakr guessed the matter at the outset; he stared at the dark-skinned boy and asked him, 'What's your name?'

'Zahiruddin.'

At this juncture, Moulana Abubakr got the joke intended all along. He asked Zahiruddin, 'Who's Ajmal?'

'I can't tell you. I don't know him.'

'Be off.'

After Zahiruddin left, Moulana Abubakr once again turned towards the razakars standing silently in his compound, and controlling his rage and agitation, he said, 'Bloody goats, hold your ears!' The razakars, who were in a state of profound confusion, couldn't understand what Moulana Abubakr meant, and when they continued to stand silently with cheerless faces, Moulana Abubakr realized that he was faced not only with the penchant of the people of Ghost Lane to play jokes, but also the crisis of his razakars not heeding his instructions. The people of the moholla say that those who peeped into Moulana

Abubakr's compound then saw him standing on the veranda facing the razakars, and they saw that after remaining silent for a while, he raised his right hand and flailed it animatedly in the air and screamed out, 'Hold your ears! Hold your ears!' And seeing him explode suddenly like this, the razakars standing in the courtyard were terrified; they shook momentarily, and then they put the lathis in their hands on the ground and stood holding their ears with their hands. The people of the moholla say that Moulana Abubakr regained his composure when he saw the razakars standing holding their ears, and leaving them there like that, he went inside the house and fell asleep, and in the evening, after he woke up, he went outside and saw the razakars still standing in the courtyard, holding their ears. The people of the moholla say that, on observing the impact of his orders on the razakars, the matter went to Moulana Abubakr's head, and he didn't let the razakars off even then. He continued to enjoy the scene; sitting in the veranda in front of the razakars holding their ears, he sipped tea luxuriously and let the evening roll along, and after that, when it was dusk and the azan for the Maghrib prayers sounded, he declared, 'Go, go and say your prayers now.' That evening, the razakars took their hands down from their ears, and instead of going to the mosque, they went to Ali Akbar's house, knocked on the door and waited outside. When the door was opened, they were very courteous and inquired after Kulsum's whereabouts. When the people in the house asked what business they had with Kulsum, they mumbled something, and that was when Kulsum, who was inside, learnt about the arrival of the razakars; she then bit a corner of her anchal with her teeth and giggled and got into the mood for mischief, so she muttered, 'Have the bullocks come looking for freedom fighters again or what?' And after saying so, when she wound her anchal on her waist and came and stood in front of the door, and in the semi-darkness of dusk, squinted at them and sniggered and asked, 'Why are you going Kulsum, Kulsum?', then, without uttering a single word, the commander of the razakars, Abdul Jabbar, raised his rifle, and from a distance of three feet, he fired at Kulsum's chest, and the people of the moholla say that when Kulsum's dead body was lifted up from near the door at the entrance of Ali Akbar's house, the mischievous smile was still lingering on her lips. The people of the moholla say that the vague sense of fear they harboured regarding the Pakistani soldiers and the razakars became distinct and tangible after the murder of Kulsum, and even amidst their own sense of insecurity, they were constantly anxious about Subodhchandra and his wife, because they knew in their heart of hearts that, even though Moulana Abubakr had been deceived by the recitation of the kalema the first time, he would definitely try once again when he got the opportunity. After Kulsum's death, catching the freedom fighters assumed greater importance for Moulana Abubakr, but the people of the moholla say that Subodhchandra's fate was already sealed; instead of the freedom fighters, it was Subodhchandra who was apprehended, and as a result of that, the most shameful incident in the lives of the moholla folk occurred. They recall that it was probably a Friday that day too, because at the time the incident took place, everyone had skull caps on their heads; that day, after the Jumma prayers, eleven people went to Subodhchandra's premises in Abdul Aziz Byapari's house, and sitting in a room inside Aziz Byapari's house they discussed whether Subodhchandra and his wife could be sent somewhere else, and then that day, Moulana Abubakr arrived in the moholla with soldiers. The Pakistani soldiers cordoned off the street, but after conducting a search, they were unable to find out who had gone from which house to join the Liberation War. When the people gathered at Aziz Byapari's house got the news of the arrival of the soldiers, at first they tried to flee, but when they saw that the soldiers were standing in the street with their rifles at the ready, they returned to the room in Abdul Aziz Byapari's house and began reciting the Milad Sharif, and wearing a cap on his head, Subodhchandra joined this group. When the Pakistani soldiers arrived at Aziz Byapari's house accompanied by Moulana Abubakr, they found a group of people performing Milad in a large room. The men standing there with skull caps on their heads kept on chanting 'Ya Nabi Salamalaika', and when, even after waiting with rifles in their hands for half an hour, the chanting didn't cease, the

Pakistani soldiers berated them and made them stop. By then, Moulana Abubakr had realized that the information about the freedom fighters could not be obtained so simply, and he remembered something from the past, because upon entering Aziz Byapari's residence, his probing eyes spotted a tulsi plant beside a wall, and it occurred to him that the person they were looking for lived here, and so, as he gazed at the men with caps on their heads standing silently, he declared, 'There's a Hindu among you lot!' The people of the moholla say that, at first, they didn't want to admit that to Moulana Abubakr, and so they retorted, 'What are you saying? Do Hindus perform Milad?', but then when Moulana Abubakr wanted to know who worshipped the tulsi plant, they remembered that it was planted by Subodhchandra's wife Swapna, and they realized that, after she broke the conch-shell bangles on her wrists and wiped off the sindoor from her forehead, she had probably forgotten about this plant; but still, these people from the moholla made a final attempt and said that the tulsi plant had probably sprouted up by itself, but Moulana Abubakr didn't believe them. That day, when Subodhchandra could not be identified from among the people of the moholla, the Pakistani soldiers lined up the twelve men, including Subodhchandra, beside the well in the compound of Aziz Byapari's house, and the moholla folk subsequently reported that Subodhchandra's fate was already sealed as he was standing at the very end of the line, grazing the side of the well. After that, when the Pakistani army captain demanded, *'Kalema bolo.* Recite the kalema,' all of them recited the Kalema Taiyeba one by one; but that day, Moulana Abubakr was prepared to see the matter through to the end, and after he spoke with the Pakistani army captain, two soldiers moved forward with their rifles drawn and ordered the first man in the line, *'Lungi uthao.* Lift up your lungi,' and then the other men from the moholla who were standing in the line saw white-bearded Idris Miya from the house on No. 18 hesitate for a while and then lift his lungi up high and expose his circumcised penis to the bright light of day, thus proving his identity, and the people of the moholla say that they then observed tears streaming from Idris Miya's eyes and running down his white beard. After that, the men standing in line lifted up their lungis one by one and exposed themselves that day, and the people of the moholla say that, even as this was going on, they were alarmed that Subodhchandra would definitely get caught now, and if he was caught then so would they. That was when, although the moholla folk couldn't say how many men had lifted up their lungis before that, one person in the line, perhaps the man standing beside Subodhchandra, grabbed him and pushed him over the low wall of the well. Because it happened so suddenly, after being momentarily startled, the two rifle-bearing soldiers panicked and fired, and three people were shot to death beside Aziz Byapari's well that day, while Subodhchandra drowned in it. The people of Ghost Lane could not forget that it was they who threw Subodhchandra into the well in 1971. The people of the moholla were confounded that day; they departed from Aziz Byapari's house with three dead bodies, and perhaps their grief and shock was so profound that they forgot all about Subodhchandra who had fallen into the well, and they later admitted that this was a fatal mistake. That evening, they performed the ritual bathing of the dead bodies, conducted the funeral prayers and took them to the Azimpur burial ground where the bodies were interred, and then they returned to their respective homes, and that was when the people of the moholla remembered that Subodhchandra's body was still in the well, so they rushed to Abdul Aziz Byapari's house and they discovered that Swapna was not in her room, and the hitherto-concealed white conch-shell bangles lay in a broken state on her bed, and on top of that was an open sindoor box, upturned; the people of the moholla then became alarmed, and after a hook attached to a rope was lowered into the well, they drew up the dead bodies of the couple. That day, the moholla folk felt dejected, endangered and upset when they confronted the dead couple, and after that, in the midst of various preoccupations, the people of the moholla completely forgot about Subodhchandra, until a person from Satkhira arrived looking for him. The people of the moholla say that one or two months after the country attained independence, on a Tuesday or a Wednesday, a person arrived in Ghost Lane and went and stood in front of Abdul Aziz Byapari's house, and Aziz Byapari opened the door and saw the person waiting there, and the people of the moholla learnt that a person had come looking for Subodhchandra; they then remembered Subodh and Swapna, and a vague sense of shame returned to their consciousness; then, those among them who went to Aziz Byapari's house saw him sitting in front of a silent young man in the same room where they remembered having eaten nimokpara earlier; on the bed in front of him was a folded shawl, and on top of the shawl lay the pieces of the broken conch-shell bangles, smeared with sindoor. The people of the moholla say that after sitting in silence for a long time, he placed the pieces of the conch-shell bangles in the palm of his right hand and shook them, as if he was examining them, or perhaps he was doing it for no reason, and after that, he took out his handkerchief, wrapped the pieces in it and put it into his shirt pocket; the people from the moholla who were standing there then were silent, and after a long time they asked, 'What's your name?' The people of the moholla later said that when they heard the answer to this question, it occurred to them that actually they already knew the answer; they say that, upon hearing their query, the man turned to them, and they could not discern what they saw in his eyes; perhaps they didn't observe any emotion at all, perhaps there was no melancholy, grief, anger, or hate in his gaze, and they say that his impassivity triggered the return of their inner sense of shame, and when they were almost reduced to helplessness, the man said that his name was Poranchandra Das.

The elderly folk of Ghost Lane could remember that, seven years ago too, Subodhchandra had fallen into the well, but they could not be certain about the circumstances behind it. At that time, there were reports of riots taking place in some localities in the city of Dhaka, and the people of the moholla learnt one day that the tenant Subodhchandra, residing in Aziz Byapari's house on No. 36, and his wife Swapna fell into the well and drowned, and they say that, at first, they thought that perhaps Subodhchandra and his wife had been murdered; but later, they heard in the moholla that it had been an accident, that Subodhchandra and his comely, dark-skinned wife had fallen into the water while trying to reach out and touch the reflection of the full moon in the well. They heard that, one night during the rainy season, because Subodhchandra's wife wasn't able to sleep, she left the room and went and stood in the open at the well-side; because it had been raining continuously, the water level in the well had risen a lot, and there was a full moon in the sky that night. The people in the moholla heard that, at some point during that night, Subodhchandra joined his wife at the well-side, and they sat on the paved wall of the well and chatted; and perhaps on account of their youthfulness and nature's joyous unveiling, they were roused to passion. Then, looking into the water in the well, which was almost within touching distance, Swapna saw the reflection of the moon, looking like a round, golden platter submerged in the water. The people of the moholla say that when Swapna gazed at this reflection in the well and exclaimed, 'Shall I touch it,' Subodhchandra responded, 'Touch it,' and they learnt that the accident happened just after that. The moholla folk could not find out what time at night the accident occurred, and who witnessed it, or who heard the conversation between Subodhchandra and Swapna, but they learnt that when Subodhchandra's wife sat on the wall of the well that night, the water level was actually not as high as she thought it to be; when she leaned down, stretched out her arm and tried to touch the surface of the water, her hand couldn't reach the water and it dangled in the air without support, and she lost her balance and fell headlong into the well. Although Subodhchandra was nearby then, because it all happened so suddenly, he couldn't prevent her fall; but he returned to his senses after that, and tucking his lungi between his legs like a loincloth, he jumped into the well to save his wife, and as a result he too perished with her. The people of the moholla surmised that Subodhchandra's wife probably didn't know how to swim, and so she began to drown after falling into the well, and when Subodhchandra jumped into the well and reached her, she grabbed him so firmly that Subodhchandra, too, inevitably drowned; the next morning, the people in the house discovered the dead bodies of Subodhchandra and his wife, both clutching each other, floating in the well. That day, the people of the moholla first retrieved the pair of bodies from the well and placed them on the platform in the veranda, and then sent word to Subodhchandra's family in Narayanganj, and that very evening, Subodhchandra's brother and two others arrived by train, and after talking to them, the people of the moholla learnt that Subodhchandra's brother's name was Poranchandra. That day, after Poran and his companions hired a lorry and departed for Narayanganj with the dead bodies, the moholla folk gathered in Abdul Aziz Byapari's house, and they spotted the tulsi plant beside the courtyard wall which had been planted by Swapna; they observed that, although there was no platform at its base, the soil had been gathered and patted down in a kind of circle. After the bodies of Subodh and Swapna were taken away to Narayanganj, the people of the moholla forgot about them, and the tulsi plant beside the wall withered and died at some point of time.

The people of the moholla say that when Subodhchandra and his dark-skinned, comely wife arrived as tenants in Abdul Aziz Byapari's house almost seven years later, for a long time they failed to notice that Swapna had planted a tulsi sapling at the old spot and gathered and patted down the soil at its base in a circle. But following the country's independence, on some Tuesday or Wednesday, Poran arrived from Satkhira, and after he put the broken pieces of Swapna's conch-shell bangles in his shirt pocket and packed Subodhchandra's belongings, he left for Kamalapur rail station, and then, the people of the moholla once again forgot about Subodh, Swapna and the tulsi plant beside the wall.

After that, the people of the moholla learnt, while sitting in Your Choice Salon for a haircut, that new tenants had arrived at Aziz Byapari's house, and that their names were Subodhchandra and Swapna, and so they went to meet them and talked to them. Sitting in Your Choice Salon, the moholla folk chatted about that; they said that Babul Miya had gone to meet the new tenants one day, and when he asked Subodhchandra, 'What's your name,' he replied, 'Subodhchandra,' and then Babul Miya declared that he already knew that.

'How is that?'

'Is your wife's name Swapna?'

'Yes, how do you know?'

'Don't you have a brother, back in the village?'

'Yes, I do.'

'Is his name Poran?'

'Yes, but how do you know all this?'

Babul Miya then said that everyone in the moholla knew all this, and he warned Subodhchandra, 'There's a well in this house, just beware of that well!' The moholla folk heard about all this as they sat at Your Choice Salon, and they felt very perturbed; they then went to meet Abdul Aziz Byapari and informed him about their anxiety lest Subodh and Swapna fall into the well again, but Aziz Byapari did not take what they said seriously, he brushed it off saying, 'Oh don't worry! Do people fall into wells again and again?' There was nothing the moholla folk could do then, so they went back, and after that, they had nimokpara and tea prepared by Swapna and listened to Subodhchandra holding forth on the furies wreaked by the Jamuna river, and that was when they once again noticed the tulsi plant beside the wall, and they observed that the soil at the base had been gathered and patted down in a circle, and sindoor had been sprinkled on the soil. The people of Ghost Lane say that, then, although they don't know exactly when, but they say that it was some time after the great floods that occurred towards the final phase of the reign of the thuggish, childless general, there was a terrible heatwave, and sparrows nesting in ventilators kept dying in the heat, and at that time, they heard for the first time about the mosque in Ayodhya being demolished and became extremely agitated, but they found that it was Subodhchandra and his wife who were even more distressed than them; subsequently, the people of the moholla remembered that they had given assurances of safety time and again to Subodhchandra, but on no occasion could they keep their word. Then one day, they learnt that the mosque had not actually been demolished, and while sitting for a haircut in Your Choice Salon one day, Subodhchandra remarked with a sombre look on his face, 'This isn't right. Does religion require mosques to be demolished?' The people of the moholla say that the other people in the salon who had come for haircuts saw in the large mirrors in front of them Subodhchandra's grimy and glum face above the neck-high white sheet wound around him, and even amidst the heatwave and the stench, they surmised the reason for his dejection, and they asked, 'Are you scared?'

'No, why should I be scared!'

'Don't be afraid, after all you haven't done anything!'

But subsequently, the people of the moholla recalled all these events with a kind of bewilderment, dejection and shame, and discovered the truth that they had perhaps not said the right thing regarding Subodhchandra for some reason that they could not fathom, because they saw that Subodh and Swapna fell into the well again. All the rumours about the demolition of a mosque continued to spread, and one day, it was really pulled down, and on the day this dilapidated and ancient mosque was destroyed following a long campaign, Subodhchandra did something they were unable to explain, and they were disconcerted. The day the people of the moholla got the news of the mosque really having been demolished, they were very morose, and two days later, when newspapers published images of fundamentalists standing atop the debris of the demolished mosque, with their hands raised in victory and turbans wound around their heads, they felt helpless, and then, that day, the matter of what Subodhchandra had done was revealed in the moholla. The rumour spread quickly through the moholla that, the day the report of the mosque being demolished in Ayodhya was received, Subodhchandra went to Nawabpur and bought sweetmeats from Moronchand's shop, and then, the husband-and-wife duo had those sweets. The people of the moholla were unable to say who witnessed this act of eating sweets, or from whom this report of their having done so was received; they later said that the source of this news was perhaps Abdul Aziz Byapari's house servant or maidservant or someone else; by that evening, this news spread through the whole of Ghost Lane and the adjacent localities, and a huge group of overwrought and agitated people gathered in front of Abdul Aziz Byapari's house, and yelling 'Allahu Akbar', they entered it. That day, the people of Ghost Lane forgot about the nimokpara served to them by Subodhchandra and his wife Swapna, and when this mass of people left Aziz Byapari's house, Subodh and Swapna were found in the well, dead; but this time, Poranchandra did not arrive, because after getting the news, the police arrived and took away the dead bodies. The people from Twin Bridge Lane and Padmanidhi Lane, and the people of the Narinda and Gaudiya Math localities, who went to Your Choice Salon for a haircut or a shave, said that after that, at some point, the people of Ghost Lane entered a complex labyrinth of time, because it was observed that they were unable to forget about having eaten the nimokpara prepared by Swapna, and they always recalled that they had repeatedly assured Subodhchandra, 'Don't be afraid,' but Subodhchandra and his wife continuously fell into the well in the moholla, or they themselves threw them in; the people of the moholla then, once again, fell into dejection and felt ashamed, and around this time, a group of moholla folk presented themselves at Abdul Aziz Byapari's house with spades in their hands, and they then entered the greatest perplexity of their lives, and it occurred to them that the frame of time in their lives had broken down.

That day, these people from Ghost Lane appeared at Abdul Aziz Byapari's house with spades in their hands, and reproached him for not sealing up the well after piped water became available in the house, and they declared that they would dig up the earth and seal the well. Aziz Byapari was flabbergasted when he heard that, and he retorted, 'Who's Subodhchandra? Where's the piped water? We're still surviving on drinking the water fetched by Nijam's mother!' And just then, they saw Nijam's mother entering Abdul Aziz Byapari's house, carrying a pitcher of water from the standpipe on the street for the family's dinner. These moholla folk could not disregard the reality of the corporeal presence of the tilawali or water carrier, Nijam's mother, and then they realized that perhaps Subodhchandra had not yet arrived in the moholla, the country had not attained independence, and the mosque in Ayodhya had not been demolished; but then, they could simultaneously remember Subodhchandra having continuously fallen into the well, and they felt very upset and ashamed, and they were at a loss. They could not figure out which plane of time they existed in, but they could not forget the taste of the nimokpara they had eaten or would eat, and the futility of the assurances to not be afraid that they had given or would give Subodhchandra tormented them so much that they announced to Abdul Aziz Byapari, 'We are going to seal up this well,' and disregarding his objections, they dug up the earth in front of his eyes and sealed the well, and after that, come evening, some of them boarded a long, green-coloured EPRTC bus with two doors from the Rathkhola intersection and went to Sadarghat. But the moholla folk say that, even before the bus reached Sadarghat, these people got upset, because they had Swapna and Subodh in mind; it struck them that if the well was sealed up, Subodhchandra was not supposed to have fallen into the well, and so their delight at riding on this new EPRTC bus was soured. The people of the moholla say that, in their state of confusion, it seemed to them that they were stuck in some place inside some dream, and within this dream, they had penetrated into the future from the past or into the past from the future, and it occurred to them that perhaps the matter of Subodh and Swapna was not true, but a dream; but they then remembered Swapna's tulsi sapling planted in the courtyard of Abdul Aziz Byapari's house, and they went to his house and saw the tulsi plant beside the courtyard wall swaying in the gentle breeze; and then they remembered the well.

(1995)

(Co-translated with Shahroza Nahrin)

Why There Are No Noyontara Flowers in Agargaon Colony

ABDUS SATTAR WAS RETURNING HOME; some people observed him after he got off the bus at Taltala and made his way towards his residence in the colony in the soft glow of evening, although this daily event of a thin, dark-skinned, middle-aged clerk returning home from office was nothing worth looking at. When he reached the road inside the colony, perhaps because it was the rainy season, or because of some unseasonal rain, the countless potholes in the rundown, brick-lined road were full of water, and where there wasn't any water the road was slippery and the treacherous slime made him hold his back high and crooked. Abdus Sattar hopped like an egret and traversed the road with the bottoms of his trousers rolled up to just under his knees, and when he reached the front of his building, he stumbled on one such slippery part and fell down; he then spread his hands behind him and sat down in the wet slime. Those who witnessed this scene burst out laughing, and then they hurried towards him and lifted him up from the mud; contemplating the incident as he sat there, Abdus Sattar's own lips too quivered a bit and he said, 'I fell down,' and thus, after a long time, solely on account of having slipped and fallen down, he got the opportunity to exchange words with his neighbours. When he returned home, he could only say the same thing to his wife Shireen Banu, 'I fell down in the muddy slime,' and then, like he did every day, he went and sat in the balcony in the grey light of dusk. Sinking into the cane chair there, he used to sit until night while his wife helped his two sons and daughter with their studies, after which they made a ruckus and then went to the flat next door and watched television, and all the while Abdus Sattar blended into the darkness in the veranda. He observed how dense and almost tactile the darkness became after the light of day was effaced; he just kept gazing, but that didn't make him happy or tired, just like he never experienced any feeling of tiredness in his clerical government job. Sometimes as he sat like this, when the southerly breeze wafted in and the green potted plants arrayed by his wife in the narrow veranda of their colony flat swayed and their leaves made a fluttering sound, the air was suffused with the faint petrichor like fragrance of the noyontara flower that had been born from the soil in a pot that was fastened with a string to the railing. Abdus Sattar used to sit on the cane chair amidst that flutter and fragrance, as if from time immemorial, and his wife Shireen Banu filled their flat with a variety of potted plants; besides the noyontara and patabahar plants, she had also planted rajnigandha saplings in the veranda. Abdus Sattar either observed or didn't observe all this, he didn't say anything about it; whether or not he was mindful of the green world of foliage that had grown inside his residence remained unexpressed until the day he died. Under Shireen Banu's indulgent tending, the sloping patabahar plants spread to every doorway of their flat; green, snake-like vines of money plants hung down from the cupboard, bookshelf and mosquito-net posts. When Abdus Sattar went to sleep after dinner, a long and clustering plant placed beside the dressing table by the head of his cot swayed as it respired; Abdus Sattar didn't notice that, he remained asleep; but his neighbours did notice, they praised Shireen Banu endlessly, and the womenfolk of the colony were beside themselves with excitement on seeing the sylvan assemblage inside the flat. Following the arrival of Abdus Sattar and his family in this colony four years ago, his wife had brought about the ultimate blooming of the artistic practice of growing plants in pots, and these plants crossed the limits of their flat and spread to their neighbours' flats. All the residents of this building in the colony – i.e., the wives of the clerks, inspectors and junior officers in various government offices – began competing with each other to fill up the space inside their flats with plants. And thus, the balance in the relationship between nature and man that had, according to knowledgeable people, apparently been ruptured in the modern age, seemed to have been restored in this building. For that matter, the estrangement that occurred every day in the relationship between the residents of this building in the colony and people at large also seemed to have been repaired somehow by the green foliage of various shrub-like plants. All these young ladies and their menfolk in the colony finally learnt to discover the beauty of life, they found arboreal significance in their meaningless and isolated lifestyles, and all of them were grateful to Abdus Sattar's wife, Shireen Banu, for that. Only Abdus Sattar remained outside this circle; nothing occurred to him when he gazed at the lovely cactus kept inside the flat, and when something did suddenly occur to him, he then felt that this plant was graceful, incomparable and entirely thorny. Green creepers descended from every balcony of the building in the colony in which Abdus Sattar lived, and a reddish-purple-coloured pattern was composed on the front side of this yellow-coloured building from the noyontara flowers planted along the balcony railings. When sunlight turned pale in the late afternoon, butterflies abandoned the shrubs at the aerodrome near Agargaon and began fluttering in front of this building in the colony, and the arrival of the butterflies and their hovering and fluttering like this continued for many days. The first day the butterflies arrived, the people in the colony were afraid that perhaps they would remain in their flats and lay eggs and build a kingdom of golden caterpillars among their verdant dreams. But their fear was at once eliminated; the butterflies didn't stay on in people's homes, as the evening light waned, they melted into the surroundings. This process continued in front of this building in the colony for a year, and through all of it Abdus Sattar sat awake, with a motionless presence, like some ageless and immovable piece of stone; when the butterflies ascended to the veranda and fluttered around there, yellow pollen from their flapping wings accumulated on Abdus Sattar's face, chin and earlobes. He gazed at them, and he wiped the pollen off his ear with his fingers, and if a butterfly entered his shirt he freed it; it seemed he had got used to living in the dominion of all these insects, it seemed he wasn't inconvenienced now, although a year ago, when the butterflies were first overwhelmed by the beauty of the noyontara flowers and began arriving there, the excitement it created in this city had interrupted the tranquillity of Abdus Sattar's life. When news of the capriciousness of the butterflies spread through word of mouth, the city's tired, sad and drowsy folk became excited, and when one day a report accompanied by a picture appeared on the last page of a newspaper, the situation took a decisive turn. Every evening, even before the arrival of the butterflies, the road in front of this six-storeyed building in the colony was crowded with all these entertainment-starved city folk leading dreary lives, and when swarms of yellow butterflies arrived and danced around the noyontara flowers and created the appearance of a moving garden of marigolds floating in the air, the people gazed in speechless wonder;

and they kept thinking that it wasn't humans but beautiful butterflies that led fulfilling lives. The middle-aged man whom these people spotted through the gaps in the railing of one veranda, sitting amidst the crowd of butterflies from beginning to end, was Abdus Sattar. Although he initially tried to remain indifferent to the comings and goings of all these people, he gradually had to become conscious of his surroundings; as the astonishment of those who came to see the butterflies was dispelled and they forsook their earlier conclusion about the fulfilment in a butterfly's life, they were once again afflicted by the fatigue of monotony. In order to drive away this annoyance, some of them began to throw clods of earth aimed at the butterflies; all these lumps of earth missed their target and fell into the verandas of the building in the colony, and one day a lump like this hit Abdus Sattar while he was sitting in the veranda. Also, given the situation, suddenly peanut and ice cream vendors arrived there for the delectation of the vexed folk and the whole place resounded with their cries and the sound of bells. The guardians of the city too were prompt in this instance, and in order that peace and order were not disrupted, a temporary police outpost was erected in a corner of the field in front of the building, and then people from the Forest Department arrived one day, and they put up a signboard on bamboo poles on the side of the road in front of the colony, on which it was written that the butterflies were only for observation and they could not be caught or harmed in any way; if anyone did that, they would be punished under the Wildlife Protection Act. When the colony took on the disarranged look of a dust-laden and noisy fair, and it occurred to Abdus Sattar for the first time that perhaps it would no longer be possible for him to sit in this spot which provided him the greatest shelter in life, the people in the colony woke up one morning and heard on the radio that the government of the nation had changed the previous night; and as a result of that, a situation was created whereby Abdus Sattar found deliverance, and he did not have to forsake his veranda. This new government of generals took many quick and significant steps in the interests of the nation and the people, and among these was the project to modernize Mirpur Zoo. A dozen chimpanzees were imported from Kenya on an emergency basis, and they were exhibited in a new cage beside the old monkey cage. When pictures and reports of these chimpanzees appeared in the newspapers, the vexed folk who were tired of monotony were shaken up, they ran towards Mirpur Zoo to see the chimpanzees, and the field in Agargaon Colony once again returned to silence; Abdus Sattar could once again submerge himself, with shallow breaths, in this silence. But most people in the world are always capricious; people are not mindful of the fact that their capriciousness is infectious, just like waves are created when a stone is thrown into a pond, and at this time one day, some caprice like this, arising somewhere, was transported and flew through the darkness, and it landed on Abdus Sattar when he was sitting in the balcony. He picked up the object that had accidentally landed there, and even before he sniffed it, he realized that it was a flower; and when he brought it close to his nose, he was certain that it was a rose; he kept the rose. The next day's rose fell about a foot away from his chair, but for the next five days no flowers landed there, and then on the sixth day, two flowers landed in quick succession; and in this way, roses kept piercing the darkness and flying into Abdus Sattar's balcony. Abdus Sattar accepted the flowers, he took in their fragrance; but he didn't think too much about it. Then one day, when Abdus Sattar went indoors to eat dinner earlier than his usual time, his wife came and stood in the balcony to enjoy the cool breeze, and that day's rose then flew in. When Shireen Banu realized that a flower had flown in from the darkness outside, she became unsettled, but she couldn't figure out this mystery; she remained seated with the rose in her hand. When Abdus Sattar came to the balcony after dinner, Shireen Banu extended her hand towards him in the darkness and said, 'Take it.'

'What is it?'

Shireen Banu didn't speak, but Abdus Sattar realized it was a rose when he received it.

'Who throws you roses?'

'I don't know.'

It then occurred to Abdus Sattar for the first time that this was definitely a mystery, but his mental inquiry in this regard did not proceed very far.

'Is this why you sit on the veranda?'

Neither of them could see the other's face. Abdus Sattar said, 'No.'

'Do you feel ashamed to admit that?'

'Ashamed of what?'

'Then?'

'Then what?'

'For the last one month, I've been clearing torn, dry flowers from the veranda.'

'What of it?'

Shireen Banu then mumbled something softly, Abdus Sattar couldn't hear it properly, but he suddenly remembered that long ago, a bluebottle had flown in from the darkness outside, and he asked, 'Do you remember the day of 18th March 1970?'

Waves of meaningless time had steadily dissipated in Shireen Banu's memory, she couldn't remember anything; she asked, 'What happened that day?'

'That was a day three months after our marriage,' Abdus Sattar replied. 'It was before your second visit to Dhaka after our wedding. I had gone to Sirajganj to bring you back, we were going to take the evening train on the 18th of March 1970; you had got ready, your luggage was packed, there was a two-horse carriage waiting in front of the gate of your house on Kalibari Road. Everything was ready, everyone was standing in the veranda or on the compound, and you were inside, just about to come out. I was standing in the darkness under the sweet-and-sour mango tree behind your house and pissing with the zip of my trouser undone; one of the shutters of the window at the rear of the house was open, and I spotted you. There were biscuits smeared with honey on a saucer, you picked one up and ate it; some honey stuck to your lip, and a big bluebottle came flying in from the darkness then, and it sat on your lip. You flicked it away, wiped your lip and went out, and I was pissing under the mango tree then; can you remember that?'

They had nothing left but darkness and silence. Then after a long time, Abdus Sattar once again asked, 'Can't you remember? I know that the bluebottle had come from the dirty latrine in the clump of palm trees behind your house; can't you remember that?'

'No, I can't remember,' Shireen Banu said. 'I'm living with a madman.'

After that, Abdus Sattar kept receiving roses in the evening's darkness, and in the mornings, Shireen Banu removed the corpses of dried-up roses from the balcony; they were unable to solve the mystery of the roses that flew in. But it seems like a very simple answer to the puzzle was soon discovered; one day, when Fazlul Karim, who lived downstairs on the first floor with his wife, two daughters and a young son, moved out of their flat in the colony, the sound of Rahimuddin Bhuiyan's young daughter's suppressed weeping could be heard from the fourth-floor flat directly above Abdus Sattar's. No flower landed that night, and after that, just like rain ceased, the hitherto inevitable process of roses flying into Abdus

Sattar's veranda too ceased. Perhaps there was a direct link between Fazlul Karim's young son departing the colony and the cessation of flowers flying into Abdus Sattar's veranda; or maybe there was no connection between these two events which happened at the same time merely by coincidence. Whatever the truth might be, Abdus Sattar remained indifferent to and removed from the mysteries that are at play in nature or within people, and all these changes did not cause any change in his life. He sat at dusk among the silent swarms of butterflies, he watched the darkness spreading, although the dance of the butterflies didn't continue for very many days after that either. Just a few days later, late in the evening one day, the city was rocked by severe tremors; cooking utensils came crashing down from all the kitchens in the colony, people screamed, they rushed down from their flats and ran towards the field. Abdus Sattar was sitting in the veranda that day as well; a few moments after the first tremor, startled, he realized it was an earthquake and he thought of going down. The building was then severely rocked a second time, and he could see that the pots of noyontara placed on the railing and fastened with string were tearing the fastening apart and about to fall down; he moved forward hastily, leaned over the railing and put his arms firmly around two displaced pots. But as he rushed forward, leaned over and then grasped the two heavy flowerpots firmly, the upper half of his body grew heavier and he lost his balance; instead of retrieving the flowerpots, his body went over the railing and descended with the pots. Abdus Sattar's trajectory was exactly like that of a bomber plane on a kamikaze mission.

Twenty-seven buildings in the city developed cracks as a result of that earthquake, a building beside the lake in Rampura tilted, and in Agargaon Colony, all the noyontara plants, and Abdus Sattar, fell to the earth. Abdus Sattar's skull was smashed and spread out like a bloody mushroom on the upper part of his neck, his brains spilled out and became one with the earth. After Abdus Sattar was buried, the grieving folk of the colony put their fallen noyontara plants back on the railings; only the widow Shireen Banu's plants lay on the ground below. After a few days, everyone's plants came back to life again and the butterflies returned, and Shireen Banu, who was a bit better now, brought back her noyontara plants and planted them in new pots; but instead of springing back to life at the railing, they died very soon. After that, everyone in this building of the colony observed with astonishment and alarm that the leaves of their thriving noyontara plants were gradually wilting; and within a week, all the plants had withered and died. The people in the colony then obtained new noyontara saplings and planted them, but all the saplings once again withered and died in the same way. The people in the colony then requested and invited a professor from the agricultural college to look into the matter and advise them. The professor tested the soil and found nothing harmful, so he planted new saplings, but they kept dying as usual. He undertook this process thrice, and all three times the noyontara saplings died for no apparent reason. The venerable professor arrived at the truth of the matter after a month of hard work, but he was unable to explain it to everyone, he merely advised the people of Agargaon Colony not to plant noyontara for the time being. However, he wrote a long note on the subject in his personal notebook. He wrote:

> I still don't know whether or not such a thing is possible. The noyontara (*Vinca rosea*) plants were thriving; but as a result of the earthquake, there was a change. The plants in two pots came in close contact with the brains of a dead man. After the earthquake, when the other plants were taken back, they were doing well; but the two clumps that the dead man had tried to save began to die, and after that the other plants became afflicted too. On examination, no infectious fungus or disease was found, there was nothing harmful in the soil; rather, it was observed that all the necessary ingredients for the plants' nourishment and growth were present. The roots of the plants were examined and they were found to be adequately healthy and strong. All the saplings that were planted at the railing, thrice in succession, are dead; but the four saplings that were planted in the earth at the spot where the dead man's head was smashed have survived

and are becoming robust. Does that mean that the plants have got into the habit of consuming some material from the brain? I am not yet certain about this, but my preliminary thinking is that perhaps this is not correct. One of these four plants was removed from there and planted elsewhere, and the elements that make up the brain, like sodium, magnesium, chloride, phosphorus and so on were added to the soil, but there was no positive result. I've tried using the fresh brain of a cow, and for that matter (something very secret), a few days ago, I brought a human brain in a polythene bag from the morgue at the medical college and tried mixing that in the soil too; it didn't work. The sapling was dying, and finally, after replanting it with the other three saplings, it sprang back to life. It's difficult to figure out why the plants thrive in this particular spot (the soil there was tested and no other special characteristics were found); there's only one special feature of the spot, which is that a person's head got smashed there, a person who, I've heard, was a bit crazy, and at the time of the earthquake, he fell while trying to save two pots of noyontara plants; in that case, is it something that's personal for these plants? It could be. But my thinking on this subject of the noyontara plants in this colony dying when they are removed from a particular spot is that the plants are simply committing suicide. That's because I have not found any real reason for their death. I cannot say anything more about why these noyontara plants die. I do know what sentient beings plants are. And in this regard, this desire for suicide first spread from one plant to another because of the close proximity of the plants, and the butterflies performed the role of messengers in this process; I suspect that subsequently the soil too might have played a role. If contact with the butterflies can be avoided, and if they are planted on soil brought from elsewhere, noyontara plants may perhaps grow again in Agargaon Colony. I was able to save one sapling by this method, inside a polythene bag. But one can only conduct an experiment in this way, not raise a garden. This note of mine is perhaps not as accomplished as a scientist's paper; but I see nothing wrong in writing down whatever I have observed and thought.

The four noyontara plants planted by the professor from the agricultural college were in the earth in front of the building in Agargaon Colony; he had thrown away the sapling that grew inside a polythene bag. But subsequently, at some point of time, people from the Public Works Department arrived and laid a metalled road in front of the building, and they paved the grassy patch between the road and the building so that no trash would be dumped there. They thus removed the final four noyontara plants and cleared that space, and ever since then there have been no noyontara plants in this colony. However, as advised by the professor from the agricultural college, if one was careful regarding butterflies and the soil, and tried hard, perhaps noyontara flowers would once again bloom here in the future.

(1991)

The Chronicle of Mohammad Selim's Life

WHENEVER THE MOHOLLA FOLK HEAR talk about Mohammad Selim, they are reminded of the day he was born, because they believe that Mohammad Selim was born under exceptional circumstances, that he paid a very high price to arrive in this world. Many people in Bhojohori Saha Street, that is, Ghost Lane, can recall the day they learnt about the deaths of Babul Miya and his wife, and the simultaneous birth of their son. They found out that the chronicle of Mohammad Selim's distressful life began even before he was born, on an overcast day in the month of Shrabon, when Babul's wife, Hajera, had crossed the ninth month of her pregnancy. That afternoon, or shortly after that, his pregnant mother slipped and fell beside the water tap while it was raining, and when Babul Miya was taking the unconscious Hajera by baby-taxi to the Medical College Hospital, just as the baby-taxi passed Phulbaria and reached the Chankhnar bridge, it collided with an oncoming bus and was wrecked. After the people there took Babul and his wife to the hospital, first Babul died, and twelve hours after that, Mohammad Selim emerged, breaking out from his unconscious mother's uterus.

Mohammad Selim's mother never regained consciousness, and according to some people in the moholla, when she died two days later, the newborn infant Mohammad Selim was in deep slumber on her bosom, with the nipple of his dead mother's breast in his mouth. These people say that, at first, the nurses in the hospital didn't realize that Hajera was dead, but after a while, they noticed that the saline in the bag hanging at the bedside had stopped flowing into the vein of her arm. When they then failed to find any pulse on her wrist, they were certain about the matter and removed the dead woman's breast from the infant's mouth. The moholla folk say that when his dead mother's nipple was removed from his mouth, Mohammad Selim was about to cry for the first time in his life, but then a thin spray of white-coloured milk from the swollen breast of the dead young woman spread all over the infant's face and he fell fast asleep again in the aroma of his mother's milk. Having lost both his parents within forty-eight hours of his birth, when the silent Mohammad Selim came home to the single-storeyed residence in Ghost Lane that lay in darkness, wrapped in a kantha and carried in his Dadi Sharifa Begum's arms, many of the moholla folk were eager to see the baby's face. The people of the moholla then heard everything from the old lady, Sharifa

Begum, who had named her grandson Mohammad Selim; they learnt that, because Hajera was unconscious when she delivered the baby, no one was aware of it. When the nurses did their rounds of the ward in the middle of the night, they discovered blood dripping from Hajera's bed, and thus they realized that the young woman had already delivered, and then they were apprehensive, certain that the newborn was dead, because he betrayed no signs of life. But when they picked the baby up from between Hajera's legs, Mohammad Selim, pale and shapeless like a bundle of cloth, opened his eyes and stared back. The people of the moholla learnt that, on seeing Mohammad Selim staring silently, the nurse broke into tears, and after the umbilical cord was severed and the infant was washed, she placed him on his unconscious mother's bosom and put the nipple of her breast into his mouth. Then, after Hajera expired, when the nurses removed the breast from his mouth, his mother's final warmth moistened his face like a fountain, and just as he was about to wake up, he fell asleep once again in that aroma.

The people of the moholla later said that Mohammad Selim had failed all his life to dwell outside that liquid aroma; growing up, he continuously heard stories about his dead father and mother as he lay in his old Dadi's lap, and the men and women and boys and girls in the moholla learnt about all this. After completing primary school, when he went and got himself enrolled in Graduates High School at the age of twelve, one day, during a discussion in the Bengali class on the kanthali champa flower, all the boys in the class wistfully realized that they couldn't identify the kanthali champa and that they didn't know what its fragrance was like; and then Mohammad Selim blurted out that he liked the smell of milk. Hearing him say that, the boys in the class burst out laughing and asked him, 'Whose milk?' Mohammad Selim remained silent then, and after he returned home, when his Dadi once again began talking about the deceased Hajera, he reiterated that he liked the smell of milk, and then after much searching, he plucked two marigolds from the moholla, and after what had been a long time, he went with Sharifa Begum to the Azimpur Cemetery. Subsequently, in order to lay flowers on his parents' graves, he filled the compound of their house with various flowering plants. Eventually, the people of the moholla observed that bees and butterflies had become more frequent in the neighbourhood, and a few people in the moholla even fell victim to bee-attacks; by the time the people of the moholla became worried about the matter, rain descended and immediately after the rain, people started sneezing continuously and their eyes turned watery. The people of Ghost Lane learnt that, one Saturday morning, Ershad saheb, the owner of the seven-storey building at the eastern end of the lane, let out a sneeze just as he was setting out for his cotton mill in Pagla and had opened the door of his car and put a foot in. After that, when he returned to the moholla in the afternoon, the people there saw that tears flowed like the showers of

Shrabon from the eyes of the goateed cotton-mill owner, and he sneezed continuously, as if he were setting off firecrackers, and kept popping yellow-coloured Histacin tablets indiscriminately into his mouth, but that didn't alleviate his condition. After putting up with the agony and exasperation for a whole day and night, he summoned Abu, Habu and Shofi. At the same time, or perhaps a day earlier or later, during an advisory meeting of the Shariat Party at the residence of the Emir of Dhaka, Moulana Abdul Jabbar let out a sneeze, and then his physical condition turned dire so quickly that he was sent home in the middle of the meeting, accompanied by two associates. At home, after drenching all the sheets and towels in the house with the water streaming down his eyes and nose, he sat upright with great difficulty and said to his wife who was attending to him, 'Get someone to call Abu, Habu and Shofi.' Even as the people of the moholla sneezed, they observed the comings and goings of the servants of all these distressed folk at the redbrick residence of the three brothers. They learnt that, while undertaking a surprise inspection of her departmental store at the intersection of Ghost Lane and Rankin Street, Maleka Banu, the widow of the late Yasin Byapari and now proprietor of the New Star Restaurant and Gausiya Departmental Store on Tipu Sultan Road, discovered that not a single employee was in the store because all of them had gone to the New Star Restaurant to eat halim. She became so agitated at this lack of common sense and dereliction of duty on the part of the employees that she felt a prickling sensation inside her nose, and even before she could call out to the employees, she sneezed loudly, making her heavy frame tremble. Hearing the sound, the employees gave up eating halim midway and returned, and escorted the agitated, sneezing-afflicted Maleka Banu to her house in the moholla. At dawn the next day, when Maleka Banu felt a prickling sensation inside her nose as soon as she woke up and water streamed down, the first thing she did was to send a person to the residence of the three brothers – 'Go and fetch Abu, Habu and Shofi, tell them to come at once.' Maleka Banu's servant went, and saw the servant of Major (Retired) Elias Khan standing in front of the iron gate outside the red-brick residence of the three brothers. The previous night, Major Elias had spoken over the telephone with his superior, Colonel (Retired) Mahmud, and sat down to write the points for the press conference to be held at the Press Club regarding the upcoming programme of the Fifth Brigade Nationalists for Resistance and Patriotism. At half past twelve at night, he got up and went to the bedroom and lay down in bed, and just as he lowered his face near his wife's armpit to breathe in the fragrance of her body, he felt an irritation inside his nose, and when that increased, he felt as if a vortex of wind had torn out a nodule in his brain which then shot through the tunnel of his nose at great speed and exploded loudly. When the sneezing didn't stop all through the night despite taking the Histacin pills stocked in the house and applying Vicks inside his nose, he sent his servant at dawn – 'Go and tell Abu, Habu and Shofi to come at once.' No matter when in the day the servants of Ershad saheb and Moulana Abdul Jabbar and the servants of Maleka Banu and Major Elias came to the residence of the three brothers, they found them busy watching Hindi movies on the VCR. Abu, Habu and Shofi got annoyed at being summoned by all these people, but after that they changed into jeans and T-shirts, with gold chains and pendants dangling from their necks, and went to Ershad saheb's residence.

They inquired, 'Is your bloody labour leader making trouble again?'

'No, I wanted to see you – just see how I'm dying of sneezing, please do something.'

'What can we do about that? After all, the bloody sneezing isn't afraid of a dagger or even a bullet! If your workers or your tenants say something, tell us. We're leaving now.'

As they sat on the well-cushioned sofa in Moulana Abdul Jabbar's carpeted drawing room, sipping tea, the three brothers inquired, 'Why did you call us? Do you have a meeting or something? Do you want us to go with you?'

Wiping his dripping nose, Moulana Abdul Jabbar said, 'Can't you see how I'm tearing up?'

'What can we do about that?' Abu, Habu and Shofi replied, 'All this isn't our work. Call us if anyone needs to be finished off, or else don't call us!'

When Abu, Habu and Shofi said the same thing to Maleka Banu, she restrained her sneezing and retorted, 'I'm dying, and all you lot say is, "What can we do?" I pay you so much money every month!'

The three brothers then became annoyed and said, 'You pay us money, we do the work, we'll do whatever work you ask us to. But what can we do if you start bloody sneezing or coughing!'

After that, the people of the moholla say the three brothers went to the Major saheb's residence, and seeing him sneezing continuously, they figured out the matter. When they said the same thing to him as well, he told them, 'Everyone in the moholla is in torment with such sneezing. Why don't you find out why this is happening?' The brothers turned silent after Major Elias said that, and then, that very evening, they themselves began sneezing and took Histacin pills like everyone else. After sneezing continuously for a day, out of exasperation or fatigue, or because of what Major Elias had said the previous day, they went to the chambers of Dr Wajed on Twin Bridge Lane and sat down on three sides of his table. After examining them, Dr Wajed said, 'Take Histacin.'

'I took it. It doesn't work.'

'Then take Avil.'

'I took Avil too. It's of no use.'

'Then tell me what you ate?'

'Rice and beef curry.'

'Stop eating beef.'

The three brothers then said, 'Everyone in the moholla is sneezing, and not everyone had beef,' and after he heard that, Dr Wajed began another line of inquiry; he asked, 'Is there any odour in your moholla?'

'No.'

'Is there a lot of dust?'

'As much as in every other moholla.'

'Are there a lot of flowering plants in the moholla?'

'No, there aren't,' the three brothers replied, and then, remembering Mohammad Selim's flower garden, they refuted what they said earlier, 'Yes, there are flowering plants.'

'Sneezing can also be due to the pollen from flowers.'

That evening, Abu, Habu and Shofi, each carrying an axe, barged into the compound of Mohammad Selim's residence, and disregarding all opposition, they worked hard for two hours at a stretch; they chopped down all the flowering plants and turned the garden into a mound of destruction. But the people of the moholla observed that even after the last flower garden in the moholla had been destroyed their sneezes didn't cease, so they became terrified then, and after a month went by in this way, one day they sensed that a kind of hush had descended upon their moholla, and then they found to their astonishment that their ailment had finally left them. The people of the moholla then learnt that, during this one month in which they had been afflicted with the enervating sneezing, the wind in the moholla had blown from the north-easterly direction, and at the same time, a defect had been detected in the furnace of the Hardeo Glass Factory. Because of the defect in the furnace, there was an increase in the volume of smoke spiralling out through the chimney, and carried by the wind, the smoke spread over the moholla to its south-west. By the time it reached Ghost Lane, the smoke had lost its colour, there wasn't any odour either, but because of its continuous presence in the air, the people of Ghost Lane felt a mild burning sensation in their noses. When the wind abated after a month, the people in the moholla stopped sneezing, and when they eventually found out about the cause, then, a few days later, Mohammad Selim once again tended to his garden and resumed his weekly visits to the Azimpur Cemetery to lay a wreath of flowers on his parents' graves. The people of the moholla later said that, approximately three years after this incident, Abu, Habu and Shofi once again remembered Mohammad Selim's flower garden when the beautiful Shireen Akhtar, the only daughter and child of Abdul Aziz Byapari of the house on No. 36, became a widow and returned to her father's home, and various incidents relating to her then transpired in the moholla. The people of the moholla said that, the day she left her father-in-law's house in Begum Bazar and returned to her father's house after being widowed, they realized that they hadn't seen the girl in a long time, and then they gazed at her face and were mesmerized. The people of the moholla learnt that, after Shireen Akhtar's return, there was an increase in the number of visitors to the house of her father, Aziz Miya, the owner of a timber mart and sawmill in Nayabazar. They learnt that, on the afternoon of the ninth day following Shireen's return to the moholla, when Aziz Miya wasn't supposed to be at home, Ershad saheb arrived, unaccompanied by his wife, at Aziz Miya's residence, and when Shireen came and stood at the door and said, 'But Baba's not at home,' Ershad saheb was at first rendered speechless, and after that he inquired, 'How are you?' On the evening of the thirteenth day, Moulana Abdul Jabbar, and on the afternoon of the fifteenth day, Abu, Habu and Shofi went to Aziz Miya's residence, offered salaams and stood there. When Shireen did not appear even after Moulana Abdul Jabbar had sat in the drawing room and conversed for a long time with Aziz Miya, he himself inquired about her and said, 'I've brought a book for her.' Aziz Miya then got up and went and brought Shireen, who had been reclining in bed, to the drawing room. When the young woman, with her hair let loose and clothes dishevelled, entered the drawing room, Moulana Abdul Jabbar looked at her and exclaimed, 'Mashallah!' and then he pointed towards an empty chair and said, 'Please sit down.' After that, perhaps because she was drowsy, or because she felt hypnotized looking at the wagging finger of the bearded Moulana who was clad in a long jobba, she sat down on the sofa beside her father and gazed at the Moulana's face. Perhaps the Moulana trembled a bit before that gaze, and so, using the fingers of his right hand, he stroked his salt-and-pepper beard; after that, composing himself a bit, he said, 'I've brought a book for you,' and he proffered the book titled *Beheshti Jeor* to Shireen Akhtar. Accepting the book offered by the middle-aged Moulana, Shireen Akhtar exclaimed, 'But I can't read!' Moulana Abdul Jabbar was then further entranced by the sound of this young woman's voice and the incandescent expression on her face; his perturbed demeanour returned, and trying to grasp the emptiness inside his fist, he said, 'Keep it.' Around that time, the three brothers, Abu, Habu and Shofi, spotted Shireen Akhtar on the terrace of her father's four-storeyed building, and they thought her face was like a full moon floating by during the daytime; they then remembered Mohammad Selim's garden. On the evening of the fifteenth day of Shireen Akhtar's return to the moholla, the eldest brother Abu arrived at the timber merchant Abdul Aziz Byapari's door and knocked, with the finest two roses from Mohammad Selim's garden in his hand, and following him were Habu and Shofi. When the entrancing young woman opened the door and stood in front of the three youths, at first the three brothers were rendered speechless, and after that, Abu said, 'Can't you recognize us? We're three brothers. We live in the house next to Ali Akbar's.'

Shireen then remembered the three boys, and a smile like a ripple on the pellucid water of a lotus pond spread across her face; she looked intently at the youths standing in front of her: gold chains hung down till the middle of the well-exercised, vestless chests beneath the shirts with their top buttons open, and all of them had the lobes of their left ears pierced, and wore a gemstone flower in each one. The young woman then said, 'Yes, I remember, please come in.' After that, as they sat in Aziz Miya's drawing room and sipped the tea prepared by Shireen Akhtar, looking at the gemstones of three different colours on their ears, Shireen asked, 'So are you three Diamond, Ruby and Emerald?' The three brothers laughed at that, and they said, 'Our names are Abu, Habu and Shofi,' and after that, they chewed their drooping moustaches, rolled up their shirtsleeves above their elbows, and flexed their muscular arms in front of the young woman; a smile returned to the face of Shireen, who had been married for eight years and was a childless widow, and then the eldest brother Abu proffered the two immaculate roses. Shireen Akhtar held the roses to her nose and asked, 'Where did you get the flowers? Do you have plants at home, or did you buy them?'

The three brothers then said that they didn't have flowering plants at home, and that they didn't buy these flowers either. They said that the roses had grown in this very moholla, in the garden of the boy Mohammad Selim, and hearing that, with a hint of a smile on her face, Shireen said, 'Then tell him to come and give me flowers every day!'

'We'll tell him at once,' the three brothers replied.

'What if he doesn't?'

'He bloody well will!'

Shireen Akhtar then recalled the circumstances of his father's demise and Mohammad Selim's birth. The three brothers emerged from Shireen Akhtar's residence and went to Mohammad Selim's house, where they found him buzzing around the garden like a bee. When the three brothers instructed him to deliver flowers every day to Shireen Akhtar, he looked beyond the wall of his house, in the direction of the roof of Aziz Miya's house on No. 36, and saw the evening clouds billowing like kolabati flowers beyond the cornice beneath the empty terrace. The following day, when Mohammad Selim knocked on Shireen Akhtar's door with two white roses in his hand, and after the door was opened, said, 'My name is Mohammad Selim,' the twenty-two-year-old woman flashed her indescribable smile and said, 'I know about you, come in.' When Mohammad Selim stood with a bunch of yellow kolabati flowers in front of the shut door on the sixth day, Shireen Akhtar was on the third floor, on the terraced roof of the house, submerged in some kind of melancholia that lasted until late into the night; she didn't hear Mohammad Selim knocking at the door, and she had forgotten all about him coming with flowers. When no one opened the door after he had banged on it for a long time, it occurred to Mohammad Selim that perhaps there was no one at home; but he realized soon after that there were people inside, because he noticed that the door was not locked from outside. He then sat on the stairs near the shut door and waited, and when Aziz Miya returned home late at night, he saw Mohammad Selim lying at the top of the stairs, fast asleep, with the kolabati flowers in his hand. When the three brothers went to Shireen Akhtar's house the next evening, and she narrated to them the previous day's incident while they were sipping tea, the three brothers, whose shirts were unbuttoned almost down to the waist, laughed in glee; when Mohammad Selim arrived just then and knocked, Shireen opened the door and brought him in. As Mohammad Selim sipped his tea with his eyes fixed on the carpet, Shireen Akhtar glanced towards the three brothers, and all of them burst into laughter; the eldest brother Abu winked, and the youngest brother Shofi asked, 'What will you do now, Selim?'

'I'll go home.'

'Do something – do you know Mada's shop? There's a koromcha tree in the house next to that; Shireen said she wants to have koromcha, so run there and pluck a few.'

Mohammad Selim looked at Shireen's face and asked, 'Really?' Shireen's eyes seemed to soften in the light then, she shook her head gently and said, 'No, you go home now.' Mohammad Selim finished his tea hurriedly and left, and the next evening he arrived with a bunch of beli buds and knocked on Shireen Akhtar's door. Shireen was on the terrace of the house that day too, but this time she was alert; when Mohammad Selim knocked at the door, she hurried down, opened the door and took him upstairs. As they sat on the terrace, the fragrance of the beli buds wrapped in her anchal suffused the air and wisps of grey-coloured clouds gathered bit by bit in the sky; after gazing at the sky for a long time, Mohammad Selim asked, 'How do you feel looking at these clouds?'

'It's very comforting.'

'My Dadi says there's a zoo in the clouds.'

Mohammad Selim then pointed towards an elephant-shaped cloud and said, 'There's an elephant!' Mohammad Selim and Shireen Akhtar then spent the entire afternoon talking about the clouds, and as it turned to dusk, Mohammad Selim asked her, 'Do you really want to have koromcha?' Shireen Akhtar blushed when she heard that and exclaimed, 'Oh no, they were simply joking!'

'Just let me know if you feel like having it,' Selim said. 'There are koromcha, kamranga, chalta and horbori trees in the Baldha Garden, just let me know if you want any.'

Shireen Akhtar then said that she had eaten all of these fruits, and that they were available in the market; Mohammad Selim then asked her, 'Have you seen a koromcha tree?'

'No, I haven't.'

'Have you seen the leaf of a koromcha tree?'

'No, I haven't.'

'Have you seen a horbori tree?'

'No, I haven't.'

'Have you seen the leaf of a horbori tree?'

'No.'

'What about a kamranga tree?'

'No.'

'Have you seen its leaves?'

'No.'

After that, Mohammad Selim kept arriving with leaves of different trees and knocked at her door, and during that time, one day Ershad saheb sent her a set of ornaments through his elder daughter from his first marriage. Shireen put the box under her cot, and after that, come late afternoon, she heard the unfailing knock on the door, and when she opened the door, she broke into a smile when she saw the boy Mohammad Selim, and she asked him, 'So what flower and leaf is it today?' Mohammad Selim then proffered the two marigolds in his hand, and taking out a small leaf from his pocket, he said, 'See this, it's a koromcha leaf.' Another day, Moulana Abdul Jabbar came and delivered a jamdani sari that he had bought, and that evening, as he sat on the terrace, gazing at the sky, Mohammad Selim took out a shoot with three leaves from his pocket and said, 'Here, it's a horbori leaf.' After that, the three brothers arrived one day with their chests puffed; they had brought along with them half a gallon of amber-musk attar in a lovely glass bottle, and when they left after having tea, Mohammad Selim arrived and gave Shireen that day's flower and leaf, and said, 'Here, this is jasmine, and this one is a leaf of the arjun tree.' The people of the moholla say that the space under Shireen's cot filled up with various gifts, while a heap of various withered flowers and leaves gathered in the large drawer on the right side of her dressing table. The people of the moholla say that, although those who bestowed gifts on Shireen Akhtar were initially unaware of one another, by and by, like everyone else in the moholla, they learnt about everything. When Ershad saheb and Moulana Abdul Jabbar found out that Abu, Habu and Shofi regularly visited Shireen Akhtar and chatted with her over tea, and that they sent flowers for her every day via Mohammad Selim, they chided their wayward hearts, and inwardly cheered for Abu: Attaboy! But the people of the moholla say that when it came to Major Elias, he initially refused to view the matter in such terms. Spotting Shireen Akhtar on the terrace one day, he sent a message through his servant inquiring after her; when he learnt that the beautiful young woman was a widow, and that she was all alone in the house when her father was absent, then, once his wife left with their two kids to visit her parents, he instructed his servant, 'Go and fetch Abu, Habu and Shofi.' When the three brothers arrived and Major Elias turned the conversation to the subject of Shireen Akhtar, they said, 'Don't bother about that.'

'Why?'

'She's my woman,' Abu said.

Major Elias then laughed and said, 'That's all right. Just share a bit with me!'

'Hey, I'm going to marry her.'

Thus did events transpire in the moholla at that time, and one day the people of the moholla learnt that Shireen Akhtar had deposited the book titled *Beheshti Jeor* in the veranda of the mosque in the moholla. At dawn the next day, when those who went there for the Fajr prayers turned the cover of the book, they saw Moulana Abdul Jabbar's name on the first page; when talk about this book spread in the moholla, Moulana Abdul Jabbar retrieved the book from the veranda of the mosque, and Abu, Habu and Shofi burst into peals of laughter as they sat in their red-brick house watching Hindi movies on the VCR. Then, one day, Shireen Akhtar donated a sari each to three female beggars. When this tale spread in Thatari Bazar and Banagram, Nawabpur and Raysha Bazar, Tikatuli and Dayaganj, then, the following day, male and female beggars from all these localities arrived in a procession at Abdul Aziz Byapari's door in Ghost Lane. That day, Shireen Akhtar pulled apart a set of matching ornaments and handed out bits of them to fifty-one male and female beggars. When news of this spread through the moholla, peals of laughter were once again heard from the residence of the three brothers. Exerting herself like this for five days, Shireen Akhtar disposed of all the things under her cot. The three brothers had kept an alert watch over the affairs, and they observed that Shireen Akhtar hadn't donated the attar, nor had she thrown away the withered flowers that had accumulated. Perhaps the three brothers exchanged glances and the eldest brother Abu's face gleamed then; they went over to Shireen's place that evening, and as they sipped tea, they inquired, 'Does Mohammad Selim deliver flowers every day?'

'Yes.'

'He isn't irregular, is he?'

'No.

When the three brothers were reassured that Mohammad Selim was still delivering flowers as instructed, they finished their tea, smiled benignly and left Shireen Akhtar's house, and then Mohammad Selim arrived. Sitting on the terrace, he handed a flower and a leaf to the woman who had been waiting expectantly for him, and said, 'This is your kamranga leaf, and these ones are guava.' After he said that, he took out two guavas and dropped them in Shireen's lap.

'Where did you get them? Did you buy them?'

'These guavas are from Ali Akbar's tree.'

'Did you steal them?'

'No.'

'If he catches you, he'll break your leg and leave you lame!'

Dusk descended and a huge full moon appeared in the sky; the moonlight fell on one side of Shireen's face and cast a hazy shadow on the white wall of the attic nearby. Gazing at that shadow, Mohammad Selim said, 'Look, here you are. Wait, I'll make another one for you,' and after saying that, he sat on his knees next to the wall, and clenching his hands together he made another shadow next to the shadow of Shireen's face. He then wiggled his folded fingers and made a nose, lips and chin on the shadow, and said, 'Don't move, look this way out of the corner of your eye.' Shireen Akhtar looked and saw two faces made of shadows looking at each other. She then sat Mohammad Selim down in her spot, and when a similar shadow formed on the wall, she sat down next to the wall, and after trying for a long time, created a second shadow. Mohammad Selim then moved towards the wall and created shadow-images by making various gestures with his fingers.

'Here's a pigeon.'

'Yes.'

'This is a duck.'

'Yes.'

'This one's a snake.'

'Yes.'

'This is a deer.'

'Yes.'

'Here's a horse, just see how he raises his leg and prances!'

'Yes.'

At the time Shireen Akhtar and Mohammad Selim were busy creating shadow-images for each other, there was a heatwave in the country, and the heat made life unbearable for all the people, as well as the birds and animals. Sparrows began to drop dead from their nests in the ventilators in the extreme heat, and after that, when pet dogs and cats began dying, not finding any place to dispose of them, the people of the moholla threw them in the drain. One day, when the air in the moholla was heavy with the odour of the decomposing bodies of dead animals, a different kind of smell spread in the moholla. After inhaling that smell for four consecutive days, the people of the moholla became aware of it; they realized that the smell, which transcended the odour of the dead dogs and cats, was the fragrance of attar. They say that Shireen Akhtar, the widowed daughter of the proprietor of the timber mart, Abdul Aziz Byapari, poured a cup of amber-musk into the drain of her house every morning, and this attar flowed from their drain and went through all the drains in the moholla; the three brothers of the red-brick house then got wind of this. At this time, Mohammad Selim's garden withered under the fierce assault of the heatwave, and one day, he observed that not a single flower had bloomed in his garden, and after several days went by with no flower blooming, Mohammad Selim's visits to Shireen Akhtar's residence ceased, and during this time, the fragrance of attar floated down the drains of the moholla and everybody learnt that this perfume had been poured into the drain by the widow, Shireen Akhtar. After they heard about that, on the fifth day of the fragrance from the drain being discerned, Mohammad Selim spent a whole day gazing at a marigold bud, but when the bud failed to bloom, then, once the light of the late afternoon turned wan, he knocked at Shireen Akhtar's door with a heavy heart. The people of the moholla say that Shireen Akhtar was busy creating shadows on the wall inside her room when she heard the familiar knock on the door, and when she hurried to open the door, she found the pale-faced, sixteen-year-old Mohammad Selim waiting for her. Observing the dejected face of the young boy, Shireen Akhtar was overwhelmed, she asked him, 'Why didn't you come?'

'No flowers bloomed,' Mohammad Selim said, 'so I couldn't bring any flowers.'

'So what if the flowers didn't bloom! Why didn't you come? Come inside!'

Shireen Akhtar stretched her right hand, drew the boy close by his shoulder, and took him inside the house. On that day of scorching heat, when they reached the drawing room and stood on the carpet, gazing at Mohammad Selim's disconsolate face, an unblemished smile, like a dew-drenched dolonchampa, lit Shireen's face; she ran her hand like a comb through the hair on Mohammad Selim's forehead, and asked him once again, 'Why didn't you come?' Mohammad's Selim face possibly turned more wilted and pitiful at that, and looking at him, Shireen Akhtar's heart melted; the twenty-two-year-old, innocent young woman embraced Mohammad Selim, and drawing him to her by placing her hand on the back of his neck, she kissed his dry, brown lips. While holding Mohammad Selim's hand and bringing him inside the house that day, Shireen Akhtar had forgotten to latch the door at the entrance of her house. So when the three brothers heard that day that Shireen Akhtar had poured amber-musk in the drain of the moholla, and they got ready and arrived at Aziz Miya's house, having forsaken watching Hindi movies, they saw that the door was ajar. They then entered the house and discovered the beautiful Shireen Akhtar in

Mohammad Selim's arms, in the act of kissing him. They were so stunned that they waited silently, and when Shireen Akhtar moved her face to take a breath, she saw the three brothers standing inside the room; she then freed herself from Mohammad Selim's embrace, and asked, 'You?' Hearing that, Abu, Habu and Shofi returned to their senses and their usual selves and leapt into action.

When Aziz Miya returned home that night, he found the three brothers, Abu, Habu and Shofi, Ershad saheb, Moulana Abdul Jabbar and Major Elias waiting for him in his drawing room; when Moulana Abdul Jabbar told him everything candidly, he stared blankly and noticed Mohammad Selim sitting in a corner of the room. Some time later that night, after the youngest brother Shofi had fetched the kazi saheb and the kazi saheb finished reciting the marriage prayers and sat in front of Shireen Akhtar and asked her whether she accepted her marriage to Abu Hussain, the son of Imarat Hussain, everyone present there heard the loud and clear 'No' uttered by Shireen Akhtar. She said 'No' thrice, and all three times the people present there said, 'She accepts,' and after that they said, 'The marriage is done, we're off now.' After the people of the moholla left, the three brothers pushed Aziz Miya out of the room, and then, the people of the moholla later said, they made the final mistake. After having detained Mohammad Selim and made him witness the marriage ceremony, once everyone left, the middle brother Habu grabbed him by the collar of his shirt and pulled him up and said, 'You son of a swine, she's like your mother! Go and offer your salaam to her,' and pushed him to the floor, where he lay at Shireen Akhtar's feet. Mohammad Selim sat on his knees and looked at the face of the woman standing before him, and he observed that there was blood on a corner of Shireen Akhtar's lips; he then prostrated himself, as if before Allah, and wet the young woman's feet with kisses.

The next morning, while going to the mosque to offer Fajr prayers, the people of the moholla observed in the clear light of dawn the dead body of Mohammad Selim, Shireen Akhtar's lover and a student of Class 10 in Graduates High School, hanging from the lamp post in front of Shireen Akhtar's house. Later that morning, the esteemed members of the moholla, Ershad saheb, Moulana Abdul Jabbar, Maleka Banu and Major Elias observed the three brothers standing in the veranda of their house with their hands stuffed in their pockets. When the police arrived at the moholla after that, Mohammad Selim's aged Dadi beat her chest and wept, and cursed the three brothers. The investigating police officer wrote everything down in his notebook, and after that when he asked Ershad saheb, Moulana Abdul Jabbar, Maleka Banu and Major Elias about the matter, they said that the three brothers were decent boys. The policeman noted down this opinion along with the details of the identities of all these people, and after that he asked the people of the moholla who had gathered around the dead body whether they had anything to say; hearing the policeman, the people of the moholla gazed at the three brothers standing with their hands stuffed in their pockets, and at all the other esteemed folk, and they couldn't say a word. Observing the people standing silently, the policeman noted down that no one had any complaint. After that, the police took the body away for post-mortem, and amidst the extreme heat and odour, the speechless people of the moholla returned with solemn faces to their homes.

(1993)

(Co-translated with Srishti Dutta Chowdhury)

Our Bakul

THE VILLAGE FOLK WERE WAITING for him to return.

Akalu reached Suhasini before dusk, and those from the village who gazed then at the paddy stalks stooping in the vast autumnal field saw him walking through the mist over the open field after he passed the faraway village of Boikunthopur. All these village folk then stood waiting, and when the hazy figure of Akalu emerged at the far end of the gently waving, golden-coloured paddy field, he looked like a solitary, white, melancholy egret; and the people of the village wondered whether Akalu's heart really wept for Fatema! Arriving near Biswaspara, he left the district board's mud road, descended into the paddy field, and walked along the earthen ridge boundary; in the weak light of dusk, his tall figure became more and more corporeal.

He had been to his father-in-law's house to search for his missing wife, Fatema.

When Akalu reached close to the village, the people looked at his face; it occurred to them that, even in the semi-darkness of dusk, the dense shadow of melancholy was visible on his face. When he arrived near Kanaibari, he emerged from the paddy field, walked past the village folk, and went towards his homestead behind the landlord's house. The people of Suhasini were really keen to call out to him and stop him and say, 'Listen dear chap, wait, tell us what happened, let's hear it!' But they couldn't say all that then, some of them gazed at his face and scratched their heads and muttered, 'Hey Akalu, are you back, dear chap,' and after that they were at a loss for words; his head tilted slightly to one side, Akalu looked at the faces of the village folk without saying anything; he walked along the edge of the landlord's compound and under the decapitated mango tree, and arrived at the rundown hut that was his homestead.

The day Fatema went missing, that morning or afternoon or evening, when everyone at home realized that Fatema had not been seen for a long time, they, that is those at home, Akalu, Bakul and Amir Hossain, looked everywhere for her.

Akalu said, 'See if she's cooking.'

They went into the kitchen and saw that it was completely empty; they realized that there had been no cooking that day, and that they hadn't eaten anything; they then felt thirsty, and so they tried to pour water from the earthen pitcher to drink but found that the pitcher was empty; then Akalu went to the well and filled the pitcher with water.

Akalu said, 'Go and see if she's doing something in the cowshed.'

They then went to the cowshed, and they saw that there was no fodder in the feeding tray; they had only one cow, it was sitting beside the bamboo-mat wall and dozing; they didn't find Fatema there and felt dejected, maybe Bakul and Amir Hossain felt scared, and they wept as they called out, 'Ma, Ma.' Akalu had no idea where Fatema might have gone, or why, and what he would do.

Then Akalu said, 'Go and see if she's gathering leaves behind the house or tending to something.'

Emerging from the cowshed, they went near the bamboo clump behind the house on the chance that Fatema was there, maybe she was gathering the withered leaves fallen there and making a broom. Going near the bamboo clump, they saw it was full of withered leaves under the bamboo trees; the leaves were fluttering randomly in the gentle, cool breeze of autumn, but Fatema wasn't there. They then went to the kitchen garden on the northern side of the house, maybe Fatema was digging the soil with a spade to plant moringa seeds there, or perhaps she was stringing plum thorns to fence around an enclosure and had forgotten all about her household as she was doing that; but Fatema was not in the garden.

Akalu then sent Bakul to the marsh. He told her, 'Bakul, go and see whether she's gone to the marsh to collect spinach.'

Bakul went running via the rear of the house, and standing near Mahir Sarkar's house, she looked in the direction of the dry, overgrown marsh, but there was no one there, not even Fatema; then leaving Bakul and Amir Hossain at home, Akalu searched for Fatema in the village; maybe she was working in someone's threshing room, maybe she was swaying her ample hips and husking paddy or flattening rice. But Fatema wasn't to be found in any threshing room in Suhasini.

The day after Akalu returned alone from his in-laws' house, the village folk saw him working in Mahir Sarkar's paddy field in the Lokkhikola field. Those who were cutting paddy in the Lokkhikola field then took a break from work and puffed on the hookah which they lit with a bit of stubble. Wiping the saliva around the opening on the hookah with their palm, they offered it to Akalu and inquired, 'Did you hear anything about your wife?'

He put his mouth to the opening of the hookah and kept it there as he took a deep puff, and then taking a few small puffs after a while, he replied, 'The slut,' and then he puffed again on the hookah noisily. The smallholding peasants and day labourers of Suhasini sitting under the sun in Lokkhikola's field couldn't understand what Akalu meant; they kept staring at his face, they asked, 'Did you find her?' And they thought that Akalu had no option but to tell them now. But Akalu fell silent once again when he heard their question, and then he squinted his eyes and cleared his throat noisily and spat and said, 'I wasted three days because of that slut, had I been working instead, I could have earned a hundred or a hundred and fifty taka.'

The matter wasn't clear to the village folk, and as they got up to go back to work, they said, 'Think about the money later, you low-born chamar, son of a swine, tell us whether you found your wife or not!'

'If I had found her, would I have left her behind? Wouldn't I have dragged the fucking whore back by her hair!'

'Your wife's been missing for three days, and you sit quietly and smoke, you bastard, and talk to us like this!'

'What else shall I do but smoke? Is my wife a cow that I'll go around the streets searching for her, asking each person, "Have you seen my wife, dear chap!"'

'Are you going to carry on sitting like this because of your wife?'

'What can I do, where shall I go looking for her?'

Akalu then wept; sitting amidst the touch of the gentle sunlight of autumn and the petrichor of the ripe paddy stalks, the landless day labourer of Suhasini village, Akalu Sheikh, shed tears. Perhaps the peasants of Suhasini sitting in the Lokkhikola field were really upset to see him suddenly breaking down, perhaps they weren't; they asked him, 'You didn't kill her, did you?'

Perhaps Akalu heard that, perhaps he didn't; he remained silent, wiped his eyes with the edge of his gamchha, and got up. The peasants of Suhasini worked continuously until the sun was directly over their heads. Lunch from their homes arrived in the afternoon, and they sat on the earthen ridge bordering the field and ate; no food arrived for Akalu, he once again lit the hookah using a bit of stubble and puffed on it.

'Hey Akalu, are you only going to smoke for your lunch?'

'Why do you people go on jabbering? What's it to you whether I smoke or eat shit?'

'Is there no more cooking in your house? What do your children eat? Can Bakul cook?'

'They'll eat the fermented leftover rice. I'll cook in the evening when I go back.'

Akalu then ate the food that the peasants in the field shared with him. After that, they once again stood in a row and bending over the crop field, they cut the base of the drooping paddy stalks, laid them on the ground, and advanced in that manner. When the daylight turned soft after the sun had set, these peasants stopped harvesting the paddy. They tied the paddy they had cut all day into bundles, took them to Mahir Sarkar's compound and deposited them there. And then they sat in the veranda of Mahir Sarkar's visiting room and prepared the final hookah of the day. Akalu sat with a glum face, resting his back against the tin fence.

'Hey Akalu, won't you have a smoke? Have a smoke and then go home, go and see how it feels when your wife's not there!'

Akalu puffed on the hookah silently, and then he said, 'But you people are saying I killed my wife!'

Another autumn, the day Akalu got married and returned from Tebariya, there was a scene in Suhasini. The peasants of Suhasini who were busy harvesting the ripe paddy in the Biswaspara field, spotted the newly-wed Akalu and his wife at the edge of the horizon, near the village of Boikunthopur. That day, the people of the village saw Akalu, wearing a dirty punjabi and a lungi, coming raising dust at his feet and dragging behind him a grey-coloured calf tied to a rope. Walking a little distance behind Akalu and his calf was a girl, stooped down and with a ghomta drawn over her head.

The next day, Akalu went to work with the village folk in the Biswaspara, Lokkhikola or Choknoor field. The peasants of Suhasini or Byangnai or Banshriya then said to him, 'Hey Akalu, you went and got married all by yourself!'

Perhaps Akalu didn't hear them, because he puffed silently on his hookah. But the peasants and landless farm labourers of the village didn't let him off, they kept pestering him.

'Hey, you got married all by yourself! You didn't invite us for the feast!'

'There's nothing to feast about!'

'What! As if we don't know about wedding feasts!'

'There's no need for a feast.'

'All right, don't feed us, but let us see your wife. You got yourself such a fine wife, and you got a calf too, let us see her! Will we eat up your wife or what?'

'Do you want me to bring my wife to the middle of this fucking field and show her to you? If you want to see my wife, come to my house and see her.'

The people of Suhasini met Akalu's wife, they also saw the female calf given by his father-in-law, Aijjal Pramanick. After coming to her husband's house, Fatema quickly shed her ghomta, and when she was busy with household work, her fulsome breasts, big buttocks and fleshy calves came to light; the people of the village saw her going around, and they said, 'Hey Akalu, a fine wife you married! Her body is like a giant wicker basket!'

After Fatema went missing and couldn't be found anywhere, the people of Suhasini remembered the former muezzin of the village mosque, Rafikul Islam, who was a secondary-level student in the Chandaikona Madrasa. He lived in a rented room in the landlord's house, and he taught Arabic to the village children and assisted the imam of the mosque, Mohsin Ali, by attending to the azan. When Fatema wanted to send her pair of twins, Bakul and Amir Hossain, to the mosque to learn to read the Holy Quran from Rafikul Islam, at first Akalu didn't pay it any heed, and Fatema pilfered from the paddy stored for food and gave Rafikul Islam two measures. Rafikul Islam sold this paddy at the weekly market and purchased two kayedas, one separa and one *Namaz Made Easy*. A few days after Bakul and Amir Hossain began learning *alif, bey, tey, say,* Akalu got wind of the matter and he hauled up Fatema.

'Where did you get the money?'

'I sold some paddy.'

'Where did you get the paddy?'

Fatema was silent.

'You slut, when the meagre store of paddy is used up, I'll see what you put there! The whole family will have to go without food then!'

'We go without food so often, it's no big deal!'

'You're never full, slut! Get food from your father's house and eat that!'

At the mention of her father, Fatema got angry, she threw the aluminium rice pot that was in her hand at Akalu; it was probably the rainy season then, and the rainwater had risen close to the edge of the plinth of Akalu's hut; when Fatema flung the rice pot with her strong, areca-palm-like arms, it missed Akalu, flew past him and landed in the water. After the squabble was over, when Fatema went to the edge of the plinth to look for the pot, she saw a very large boal fish floating on the water. It was lying on its side; perhaps the boal had been carried by the floodwaters and was feeding on something near Akalu's plinth, and then this venerable fish's head was smashed by the force of the aluminium pot flung by Fatema. Akalu went to the weekly market, sold this two-and-a-half-foot-long fish for one hundred and fifty taka and bought half a maund of paddy; he also bought aatap or sundried rice, cooking oil and jaggery, and he instructed Fatema, 'Make pithas.' The following evening, Fatema ground rice, and after that she prepared chitoi pithas. She then sent Bakul to invite Rafikul Islam over, saying, 'Go and bring that lad who teaches you Arabic.'

Bakul went to the landlord's house and fetched Rafikul Islam, and in the kitchen, Fatema ladled out the pithas from the clay pan for Bakul, Amir Hossain and Rafikul Islam; they dipped the pithas in jaggery syrup and ate them and chatted. Rafikul Islam said, 'Ma'am, I'll take you once to our house in Baghber. There's a date tree in our house. When it gets juice during the winter, the doodh pithas made with the juice are truly wonderful. I'll take you once during winter. My Ma makes wonderful pithas.'

Perhaps this evening's programme was enjoyable in another way for Fatema, perhaps she liked Rafikul Islam's company; she prepared pithas, and Bakul, Amir Hossain and Rafikul Islam ate them. Fatema urged Rafikul Islam, 'Eat it, don't feel shy.'

In the course of preparing the pithas, Fatema's ground-rice batter finished, and then she remembered that Akalu was still left. So she soaked rice in water and sat down once again to grind it, and that was when Akalu returned from the gathering of smokers in the visiting room of the landlord's house; on his return, he saw that there wasn't a single pitha left, and Fatema was grinding away on the grindstone.

'What are you doing?'

'I'm grinding rice.'

'Why are you grinding rice now? When will you make the pithas?'

'I had made them, they've been eaten.'

'Who ate them?'

Then, after hearing everything, Akalu quarrelled with Fatema. He said, 'Did I ask you to make pithas for this lover of yours!'

After the village folk found out about the incident, Rafikul Islam, the secondary-level student at the Chandaikona Madrasa, left his rented room in the landlord's house one day and went away, but the people of Suhasini did not forget about Fatema having treated him to pithas. After Fatema went missing and Akalu was unable to find her, one day, sitting in the Rouha field during a break from harvesting paddy, the peasants and farmworkers of the village inquired, 'Did you find your wife?'

Akalu did not reply.

'Try to find out if your wife's run away.'

'Where would she run away to?'

'That student at the Chandaikona Madrasa, she hasn't gone to him, has she?'

Akalu fell silent once again.

'Go and find out.'

'The things you people say!'

When Akalu married Fatema and brought her home from Tebariya, the female calf given by Fatema's father accompanied him to Suhasini. Fatema prepared the fodder and fed the calf, she tied a rope around its neck and took it to the road near their house, tethered it to a post and left it there to eat grass; with all the eating, the calf turned lovely and plump. When the people of Suhasini joked with him and said, 'You got married and brought such a fine wife, you got married and brought such a fine cow, both are similar,' Akalu then responded, 'I'll sell off the cow.'

'Do that. When one gazes at your cow one's fucking clothes get soiled.'

But it wasn't possible for Akalu to sell off the cow, because when he told Fatema this, she sobbed as she lay in bed at night. Seeing his new bride's tears, he was silent for a few days, and then he again said one day, 'Let me sell off the cow and thatch the roof anew.' When Fatema heard that and once again sobbed as she lay in bed at night, Akalu gave up this plan for the time being. But when both Fatema as well as the cow brought from her father's house failed to conceive even after a year had gone by, Akalu then thought that perhaps both the creatures bestowed upon him by his father-in-law, Aijjal Pramanick, were barren.

The village folk teased Akalu, 'Hey Akalu, your father-in-law gave you a barren cow!'

'Why should it be barren?'

'What else is it? How many teeth does it have, and when will it get pregnant?'

Akalu spoke about the matter with his wife that night, 'This cow your father's given is barren, I'm going to sell it off.'

'Why do you say it's barren?'

'Why isn't it in heat otherwise? I don't need this cow. I'll sell it off!'

There was nothing Fatema could say; she wept once again at the possibility of the cow, given by her father at her wedding, being sold off. So Akalu once again deferred selling off the cow. The village folk then asked him, 'Hey Akalu, how many years has it been since you got married?'

'What?'

'Your father-in-law didn't marry you off to a barren girl, did he?'

When Akalu spoke about the matter with his wife at night and told her, 'I hope you're not barren too, like the cow your father gave,' she turned silent with humiliation and sorrow.

'Why don't you say something?'

'What can I say?'

'What did I ask you?'

'What's all this you're saying?'

'Don't you understand what I said?'

'No, I don't.'

'Your father has dumped a barren girl and a barren cow on me! You understand so much, you whore, don't you understand this?'

After that Akalu waited for close to a year, and then the female calf given by Aijjal Pramanick was in heat; Fatema observed it when she went that evening to bring the cow home from its grazing spot beside the road. The next day, Akalu took Fatema's black cow to Pangasi village and showed her a bull to mate with, and a few days after that, Akalu got the news that Fatema was pregnant. Perhaps Akalu wasn't surprised at these two young creatures becoming pregnant at the same time, or perhaps he was; but when, after the stipulated time, both of them gave birth to twins, not just Akalu, but all the people of Suhasini were astonished; they said to Akalu, 'Hey, it seems your father-in-law gave you a fine girl and a fine cow, both of them look the same, and both of them produced two babies at a time!'

Akalu then thought more deeply about the matter; Fatema had two babies, a boy and a girl, the black cow too had two calves, one male and one female. He said, 'Indeed!'

Akalu named his son Amir Hossain, and his daughter Bakul; when he had some spare time, he would call out to his daughter, 'Come here, my bakul flower.' Fatema named the black cow's two calves Moyna and Tiya; after mixing the fodder in the feed tray, she would call out, 'Come my mynah and parrot.'

But Moyna and Tiya got lost one day with their mother; when Fatema went to clean the cowshed after waking up in the morning, she found the black cow and Moyna–Tiya missing, the cowshed was empty. At first, she thought that perhaps Akalu had taken the cows to thc field, but Akalu said that he hadn't. Akalu and Fatema then searched, muttering, 'Where did the cows go?' They looked in houses, fields and marshes, but the black cow and Moyna–Tiya couldn't be found. Fatema sobbed all night long, she wept the next day too, and the day after that as well; Akalu heard her weeping and berated her, 'Don't sob next to my ear!'

Then, during a respite from the weeding work in the ripening crop field, or from stacking the jute stalks they had cut, or from ploughing the land for the late autumnal paddy crop, the peasants of Suhasini puffed on the hookah and chattered among themselves.

'Hey Akalu, so the cow given by your father-in-law got lost!'

'Yes, I couldn't find it.'

'Where did you look for it? Have you ever heard of anyone in the entire village losing a cow!'

'What can I do if it's missing!'

'You've lost as many as three cows and you're sitting and smoking, and saying, "What can I do?"'

'I looked everywhere in the village, but I couldn't find them. I went to Pangasi and looked in the cattle-pound there, but they weren't there. What am I to do now? Where can I go now to look for the cows?'

'Does anyone lose cows like this?'

'Don't they?'

As the peasants of the village got up to return to work, they asked Akalu, 'You didn't sell them off, did you? Some trader from the weekly market in Pangasi didn't come at night and take them away, did he?' Akalu was silent then, perhaps he thought that there was no answer to such questions. When the peasants of the village needled him once again by asking him, 'Why are you so greedy,' Akalu got infuriated, 'Why do you chaps talk so much? If I wanted to sell my cows, why would I do it on the sly?'

After Fatema went missing, the peasants of the village encountered Akalu in the crop field every day; they remembered Akalu's wife's body, and when they remembered that they also remembered the black cow given by Akalu's father-in-law; when they gazed at the rump of the cow, they thought their ritual ablution would be sullied; and at the mention of this cow, they remembered Fatema, who was strong and overwhelmingly youthful; and there was a relationship between this woman and the black cow from her father's house. They once again asked Akalu about his missing wife during their smoking break, 'Hey Akalu, did you hear anything about her whereabouts?'

'No.'

'A person disappearing like this, it's simply incredible!'

'You people tell me what I ought to do!'

'After all, what can you do? Just carry on with your labours and then sit and smoke, what else can you do?'

Akalu then wept once again, and perhaps the peasants of the village were filled with compassion when they saw that, or perhaps they weren't; they remarked, 'You didn't sell off your wife, did you?'

'I sold off my wife! And where did I sell her?'

'You took her to Sirajganj and sold her off to a rich man! What with the body your wife has, he must have given you a good amount of money!'

'Yes, I'll sell off my wife for money!'

'Why, didn't you sell off your wife's father's cow on the sly for money too?'

'Are a cow and a person the same? Sell off my wife because I'm poor – does anyone do that?'

'Don't they? All right, if you didn't do that, don't sit on your backside like a cow, get up and go to the police station; if you don't feel brave enough to go on your own, take the landlord's younger son, Chhoto Miya, along with you.'

'Will Chhoto Miya accompany me?'

'Why won't he? After all, Altaf Hossain liked your wife very much, so why wouldn't he go now!'

Heeding the advice of the village folk, Akalu went to the Raiganj police station; but Altaf Hossain, the younger son of the landlord, didn't accompany him, he became furious when he heard Akalu's request and retorted, 'The fuck I'll go to the police station!' And after that, he disappeared from the village, and so Akalu had to go all by himself. After hearing everything, the duty officer at the Raiganj police station was silent. He was faced with a dilemma: if he registered the matter, it could become a case of kidnapping or murder of a woman, and that would damage the immaculate record of the police station. He asked, 'So do you want to register the matter?'

'Whatever you say, chhar.'

'I don't understand what's happened to your wife.'

Akalu was silent.

'What's your name?'

'Akalu Sheikh.'

'What's your father's name?'

'Jahiraddi Molla.'

'What do you do?'

'I work, chhar.'

'What work?'

'I do agricultural work.'

'How many bighas of land do you have?'

'I don't have any land, chhar, I work as a farm labourer on other people's lands.'

The duty officer in the police station, who was also the chhoto daroga or second officer, had nothing more to ask; after ascertaining that Akalu was a mere landless agricultural labourer, he was certain that there was nothing more to be done regarding this missing woman. He then explained the matter to Akalu; he said that if a case was registered, it would have to be investigated, and if that was done, people would have to be questioned, several people may have to be taken into custody, maybe Akalu too would have to be in custody; this would then lead to a lot of trouble. He advised Akalu, 'Wait for a few days and see, maybe she went somewhere and will return now!'

But Fatema didn't ever return.

Akalu worked dejectedly in the field, while Bakul and Amir Hossain wandered around the compound of their house all by themselves; after waking up in the morning, they performed the ritual ablution and went to the mosque to learn the kayeda and separa. After Rafikul Islam, the secondary-level student at the Chandaikona Madrasa, left, Mohsin Ali, the imam of the Juma Mosque, took up this additional task of teaching Arabic. The boys and girls of the village sat in front of him and bobbed their heads up and down as they read out, *alif*, *bey*, *tey*, *say*; they read out, *alif jabar aa*, *alif jer ee*, *alif pesh oo*, *aa ee oo*; they read out, *kul hu allah aahaad*, *allah saamaad* … Mohsin Ali, the imam of the Juma Mosque, who was an elderly peasant of the village, exclaimed, 'Hey Bakul, why are you reading so softly, read loudly!'

Bakul then began to cry.

'Why are you crying, what's the matter, girl?'

'My mother went missing, Dada Miya, and she hasn't come back.'

'She'll come back, just you see, don't cry.'

'When will she come back? I think Ma's dead!'

Compassion for the boy and girl then arose in the heart of Mohsin Ali, he wiped the tears streaming down the cheeks of Bakul with the fold of his punjabi.

'Who told you that your Ma had died?'

'Then why hasn't she returned?'

Mohsin Ali then commenced a ruse with this seven-year-old girl; he told her that he could say whether her Ma was alive or dead; and when Bakul said, 'Tell me then, Dada Miya,' Mohsin Ali explained the ruse to the boy and girl.

'A plant has to be planted in the soil now, got it?'

'All right.'

'Tell me which plant can be planted?'

'Plant a mango plant, Dada Miya.'

'No, not a mango plant.'

'Then a jamun plant.'

'No, not a jamun plant either.'

'Then a persimmon plant.'

'No, not persimmon.'

'Then you say which one.'

'No, you have to tell me.'

'Then let it be areca nut.'

'No, not areca nut.'

'A lemon plant then.'

'No, not lemon either.'

'Then a banana plant.'

'Yes, we'll plant a banana plant.'

After that, Mohsin Ali went to Akalu's homestead that evening; he observed that Bakul and Amir Hossain were sleeping on a bamboo machan in Akalu's thatched hut; he woke them up, 'Hey Bakul, hey girl, aren't you coming?' Mohsin Ali then left the hut with Bakul and Amir Hossain. The people of Suhasini saw the imam of their Juma Mosque, Mohsin Ali, accompanied by the children of the missing Fatema, roaming around the village for a long time, after which they collected a sapling from the clump of seeded bananas in Dr Robbel's house. Mohsin Ali looked for a soft, damp spot near the edge of the plinth at the rear of Akalu's hut and planted the banana sapling there, and Bakul and Amir Hossain were with him all the while. Mohsin Ali said, 'Recite the Al Hamdu surah, recite it thrice and then blow on the plant.'

The three of them then stood amidst the shadows of the trees at the rear of Akalu's homestead with their hands on their chests and recited the surah: *Aaujubillya hi minash shaytaner raajim, bismillah hir rahamanir rahim … Al hamdu, lillaahi rabbil alameen* … Mohsin Ali then explained the rules once again to Bakul and Aamir Hossain; he told them the plant must never be watered, and if the plant survived despite that, it would mean that Fatema Ma was alive and she would return; and if the plant died…

But the plant didn't die.

The people of the village saw through the ruse of the elderly imam of the Juma Mosque, but Bakul and Aamir Hossain did not; they kept gazing at the plant. The seeded banana sapling withstood the dry season, drooping silently, and come the next rainy season, it seemed to awaken at once; within a few days, the plant became so robust and tall that whenever anyone from the village observed it they were at a loss; they wondered whether it was for this reason that the elderly moulovi had set aside every other plant in the world and chosen to plant a seeded banana sapling in the name of Fatema! When they gazed at the circular and bulging base of this plant, and looked at the profusion of leaves hanging down, it reminded them of a woman; they were certain that the woman was Fatema, and sometimes the people of Suhasini looked at the seeded banana tree at the rear of Akalu's homestead and felt sad for the missing Fatema. Bakul and Aamir went near the banana tree at the rear of the homestead in the morning or in the afternoon or in the evening, and by and by they began talking to this tree.

'Hey Ma, won't you ever come back?'

'Why, why won't you return?'

'Do you think we don't feel sad for you?'

As time went by, the banana tree sent out suckers and it turned into a clump, and Akalu was annoyed; and when he said, 'Seeded bananas can't be sold, they don't fetch a price, I'm going to cut this tree,' Bakul began sobbing, as did Aamir Hossain; Akalu then had to give up the plan of cutting down the banana tree. He said, 'Mohsin Ali Chacha Miya tricked you, the sapling you planted died long ago.'

'No, it didn't die.'

'Didn't it die? How many saplings did you plant?'

'One.'

'How many plants are there now?'

'Many.'

'Is the plant that you planted still there?'

'Why? Isn't it there?'

'That plant died long ago after bearing fruit, the ones you see now are different plants, not the original one.'

Many days then went by, Mohsin Ali died, Akalu got married again, and everyone forgot about Fatema. The day Akalu returned from Chandaikona after getting married again, the village folk observed an old scene; this time as Akalu came walking through the Lokkhikola field, he held a rope tied to a black cow in his hand, and behind the cow was a girl with her ghomta drawn, Sakhina, Akalu's new wife.

The day after getting married and bringing her home, Akalu encountered the peasants of Suhasini in the village field, and like before, they worked and took a break to puff on the hookah and chatter.

'Hey Akalu, you're lucky indeed! You got another wife, and you got a cow as well.'

'Why do you people jabber so much?'

'All right, you got married, let's see your wife.'

'Do I have to bring my wife to this fucking field so you can see her?'

'Won't you let us see your wife?'

'If you want to see my wife, come to my house and see her.'

Akalu then tried once again to cut down the clump of seeded bananas, but Bakul and Aamir Hossain began to sob again; after hearing everything, Sakhina said, 'Let it remain.'

'Do seeded bananas fetch any price? Mohsin Ali Chacha Miya played a trick, and these kids are holding on to that!'

'Why not let it remain? It's on one side of the homestead, let it be.'

'But these aren't even the original plant! That one died long ago!'

But seeing the palms in the clump of seeded banana trees, Bakul and Aamir Hossain thought that these were the original plant; they looked the same, green, robust and beautiful; they grew up talking to the plant. Then, after Bakul began wearing a sari, the village folk once again remembered Fatema after a long time; Bakul began growing tall, even before she was eleven or twelve years old the bare calves of her legs were as plump as the stem of the seeded banana planted by the imam Mohsin Ali, and the various parts of her body began to bulge and spread out. When the village folk remarked, 'Hey Akalu, your daughter looks just like your lost wife,' perhaps Bakul understood, or perhaps she didn't understand anything; but when she lay down on the machan in the kitchen, her body wasn't fully covered by her sari, and when she soaped herself with her palms while bathing, her astonishment at her own dark-skinned body steadily expressed itself. Then one night, as she lay on the machan, she felt an ache in her stomach, the pain gradually increased, and after that she felt as if her abdomen was tearing apart; and then Bakul's clothes got wet. That night, Bakul got down from the machan in the kitchen in a state of bewilderment and went to the seeded banana clump at the rear of the homestead; there, she clung to the thick base of a banana palm and lay on her side on the earth; she wept, calling out, 'Ma, Ma!' Red ants were lying in wait there. They left their anthill and emerged.

The next morning, the village folk who went to the rear of Akalu's homestead saw Bakul's bloody sari lying near the seeded banana clump; the red ants of Suhasini were devouring Bakul.

(2000)

The Monkeys in the Moholla, Abdul Halim's Ma and Us

THE PEOPLE OF GHOST LANE were preoccupied with monkeys; they looked up at these brown-coloured creatures that sat atop walls or high up on roof parapets with their tails dangling, and shouted out, 'A monkey, a monkey! There's a monkey!'

Perhaps sometimes the people of Ghost Lane then spoke about the War of Liberation, perhaps they spoke cheerfully, or perhaps, exhausted in these difficult times, they spoke with annoyance. When the events of 1971 began unfolding in the country after the 2nd of March, when night curfew was imposed on the city of Dhaka, when the sounds of the screeching tyres of heavy military vehicles racing down Tipu Sultan Road and of gunfire shattered the silence, and when on the night of 25th March the timber marts on Nayabazar began to burn, Ghost Lane was not unaffected by all that; 1971 inevitably descended upon Ghost Lane, and then Abdul Halim got caught in the whirlpool of the time; perhaps his Ma wept, crying, 'Oh Abdul Halim, oh my child,' or lamented in silence, perhaps the people of the moholla heard the sound of her weeping, or perhaps they didn't. Or perhaps his Ma didn't weep any longer; perhaps, after so long, the people of Ghost Lane too forgot about Abdul Halim, or perhaps they did not entirely forget, perhaps they retained the memory of Abdul Halim's expedition. The long stream of time flowed over the moholla, just like water flowed in the nearby Buriganga, but nonetheless, perhaps sometimes the moholla folk remembered Abdul Halim, and they then exclaimed, 'The fucker was a crazy one'; the people of Ghost Lane called everyone 'fucker' and 'crazy' and engaged in meaningless uproar in the changed times; they worked lathe machines or ran shops on the streets of Dholaikhal selling spare parts of old motors cars, and perhaps in the evening, they sat at old Bihari's shop and sipped tea and chatted, 'Hey you fucking son of a swine…!'

The moholla folk say that there were monkeys in Ghost Lane in the past as well. The aged residents of Ghost Lane remembered seeing lots of monkeys in the moholla at one time; these creatures with bright red backsides used to clamber down the wall from roofs and pilfer bottles of Horlicks from unguarded kitchens. The small boys and girls of the moholla used to then run after the monkeys; they used to gaze at a monkey sitting on the parapet of some distant house, stick out their tongues and make faces, and sing ditties like 'Oh my monkey chum, I've seen your red-red bum!' But gradually monkeys disappeared from Ghost Lane, the people of the lane didn't know why that happened; they later said that, in fact, they didn't even realize that there were no more monkeys in the moholla, and that they had not seen monkeys there for ages. After a long time went by in this way, a monkey returned to the moholla and the moholla folk became aware of that, and when they realized that one or more monkeys had arrived in the moholla, they couldn't figure out where these monkeys came from; they then remarked, 'Where did these fucking monkeys come from?' Thereafter, they thought that perhaps the monkeys had come from Dayaganj, perhaps they had come from the lane called Dinanath Sen Road in Gendaria; but because they had got accustomed to the absence of monkeys in the moholla for so long, it seemed that even after first becoming aware that monkeys had arrived, they chose to remain unaware of it. Then one day, hearing her baby boy crying, the young wife of Noorul Haque, who was a tenant in the house beside that of Chandrakant's family, left a pot of vegetable curry cooking on the stove and went to the bedroom, and when she pacified him, put him to sleep and returned to the kitchen, she wasn't very attentive; she finished cooking the vegetable curry and took it off the stove, prepared dal, and after that, she hauled up water from the well using a bucket tied to a rope, had a bath, and then went to the bedroom and waited. When the sun was directly overhead, her husband came home for lunch from his office in the Food Department in

Postogola. Spreading a mat over the cot in the bedroom, he got ready to eat, he brought a bowl of vegetable curry from the kitchen, he brought the dal, and when he went near the shelf on the wall to bring down the pot of rice so that he could take some, he saw that the shelf was empty; the pot of rice wasn't there. Exclaiming, 'Where has the rice pot gone, where has the rice pot gone,' he looked for the pot of rice. That afternoon, both husband and wife thoroughly searched every nook and cranny of the kitchen, all around the well and in the alley beside the house, but there was nothing anywhere; neither was there any rice, nor the aluminium pot. At first, the matter seemed ghostly to them, and after that, they thought that when Runu had left the kitchen and gone to the bedroom to pacify her son, some thief, or beggar must have got into the house from the alley, quickly taken down the rice pot from the shelf and carried it away. When Noorul Haque realized what had happened, he swore at her for her inattention and called her an idiot, and then Runu once again put a pot on the stove to prepare rice afresh.

The night the sky on the western side of the moholla was lit up by the ghostly red glow of the fire in Nayabazar, and the moholla folk woke up from their sleep in a state of fear and bewilderment and heard the sound of rifles and machine guns and the screams of faraway people in danger, they were at a loss as to what they ought to do. Disregarding the curfew, they came out into the street of the moholla and asked one another, 'What's going to happen now?' No one could be found who could answer this question of theirs; it seemed they didn't ask this question so as to get an answer, they said it because they had sensed the terrifying nature of the incident and become perturbed. The people of the moholla spotted Abdul Halim in the lane of their moholla, in front of the gates of their houses, and they remarked, 'What's up, Miya? You were parading with a staff in your hand all these days, what are you going to do now? They're going to shoot and finish us off!' Abdul Halim heard them and was silent; perhaps, seeing the fierce, angry, red glow of the distant blazing fire, he was scared; perhaps there was nothing he had to say. There was a kind of fun in marching together with his fellow students from Salimullah College, with lungis folded up and bamboo staffs carried like rifles on their shoulders, perhaps there was also an expression of rebellion in that; but now, in the face of this question by the moholla folk, he remained silent. That night, the people of the moholla returned to their respective houses, and perhaps fell asleep again just before dawn. After that, when they woke up in the morning, they realized that they had missed the Fajr prayer because the muezzin of the mosque in moholla had not used the mic for amplification while reciting the azan out of fear of the Pakistani army, and the imam of the mosque, Moulana Nuruzzaman, concluded the Fajr prayer accompanied only by the muezzin. When the people heard about this, they went to Moulana Nuruzzaman's residence behind the congregational hall and said, 'Hujur, you too did this? You too were scared!'

Moulana Nuruzzaman's face then turned woeful; he said that, actually, he too had been scared, because he was only human, and it had occurred to him that perhaps silence was the best policy when confronted with these agitated and enraged animals. Those of the moholla folk who then made their way furtively through alleyways and headed to Nawabpur Road, at the end of Lalchan Mokim Lane, saw that, despite the curfew, a flood of people was proceeding towards the Buriganga. Within a couple of days, Ghost Lane too was almost evacuated, and the people of the moholla say that, one day during this time, Abdul Halim gazed at Hasina Akhtar Jharna.

That was when the moholla folk first heard about the disappearance of the rice pot from the kitchen of Noorul Haque, the tenant of Nepal Chandra, and they too were of the view that this was the handiwork of some beggar, that because of the inattention of the stupid wife, someone had slipped into the empty kitchen, taken the pot and hurried away via the alley. But then, there was a theft in the house with a stone tiger at the gate one day, either in the afternoon or evening; the owner of the house, Abdur Rahim Miya, returned home from his Rahim & Co. Plastic Industries Ltd. in Juginagar and went to the tap to wash his face; he took off the Citizen automatic quartz watch on his wrist and placed it on top of a low wall beside the tap, finished washing himself and went inside the house, but he forgot about his watch. When he woke up in the evening after his nap, he remembered his watch, and when his wife Parveen then went to the tap and couldn't find the watch on the wall, she screamed, 'I can't see any watch here, there's nothing here!' Abdur Rahim emerged from the house. Everyone then searched the entire compound, inside the house, the pockets of his shirt and trousers, the drawers of the desk and cupboard, everywhere; together with Abdur Rahim and Parveen, their young servant Akbar, too, searched all over. After that, when it was clear that the watch was nowhere in the house, and Abdur Rahim could convince his wife with certainty that he had not lost the watch somewhere else, the question that arose was: Where had it gone? Abdur Rahim exclaimed, 'Has it flown away from the house, or what?' And then they suspected Akbar and the maidservant, Basona's Ma. As soon as Basona's Ma heard the accusation, she began to weep, 'I haven't stolen it. If I've stolen it, Allah will judge me, I'll get leprosy and my arm will decay.' But Parveen was not convinced by all this; she said, 'Don't give me all that talk. There's no one else at home, you stole it, or else Akbar stole it. It's you people who have stolen it, and you're the ones who will have to give it back if you know what's good for you.' But Akbar paid no heed to such accusations; he said, 'I don't steal such two-hundred- or four-hundred-taka watches.' And when he said that, Abdur Rahim was enraged; he screamed, 'You bastard, son of a swine, you're showing me attitude! If you didn't steal it, then your father stole it! Give the watch back!' When the moholla folk got the news about the theft of Abdur Rahim Miya's watch, they wondered whether thefts had gone up in the moholla, and after that, they thought that perhaps this was the handiwork of none other than Akbar, or perhaps that of Basona's Ma; they said, 'The moment you thrash them, they'll bring it out, wailing for mercy.'

But just two days after the timber yards in Nayabazar burned through the night, all the people of Ghost Lane left the moholla fearing the arrival of the Pakistani soldiers, and fled across the river, towards Jinjira and Nawabganj. Abdul Halim stayed on in the moholla for another day with his Ma and two younger sisters. But after that, his Ma, Amena, didn't want to remain in the moholla that had turned silent and desolate; she said, 'I feel terrified.' Abdul Halim then took his Ma and two sisters, Renu and Benu, to his younger aunt's house in the village of Chorail in Jinjira. The family of Abu Haider, from the house on No. 34 at the very end of their lane, accompanied them. Abu Haider's wife had gone to Abdul Halim's house the previous day, and with her was her elder daughter, Jharna, who was a student of Class 10; sitting in a chair in the outer veranda of their residence, Abdul Halim observed the girl, wearing the shabby, pink-coloured uniform of Kamrunnesa Girls School, coming walking with her mother amidst the gathering shadows of dusk under the canopy of their kamini tree with a kind of trembling air. Abdul Halim then gazed at the frightened face and eyes of the shadow-wrapped Jharna and wondered whether he had ever seen this girl before in the moholla. When Jharna's Ma entered the house and said to Amena,

'Aapa, I heard that you people are leaving too. I'm scared to death, where are we to go,' then Abdul Halim said, 'You can all come with us, there's no problem. There's lots of space in my aunt's house, there won't be any difficulty. All of you come along with us.' The people of Ghost Lane later said that, actually, as soon as Abdul Halim glimpsed Jharna's distraught face beneath the kamini tree, he knew that he would ask Jharna and her Ma to go with them to Jinjira, and perhaps as a result of that, eventually disaster descended upon Abu Haider's family; or perhaps that wasn't so, because this was a time when no one knew what would happen to whom, and where.

After that, when the moholla folk heard that Abdur Rahim's lost wristwatch hadn't been found, and that even after Basona's Ma was slapped a few times and Akbar was issued the dire threat of being dismissed from service the watch couldn't be recovered from them, they were terribly dejected; because they were sure that one of them must have stolen the watch. They then felt perturbed once again about the rise in thefts in the moholla, and after that, when they were unable to come up with any solution regarding the watch, they said that if Abdur Rahim was telling the truth and that if he had really taken off his watch and placed it on the low wall as he was washing his face and hands at the tap, then Basona's Ma must certainly have taken the watch, or else Akbar did. They said, 'It will emerge as soon as they're thrashed properly,' but nothing came of all such talk by the moholla folk. Parveen Sultana hit Basona's Ma once again one day with a ladle, and Basona's Ma once again wept as she was hit; she declared Allah was witness to her innocence, she said, 'If I've stolen it I'll vomit blood and die, I'll get leprosy. And if I've not stolen it, since you hit me, you'll bear dog-pups in your womb, your arm will be paralysed, Allah will judge you, because I've been judged by Allah!' Perhaps Abdur Rahim's wife got scared by this threat. The moholla folk heard about all such incidents, but they didn't really want to get involved in this family matter of Abdur Rahim's. Later, people in the moholla said that they were actually fools, and the reason for this foolishness on their part was that they had not seen monkeys in the moholla for a long time, and it was because they had forgotten about the monkeys that this confusion entered their lives.

This confusion on the part of the moholla folk remained lifelong. But they did eventually find out about what had actually happened to Jharna in Jinjira. Those from Ghost Lane who got caught in the military operation in Jinjira on the first Friday of April 1971 were the ones who were most uncertain in this regard, because they had witnessed everything and knew that just anything could have happened to anyone; any person trapped within the encirclement of rifle-toting Pakistani soldiers could have been shot or bayoneted and killed, if the person was a woman she could have been raped, she could also have been killed after being raped. The moholla folk had not known what happened or didn't happen to Jharna because neither

Abu Haider nor anyone from his family spoke about this, perhaps Abdul Halim knew the details, but he too didn't say anything, and after that he died as well. Perhaps somewhere around the village of Chorail, Jharna had got separated from the others while fleeing the pursuing soldiers, perhaps Abdul Halim was with her then, and in the courtyard of some house or in some field the two of them saw soldiers in front of them; and the moholla folk were at a loss about how Abdul Halim survived! The people of Ghost Lane were of the view that perhaps Jharna had understood, perhaps she had understood that there was no way she would survive, and she had then played a trick and saved Abdul Halim; perhaps Abdul Halim lay limply on the earth pretending to have been shot and Jharna held him, pretending to weep, and the soldiers who had encircled them advanced. What did the soldiers do after that? The moholla folk don't know; what they do know is that the soldiers killed Jharna, but Abdul Halim survived. Perhaps Abdul Halim then lay beside the dead girl in some field near the village of Chorail and wept silently, and after that, when the army concluded its operation that evening and crossed the river and returned to Dhaka, and Abdul Halim and Jharna's family members recovered their faculties, they discovered that those two were missing. Abdul Halim's cousins and Abu Haider set out in search of them, and after a lot of searching, they found them lying in a field; perhaps Abdul Halim was then sitting, holding Jharna's bloodied body in his lap, or perhaps he lay distraught on the earth beside Jharna's body, assailed by terror and grief. Perhaps Abdul Halim was the sole witness of what had happened to Jharna; but he didn't tell the moholla folk anything, Abu Haider too remained silent. The day following the military operation in Jinjira, Abu Haider returned to the moholla with his family and found that many others had returned before him. Those in the moholla who saw Abu Haider then later said that in the space of two days Abu Haider had become almost unrecognizable, his face was black like the smoking, smouldering embers of the timber yards of Nayabazar, and looked like solidified lava; they inquired, 'Haider Miya, what happened to you?' Gazing blankly at those moholla folk, he only said, 'I left my daughter behind in Jinjira.' But it seemed the moholla folk didn't understand him, and then Abu Haider spoke again: 'I buried Jharna in Jinjira!'

However, after a time everything became clear to the people of Ghost Lane, and they say that they wonder why they hadn't been able to figure it out. When Abdur Rahim's missing watch was not found and the moholla folk reflected upon the rise in the nuisance of petty thefts, then Bahima Begum Rita, the wife of Ali Reza Byapari's middle son, Major Mujibur Rahman, came from Jessore Cantonment with her young son and daughter for an outing to Dhaka. One day, after preparing Horlicks for the children in the kitchen, the maidservant left the glass jar on the kitchen table, and when she returned she found the jar missing; the young girl was flabbergasted, she said, 'Where on earth has the bottle gone,' and she scoured the kitchen, searched the room; she thought she had absent-mindedly carried it with her and left it somewhere else, but the jar of Horlicks was not to be found anywhere; after that, everyone in the family looked for it, but the jar was nowhere. The moholla folk say that actually they were fools, they were too late in figuring out the meaning of the arrival of monkeys in the moholla, because they were unprepared for it; they then found out that, when the Horlicks jar could not be found in Ali Reza Byapari's house after much searching, Ali Reza's aged widow, Zarina, asked, 'Could a monkey have taken it?' The people in her household were surprised to hear her say that; they retorted, 'Where are the monkeys? How can a monkey carry away such a large glass jar?' But when the people of Ghost Lane heard about this, those among them who were elderly or aged remarked that they couldn't figure out why the thought hadn't struck them earlier, because it was only monkeys who pilfered Horlicks bottles from homes; perhaps the monkey was lying in wait, and the moment it saw an opportunity it entered and tucked the jar under its arm and scooted. The people in the moholla then realized that perhaps monkeys had returned to Ghost Lane after a very long time, and they waited to spot the monkeys that had secretly arrived in the moholla; they said, 'Have monkeys really arrived? Why haven't I spotted the fuckers?' After that, the moholla folk tired of it all, but they still never spotted any monkeys. Then one day, Runu's rice pot was found; Chandrakant's younger brother, Chandrashib, went up to their rooftop with a red-and-green kite and a string reel to fly it, when he spotted the aluminium pot lying on the roof of the adjacent house; after that, the people of Ghost Lane were certain about the presence of monkeys in the moholla, they knew that the monkeys would definitely be sighted now.

The moholla folk then encountered Abdul Halim; after getting the news of Biharis breaking into and looting the vacant houses deserted by Hindus, fearing their house would be looted too, Abdul Halim had left his Ma and two sisters in Jinjira and returned to the moholla. The day he returned, or the following day, he heard knocking on their door at night; at first, he was scared, he lay quietly, not responding. Then Abu Haider called him from outside the door, 'Abdul Halim, I am Jharna's father,' and then Abdul Halim opened the door and stepped outside. Abu Haider took Abdul Halim to his house that night, he told him that, at this time, being all alone at home in the night was not safe; and the moholla folk say that he stole from Abu Haider's residence on the very first night! The moholla folk say that perhaps no one would have learnt about this incident, but they say that the incident took place so that it would be known, it came to be known through whichever way because no incident was really an incident unless it got known. That's why, after the country became independent, the moholla folk can't say exactly how many years later, one day, Nimphol Dasi, the female sweeper assigned to carry the garbage from the lane and throw it into the bin on the main road, was clearing the garbage beside the wall in front of Abdul Halim's residence, when Amena Begum took Nimphol's little girl, Jabakusum Dasi, who had accompanied her mother, inside her residence, and that was how the matter of the theft by Abdul Halim came to light.

The people of Ghost Lane were certain about the arrival of monkeys, but they never spotted them; the moholla folk became desperate to sight the monkeys.

The day Amena Begum took Jabakusum into her house, that night, or at some other time, the moholla folk learnt about this incident; Nimphol Dasi brought Jabakusum along every day when she went to work, she worked while Jabakusum hovered around her or stood somewhere nearby and bit her nails. Perhaps she was standing like that near Abdul Halim's entrance that day, perhaps she was bothering Nimphol Dasi, saying, 'Hey Ma, Ma!' The aged Amena Begum then stepped out and took Jabakusum inside. After that, when Jabakusum returned to the road outside, her Ma observed that her hair was neatly combed, and a red satin ribbon had been knotted like a flower on the plait behind her. The people of the moholla say that Amena Begum had preserved this ribbon for a long time, and that this ribbon actually belonged to Abu Haider's daughter, Jharna; Abdul Halim had stolen it and kept it in his own room!

When the moholla folk heard that the lost rice pot belonging to Nepal Chandra's tenant had been found on a roof, they realized that Abdur Rahim's missing Citizen wristwatch too would certainly be found, and they waited to hear about it; but they waited even more eagerly on the rooftops of the houses in the moholla to spot a monkey on some parapet or wall. They couldn't figure out why the monkeys that had eaten up rice, run off with a watch, and pilfered a Horlicks jar could simply not be sighted. They waited to hear about monkeys being spotted; they were certain that they would hear about it.

After Amena Begum tied the red ribbon on Nimphol Dasi's daughter's hair, the moholla folk heard about it, and they said that the ribbon belonged to none other than Jharna, and that Abdul Halim had stolen it from Abu Haider's residence. After returning to the moholla from Jinjira following Jharna's death, Abu Haider took Abdul Halim to his house, saying, 'Come and stay at our place at night.' But there was no cot for Abdul Halim to lie on in Abu Haider's residence; Abu Haider's two young sons slept on the only cot in the outer room, so a bed was laid out on the floor for Abdul Halim; he said, 'It's no problem.' And then the mosquito net was being put up and perhaps there was a power cut then, or perhaps the lights had been turned off earlier from fear of the Pakistani army; as the mosquito net was being put up in the darkness or semi-darkness, it was observed that the string in one corner was missing, so then a string or something like that had to be looked for. Abu Haider, his sons and Abdul Halim searched inside the room, but nothing suitable was found. After a while, Abdul Halim found Jharna's ribbon on top of some table or under the mattress on some cot; on examination, it was clear that this was a ribbon, and because there was no one in the house who would use such a ribbon, he was certain that this belonged to Jharna, and the people of Ghost Lane say that, right then, or later, when he lay in bed in the darkness, he decided that he would take it. That night, when Abu Haider figured out that Abdul Halim had found something, he said, 'Let's see that. Give it to me.' But perhaps Abdul Halim did not want to use Jharna's ribbon to tie the mosquito net, or perhaps because he had decided that he would steal it, he said, 'This won't do.' While returning to his own house in the morning, he brought the ribbon along furtively, and wrapped it in paper and kept it in the drawer of his study table or under the mattress on his cot. Perhaps he wanted to keep this personal item of Jharna's as a keepsake, but he himself didn't live for much longer.

The people of Ghost Lane had for long thought that there were monkeys in the moholla, and when they couldn't spot them, they were baffled once again as they waited. 'So then is it not monkeys but something else, someone else?' But their bafflement and waiting period rapidly ended, and they got news of monkeys being sighted.

When the people of Ghost Lane heard about Abdul Halim, they were filled with sadness, because those in the moholla who were elderly now said that, at that time, they were young, and after returning from Jinjira, they lived in the moholla in terror. Abdul Halim went to Jinjira after a few days and brought back his Ma and two young sisters to Ghost Lane, and then after a few days, there was continuous talk in the moholla about the freedom fighters. The people of Ghost Lane heard about the various achievements of the freedom fighters, and then when they met Abdul Halim, they thought that perhaps he would join the War of Liberation; perhaps they asked him, 'Hey Miya, aren't you going to fight the war? You only marched with a bamboo staff!' But there was no sign of Abdul Halim going to war, and then finally, one day, in the month of Asharh, on a night of heavy rain, he left home; and the moholla folk learnt that Abdul Halim was nowhere to be found, he had had gone missing, and he had left behind a small note for his Ma. When the moholla folk got this news and then they secretly listened at night to the news regarding the war on BBC and Free Bangla Radio, they thought that perhaps Abdul Halim was fighting in some battlefield in some sector somewhere. And then one day, they heard about his death, and they lamented, 'Oh poor Abdul Halim!' A month or two after leaving a note for his Ma on the table, on the evening of the sixteenth day of the month of Bhadra, a Thursday, a stranger, a youth, arrived in the moholla; he walked briskly and entered through the front door of Abdul Halim's residence, and then, after speaking to Amena Begum, he exited through the rear entrance and left; the youth brought news of Abdul Halim's death. The moholla folk learnt that, just before dawn on the 23rd of Asharh, a Wednesday, Abdul Halim left his house and made his way through lanes and alleys to a residence in Hazaribagh, and from there, four of them, among whom this news-bearing youth was also present, went via Kamrangi and reached the bank of the Buriganga, where a medium-sized wherry with a straw covering was tied at the riverbank; many other people were waiting in the boat, in complete darkness, for this band that Abdul Halim was with. That Thursday, this strange youth looked at Abdul Halim's Ma's pale face and said that, when they were getting into the boat, Abdul Halim slipped and fell into the water below. It was raining heavily then, with a gusty wind and eddying waves, and Abdul Halim didn't know how to swim either; he was lost in the bosom of the river in that darkness, and it wasn't possible for the others to wait too long in order to search for him. The people of Ghost Lane say that they couldn't remember whether or not they heard any sound of Abdul Halim's Ma weeping.

Soon after that, the moholla folk encountered the monkeys. The first day, workers in Haji Abdur Razzak's lozenge factory spotted two monkeys drinking water from the large pan in the rear courtyard, and the moholla folk found out about this. After that, these monkeys were continuously sighted. After a few days, the moholla folk were certain that the two monkeys they had spotted in different places in Ghost Lane, on rooftops, on walls or some parapets, were actually a monkey couple, and they were even more certain that one of the two monkeys, which was bigger, was a male monkey, and the other a female one.

All the incidents in Ghost Lane involving monkeys then kept happening, and the moholla folk sat at Bihari's shop and had aloo puris and tea and talked about monkeys. Then one night, there was a burglary in Ershad saheb's residence; the thieves broke open the door and entered and took away all the gold ornaments and money, and when Ershad saheb's wife screamed as they were leaving, they stabbed her in the stomach, exploded country bombs on the street outside and left in a microbus. The next day, the police arrived, carried out investigations, and noted down all the details. The people of Ghost Lane heard about the burglary in the moholla; they were perturbed, and they remarked, 'Where do these two monkeys live? On a tree, or on the roof of some house?' This remained a matter of mystery to them for many days; there were two monkeys, one followed the other, they walked and swung on walls, they leapt from the roof of some house to that of another house, or else lay in the afternoon on some parapet with their tails dangling. The men and women in the moholla, the children, the youth and the elderly folk, everyone, whoever had the time, halted and gazed at the monkeys; everything about the monkeys seemed like a game to them. But they never found out about the dwelling place of these monkeys.

After Abdul Halim wrote a note to his Ma and left, Amena Begum discovered the red, satin ribbon. She came upon it, as she was tidying up the room one day, wrapped in a piece of paper in the drawer of Abdul Halim's study table, or under the mattress on the bed, and she first wondered whether it might belong to Renu or Benu; perhaps she was surprised that someone had folded and wrapped her daughter's ribbon so neatly, and she suspected that perhaps the ribbon did not belong to Renu or Benu, but to someone else. Amena Begum then brought the ribbon close to her nose, smelt it, and at once she knew that it belonged to Jharna, because she got the smell of hair oil from it; perhaps Jharna used to apply perfumed oil on her hair. The moholla folk say that they heard about this ribbon only after Abdul Halim's Ma gave it to Jabakusum Dasi, and thus learnt that Abdul Halim had stolen it; they say that, as Amena Begum looked at this ribbon, her heart was filled with anguish, perhaps for the dead girl, Jharna, or perhaps for her crazy son. After that, she put away the ribbon safely, in its paper wrapping, in her personal vanity case made of cane, in the hope that, when Abdul Halim returned from the War of Liberation one day, she would put it back in its former place before he could notice it was missing; and that when Abdul Halim remembered the ribbon, he would look under the mattress and be astonished that the ribbon was still there, and then perhaps he would remember Jharna and his eyes would turn moist. The possibility of there being tears in her son's eyes as he remembered the dead Jharna made Amena Begum's eyes moist; she put the ribbon away in the vanity case and counted the days.

Tales about the monkeys were heard in Ghost Lane, and the moholla folk said, 'Did you hear about the fucking monkeys? I tell you, they're fucking rogues,' and they were immersed in that talk. Then one day, the wristwatch that Abdur Rahim had lost was found, and Akbar, who was an employee in Abdur Rahim Miya's plastic factory as well as his domestic servant, discovered the monkeys' dwelling place. The moholla folk found out that, when Aslam climbed up his family's chalta or elephant apple tree one day to pick the fruit, he found the watch lying in a smashed and broken state in a hollow of the tree, and as soon as he spotted it, he realized that it was Abdur Rahim's lost watch. Aslam then went to Abdur Rahim's house and handed over the damaged watch; when Abdur Rahim came home at noon for lunch, he and Akbar saw the watch, Parveen showed it to them, saying, 'The monkeys had taken it away. How they've smashed and destroyed it!' When Parveen said that, Akbar burst out in rage; he said, 'Rats and monkeys take away your watch and you have no clue, and you call us thieves, you abuse us!' It then turned into a heated argument, and after a while, Abdur Rahim took off the sandal on his foot in rage and beat Akbar with it; Akbar became even more enraged after being hit with the sandal, and he set out in search of the monkeys with a lathi in his hand. After that, when he spotted the pair of monkeys on the roof of the attic on the first floor of Fakhrul's house, he concluded that this was their permanent dwelling place; but ultimately, the monkeys bit Akbar on his backside that day! At first, Akbar went around the rooftops of the houses in the moholla looking for the monkeys, and after that, in the evening, when he climbed up to the roof of Ekhlasuddin's four-storeyed house and looked from there, he spotted the pair of monkeys lying under the water tank on the roof of Fakhrul's attic. He observed discarded tin containers, glass bottles, and bits of crumpled, rolled-up cloth strewn around there; seeing all that, Akbar realized that must be the monkeys' den, and then he did something, as a result of which the monkeys bit him. The moholla folk found out that, after spotting the monkeys' dwelling place from afar, he went to Fakhrul's house, and without telling the people in the house anything, he went up to the roof on the first floor, and he held the lathi between his teeth and began climbing up the drainpipe. Perhaps there was some sound as he climbed up the pipe, and so the monkeys were alerted, and as soon as Akbar's head was visible from the roof of the attic, the two monkeys bared their teeth and pounced upon him. Akbar got no chance to use his lathi; in the face of the attack by the monkeys, he released his grip on the pipe and fell on the terrace, and he had no clue where the lathi he had been holding between his teeth landed. But the monkeys didn't spare him; they jumped down after him and Akbar desperately ran towards the door to the stairs, and just as he had crossed the door and was almost inside, the male monkey bit him from behind, below his waist, on his bottom; but because the pair of shorts he was wearing was made of thick cotton cloth, he was saved, the teeth didn't touch his skin. But when the moholla folk got this news, they couldn't believe that, even after such a big creature got enraged and bit him, there were no teeth marks on him; they then decided to annoy Akbar, and said, 'Are you sure there's no wound on your arse? Look properly and see whether you've been bitten, show it to Basona's Ma!' But Akbar merely said, 'Why are you people so worried?' And then he told the moholla folk that he had no problem. But the people of Ghost Lane didn't want to let him off so easily; when they spotted Akbar as they sat at Bihari's shop, they shouted out to him, 'Hey Akbar, hey you fucking bastard, come here,' and after that, they tried to frighten him. They said that, just like a person bore dog-pups after being bitten by a dog, and twisted up like a jute-string and foamed at the mouth and died, the same thing happened if one was bitten by a monkey; after that they said, 'You've been bitten by a monkey. Don't try to be too clever, go and see a doctor, show him your arse and get an injection, or else you'll die.' But Akbar turned his face away, he didn't pay them any heed. Abdur Rahim then found out about the matter, and in the evening, he took Akbar to Dr Wajed's clinic on Twin Bridge Lane. Dr Wajed questioned him and learnt everything, but he thought that, in order to be certain about the matter, he ought to examine the spot; and then when he asked Abdur Rahim to leave the chamber and said, 'I need to see the spot,' Akbar dropped his shorts and held his backside up high under Dr Wajed's spotlight. Dr Wajed examined him properly to see whether there was any injury from the monkey's teeth on Akbar's skin, and then he turned his head away and said, 'Nothing's happened to you.' When Akbar then encountered people from Ghost Lane, they exclaimed, 'So you showed your naked arse to the doctor!'

Perhaps some day after Amena Begum received the news of her son's death, she remembered the red ribbon she had kept in her cane vanity case, and the people of Ghost Lane say that this little strip of cloth assumed much greater significance than something that merely reminded her of her son. And then once again, the ribbon lay inside the vanity case for a long time; Renu and Benu got married, they had children, these children grew older, and Amena Begum became feeble and withered. Perhaps during this time, she remembered the perfumed ribbon and became upset, and standing one day at the outer veranda, she spotted Nimphol Dasi's daughter; and on that day, the history of the red ribbon came to light in the moholla.

The monkeys then did yet another dastardly deed: they stole a real pistol. Some people saw the monkeys playing with this weapon, and when the moholla folk got this news, they thought that perhaps it wasn't a real pistol, only a toy one. After that, it occurred to them that perhaps it was a real one, but they could not figure out who the weapon belonged to, and they said, 'It must be someone's. People in the moholla have so many kinds of pistols.' After that, they thought that the owner of the pistol would certainly try to recover his weapon, and that they would then come to know who the owner of the pistol was; but no one came forward to recover the pistol, or perhaps someone did and recovered it secretly and took it away without the moholla folk knowing; the only thing the people of the moholla learnt in this regard was that, after keeping it in their possession for two days, the monkeys threw it away somewhere. After that, perhaps the police in the Sutrapur police station got word about monkeys roaming around with an illegal firearm on the roofs of the moholla, because they suddenly arrived at the moholla one day and asked the moholla folk about the pistol. But the people in the moholla who spoke with the police didn't want to get involved in any trouble; at first, they were silent, and after that they said, 'What would we know about pistols? We haven't seen any pistols or suchlike,' and they then saw Akbar walking along the road. The people of Ghost Lane felt grateful to this servant of Abdur Rahim's, Akbar, for discovering the monkeys' dwelling place, but when they saw him, they suddenly felt like joking with him; they looked at him and laughed, and said, 'Hey Akbaira, you couldn't handle the monkeys could you? They bit your arse!' After all these days, it now seems that Akbar felt pleased then; he didn't get angry at the moholla folk's words, rather he laughed and said, 'Just you wait and see, they'll come and bite your arse, too, any day!'

The people of Ghost Lane then remembered Abdul Halim, and it occurred to them that it had been a long time since they met Amena Begum and inquired after her well-being. Perhaps in this long while, Amena Begum's life had run its course, perhaps she had faded like the leaves of the aswath tree during autumn, and trembled in the cold wind, having arrived at the point of dropping off.

Some of the moholla folk went to Ekhlasuddin's residence sometimes to spot the monkeys; they climbed up to the terrace above the third floor and gazed at the two monkeys in the distance, romping around noisily atop Fakhrul's attic; they found it very amusing. Manowara, the wife of Ekhlasuddin's elder son, was a nice girl; she was pretty, plump and good-natured, and lived with her husband on the third floor. Whenever her husband swore at her for some reason, or for no reason, she was very sad, and she then stood near the window and gazed at the sky. On a day like that, Manowara's husband, Abdul Quddus, scolded her for some reason, or for no reason; he swore at her, calling her a whore, and that made her very sad, and she went and stood at the window; she then spotted the pair of monkeys gambolling noisily atop the roof of Fakhrul's attic. She thought that the two creatures never tired, they kept on jumping, hugging one another and biting one another; then, after that, before Manowara knew it, all of a sudden, the female monkey stood still atop the roof and the male monkey penetrated her from behind, and in the soft light of the evening descending upon the moholla, they jerked their hips and mated. Manowara thought she ought to move away, but she didn't, and gazing further into the distance, she saw the sun setting over the moholla.

(2000)

Translator's Afterword

I FIRST READ SHAHIDUL ZAHIR in 2019, and the very first sentence of the very first story by him that I read had me ensnared. That was the story titled 'Where Is My Heart's Wanderer', and the next story I read was 'The History of Our Cottage Industry', which spun me around altogether. Was there any short story like this in the world, I wondered.

Before that, my friend Iqbal Hasnu, in Toronto, editor of the bilingual literary journal, *Bangla Journal*, had written to me, urging me to translate Zahir, and he had an omnibus of the author's short stories sent to me from Dhaka. But it was only after another friend, Ajmal Kamal, in Karachi, also sent me soft copies of Zahir's entire oeuvre a couple of months later – towards translating a story for *City*, the journal he co-edited, for its issue on 'Contemporary Writing from Bangladesh' – that I woke up, as it were, and began reading.

Zahir is the first Bengali writer that I read in the Bengali language for the sheer joy of reading. It was an exhilarating experience, and all the more so because I was deriving the exhilaration from reading in Bangla a mostly unknown writer, who, as far as I could see, belonged to the world of literature, to world literature, whose work transcends language, geography and culture. It was a discovery, and as a translator devoted to translating 'voices from the margins', I immediately wanted to share Zahir's work, and saw this as an exciting new chapter in my translation journey, something I ought to embrace and devote myself to.

This volume is the second of three books that comprise my Shahidul Zahir translation project. I was galvanized into taking up this project after living for two weeks in the pages of his books. And I wanted to pledge this labour for the fiftieth anniversary of Bangladesh's independence. Reading Zahir also prompted me to begin an engagement with Bangladesh, and I am fortunate to have been able to do that since 2019, with yearly visits, every visit ever richer.

In translation, I am primarily a translator, not a littérateur, and so I requested Iqbal Hasnu to provide me a list of short stories by Zahir to translate. The ten stories carried in this volume were suggested by him. After my own reading of Zahir's three short story collections, I could only concur with his selection.

Zahir is a kind of magician who, through his prose, creates a maze-like fictional universe and landscape that seizes you and carries you away – and then he delivers a political punch in your face, and you realize that all his artifice and magic is only a means towards that end. He writes about history and politics, especially through the device of memory. His narrative, which is peppered with sardonic humour, goes back and forth in time, leaving the reader in confusion between past and present.

Zahir is also a kind of ambassador of the soil of Bangladesh, its people, and their language. Language is the very basis, the raison d'être, of Bangladesh. So translating Zahir has been a means for a beginning, a process of learning about the many speeches, or dialects, of Bangladesh.

Zahir's stories invoke a collective, especially a 'moholla' or small neighbourhood, where everyone knows everyone, where there is an almost corporeal entity called 'mohollar lok' or moholla folk, among whom word spreads when anything happens, where rumours, gossip and hyperbole are as much a part of collective memory as are facts and chronology. He is a keen observer of people, and a sensitive human being with an eye and sensibility that is touching, moving and awe-inspiring.

Reading Zahir brought diverse writers to my mind – like Isaac Bashevis Singer, R.K. Narayan, Jose Saramago – nonetheless, Zahir is uniquely original, and Bangladeshi. Debesh Roy, the acclaimed Bengali writer, had written in Zahir's obituary that reading Zahir had given him the sense that a truly independent literature of Bangladesh had emerged.

Zahir employs people's dialects in their speech, most notably that of Puran Dhaka, or the old city, which he has memorialized through his fiction. While that speech forms part of the reading and cognitive experience of the reader of the original text, as a translator I have no means to convey the polychromatic qualities of the original; all I have done is reproduce the original speech through transcription in places, following it with the meaning.

Regarding the stories themselves, I would like to comment about three in particular.

In translating Zahir, I do not take any liberties, or make any arbitrary presumptions. His writing is the work of an evolved master, the prose highly crafted. And that is what defines him, as I see it. So as a translator, I must simply provide the words and sentences in English that exactly convey the author's work. No more, and no less. The author's text is sacrosanct, as it were. I began my translation engagement with Subimal Misra, who is known as an 'anti-establishment' writer. His text was also highly crafted. So unwavering fidelity to the text is a fundamental aspect of my practice. In this connection, I might mention that Zahir himself translated the story 'The History of Our Cottage Industry', and his unpublished translation is included in the omnibus of his short stories. I thought I would simply reproduce that in this book, with a note that it was the author's own translation. But when I read that closely, comparing it to the original – although Shahidul Zahir as the author was free to translate the story in whichever way he wanted to – I thought I had to stand apart from his translation. That was not the way I would have translated it. For that matter, he could similarly have tried his hand at translating, say, the novella, *Life and Political Reality*, which Shahroza Nahrin and I painstakingly translated, to our satisfaction, with utmost fidelity to the text. Our translation did not need any subtraction from or addition to the original text. So I translated 'The History of Our Cottage Industry' anew, in my own way. I imagine an encounter with the late author, in which I read to him my translation, and am suitably equipped to tell him that I am his translational trustee!

The story 'The History of Our Cottage Industry' also brings to mind Shahaduz Zaman, an acclaimed Bangladeshi writer, also a physician, and now Professor of Medical Anthropology in Sussex University. He knew Shahidul Zahir, and was supposed to have a long conversation with him for the *Bangla Journal,* which was not to be because of the author's sudden demise. After my spell of immersion in Shahidul Zahir's works, among the literary obituaries for Shahidul Zahir that I then read was Shahaduz's '*Theme Gelo Dokkhin Moishundi Aar Bhuter Golir Golpo*' (The End of Stories of South Moishundi and Ghost Lane). In this piece, he had written about the story 'The History of Our Cottage Industry' ending with a comma. He wrote: 'Shahidul Zahir's short story "The History of

Our Cottage Industry" comprises a single paragraph. In a story that is almost twenty pages long, there is no caesura, no stop, and he advanced the story using merely commas and semicolons. The story ends with a comma. He had told me that he had done that in order to capture the vicious circle of life in the moholla. He said that when this story was being printed for the book, *Dumurkheko Manush O Onyanno Golpo,* he was simply unable to explain the matter to the people in the press. Every time he deleted the full stop at the end of the story and replaced it with a comma, the proofreader changed it back to a full stop; he asked, "Does any piece of writing end with a comma – don't you have to adhere to grammar?" And despite being forbidden, they finally printed the story with a full stop. Shahidul was anguished and pained on account of that comma, he agonized about it. And in order to ensure an authentic version of the story, he republished it – with the comma – in his next book, the collection of stories titled *Dolu Nodir Haowa O Onyanno Golpo.*'

In the story 'Where Is My Heart's Wanderer', the title is somewhat modified. The Bengali title, 'Kothay Pabo Taare', means 'where shall I find him/her?' When I first read it, for some reason I remembered the title of an American novel I had read over forty years earlier, *Where is My Wandering Boy Tonight?* by David Wagoner. So the title I gave to my translation was, 'Where is My Wanderer?' But I realized the author's title actually had deeper resonances.

'Ami kothay pabo taare' (where shall I find him/her) is a song by the Baul singer Gagan Harkara (1845–1910). In his song, the him/her being sought is 'moner manush', the person of one's heart, or God almighty in Sufi philosophy. And it was to the tune of Gagan Harkara's song that Rabindranath Tagore set his song, 'Amar sonar Bangla' (My golden Bengal), which became the national anthem of Bangladesh. So, I altered my title and gave it its present form, which I thought would suit the story.

The story 'The Thorn' – I translated this in mid-2021 – is a story about the unfailing recurrence of communal violence against Hindus in East Pakistan/Bangladesh, which makes the moholla folk think they are caught in a time warp. In October 2021, during Durga Puja, communal violence against Hindus broke out in parts of Bangladesh. Meanwhile, in my own India, the drumroll for the final march to making India a Hindu state was proceeding at full pace. My friend Shafiqul Alam, a senior journalist in Bangladesh, posted on Facebook, saying that that there had been violence in some of the very same places that had witnessed communal terror in 1946 – like in Hajiganj in Chandpur district (then part of Tippera). He had learnt about that from reading Nirmal Kumar Bose's *Chhechollisher Diary* (1946 Diary), edited by Aveek Kumar Dey. Bose was the interpreter and personal secretary of Mahatma Gandhi, and had accompanied him during the latter's tour of the riot-torn areas of East Bengal in 1946–47. In 2021, Bangladesh witnessed public rallies against this violence, and the government was quick to take action; while in India, a new majoritarian society-state-culture-politics is being erected with every passing day. As it happened, that post by Shafiqul prompted me to propose (together with Amlan Biswas) Bose's 1946 and 1947 diaries for the New India Foundation's inaugural translation fellowships, and we were eventually selected. Perhaps the story 'The Thorn' could be the 'national story' of our part of the world.

In 2017, mysterious graffiti – the work of some anonymous Banksy-like artist – began appearing on the walls along streets in parts of Dhaka. The captions '*Subodh tui paliye ja, ekhon somoy pokkhe na.* Flee, Subodh, the time's not right for you' and '*Subodh tui paliye ja, tor bhagye kichhu nei.* Flee, Subodh, there's nothing in your fate' accompany two such images of a bearded man with dishevelled hair who holds a shopping trolley with a sun caged inside. Apparently, this was a matter of concern for security and intelligence authorities, who then sought to investigate the matter. I was reminded about this by Tokon Thakur during my visit to Dhaka in May 2022. Tokon, a well-known poet, has spent the last seven years working on a film based on the story, 'The Thorn'. He told me that, as far as he knew, the Subodh in the graffiti was none other than the Subodh in the story. I thought that was incredible! Such has been the impact of Shahidul Zahir's writing.

Finally, I would like to acknowledge the keen interest taken by Rahul Soni, my editor at HarperCollins, in my Shahidul Zahir translation project. This book would not have been complete without his painstaking copyediting and general companionship. *Here's looking at you!*

V. Ramaswamy
Kolkata, May 2022

SHAHIDUL ZAHIR (1953–2008) completed his post-graduation at the University of Dhaka and the American University, Washington, D.C., and joined the civil services in Bangladesh. He is best known for his novella, *Jibon O Rajnoitik Bastobota*. Shahidul Zahir's oeuvre includes the short story collections *Parapar*, *Dumurkheko Manush O Onyanno Golpo*, and *Dolu Nodir Haowa O Onyanno Golpo*, the novels *Shey Raate Purnima Chhilo* and *Mukher Dike Dekhi*, and the novella *Abu Ibrahimer Mrityu*.

V. RAMASWAMY has translated Subimal Misra's *The Golden Gandhi Statue from America: Early Stories*, *Wild Animals Prohibited: Stories, Anti-Stories*, and *This Could Have Become Ramayan Chamar's Tale: Two Anti-Novels*, Manoranjan Byapari's novel *The Runaway Boy*, and *Memories of Arrival: A Voice from the Margins* by Adhir Biswas. His translation of Shahidul Zahir's *Life and Political Reality: Two Novellas* was published in 2022.